MW00577466

A GRIM TELLING

A RAVENWOOD MYSTERY

SABRINA FLYNN

A GRIM TELLING is a work of fiction. Names, characters, places, and incidents are either the product of the author's overactive imagination or are chimerical delusions of a tired mind. Any resemblance to actual persons, living or dead, events, or locales is entirely due to the reader's wild imagination (that's you).

Copyright © 2022 by Sabrina Flynn

All rights reserved.

This book or any portion thereof may not be reproduced or used in any manner whatsoever without the express written permission of the publisher except for the use of brief quotations in a book review.

Published by Ink & Sea Publishing
www.sabrinaflynn.com

Book 9 of Ravenwood Mysteries.

ISBN 978-1-955207-27-0
eBook ISBN 978-1-955207-28-7

Book cover by MerryBookRound
www.MerryBookRound.com

A novel of suspense in Victorian San Francisco

A RAVENWOOD MYSTERY

A
GRIM
TELLING

SABRINA FLYNN

ALSO BY SABRINA FLYNN

Ravenwood Mysteries

From the Ashes

A Bitter Draught

Record of Blood

Conspiracy of Silence

The Devil's Teeth

Uncharted Waters

Where Cowards Tread

Beyond the Pale

A Grim Telling

Spark of Chaos

Flame of Ruin

God of Ash

Untold Tales

Bedlam

Windwalker

www.sabrinaflynn.com

To Brothers
the good, the bad, and the ugly
3/28/2022

There is a battle of two wolves inside us all. One is evil. The other is good. The wolf that wins? The one you feed.
—Cherokee Proverb

AUTHOR'S NOTE

This book contains racial terms from the early 1900s.
What may be accepted today may not be next year, so
I've opted to use the racial self-identifiers of the time.

FLIGHT

1901

Moonlight slipped through cracks in a boxcar. Shadow and light danced on the walls, playing over the huddled forms of her children. It reminded Lily of a child's rotating picture lamp. Tobias had taken refuge in her arms, his head nestled against her breast as he slept. Maddie rested on their sparse belongings, and Josiah slumped against the far wall, his elbows on his knees and his head in his hands.

Josiah looked up to meet her gaze. His rich black skin blended with the shadows, but his eyes fairly glowed in the moonlight. They were the color of amber, and when joy entered those eyes, they turned to honey. But not lately. The past haunted her older son and tore at his soul.

Lily turned her face to the distant moon as if it were a touch of sunlight. With the past came memory: a ghost of a caress over her cheek, the scent of summer grass and honey soap, and a deep voice murmuring in her ear. A memory of happiness.

Josiah Shaw had the eyes of his father. Only they were as grim as his nickname—full of pain and apology. But mostly regret.

PRIDE AND JOY

1892

"I DO BELIEVE YOU'VE GOTTEN MORE BEAUTIFUL, MRS. SHAW."

Lily smiled at the voice in her ear. "You said that yesterday, Mr. Shaw."

"Did I?"

"And the day before that."

"I do not lie." His voice was rich with warmth. "I was never any good at it."

"You haven't ever tried."

Nathan Shaw stared down at her with more love in his eyes than she knew what to do with. Tall grass swayed above the couple. The sound of children's laughter drifted from a nearby stream, and sunlight sprinkled through leaves overhead, playing over the ebony skin of the man stretched by her side.

Lily cocked her head. "Is there any sort of disease that makes a man delusional?"

Nathan sobered with an expression she knew well. She saw it every time a patient came in with some dire illness. The gray at his temples became severe, the creases on his forehead deepened into a scowl, and frown lines emphasized his broad and crooked nose.

"There is," he confided. "I'm afraid it's deadly."

She raised her brows as he slid his palm to her pregnant belly. The baby within gave a kick, and Nathan laughed.

It was a soothing sound that she felt in her bones.

"It's called love," he whispered, leaning down to kiss her.

"You're a goner," she murmured against his lips.

"I've made peace with it, Mrs. Shaw."

Her stomach lurched, and she groaned against his lips, shifting onto her side to sit up and lean back into his arms. "I haven't."

"How about… Basil?"

Lily snorted. "No."

"Consider the name for a moment," he urged. "Basil Tiberius Shaw."

"You're crazy."

Nathan moved his hand to feel the energetic infant kicking a foot against her insides. "He's trying to break out again, isn't he?"

Lily grunted.

"All right, here's a name: Atticus Shaw."

"How do you know it's going to be a boy?"

"I know."

"And if you're wrong?"

"We'll name her Angela."

"For the sake of our child, I hope it's a girl."

"You got to name Josiah," he defended.

"And you gave Grace Madeline Shaw a beautiful name."

"But you got to name the hotel."

Lily leaned more heavily into him. "If the kicking is any indication, this baby is looking to be more work than running that hotel."

"I'm sorry I haven't been around to help you."

"You haven't been around to sleep," she pointed out.

"Rude of people to get sick on Sundays and in the middle of the night, isn't it?"

"They should wait," she agreed with a laugh. "Josiah has been help enough."

A splash attracted their attention. Nathan looked over the swaying grass to where his children played in a stream. Josiah was ten and Maddie was seven, and he couldn't account for how quickly time flew.

Maddie had slipped on the rocks and was fighting tears, while her brother tried to drag her out of the water. Nathan trotted over to pluck his daughter from the rocks. "Now what's this?"

"A frog scared her, Pa," Josiah said with a roll of eyes.

"You said it was poisonous," Maddie cried.

"Why would you go and believe anything I say?"

"Because you're her older brother," Nathan said.

His son looked down at his toes.

Nathan carried his daughter to the bank and set her down to look at the gash on her knee. He clucked his tongue at blood streaming down her shin. "It's going to need something real special."

Maddie fought back tears as her father dabbed at the gash with a clean handkerchief.

"It's not that bad," Josiah said, crouching by the pair.

"Are you the doctor here?" Nathan asked.

"Enough to know she ain't gonna die."

"She *isn't* going to die," Lily corrected.

"See now," Nathan said. "You both made your mother haul herself up to see what the fuss was about."

"I'd choose your words with more care, Mr. Shaw."

He winked at his wife.

"So what's it need, Pa?" Josiah asked. "Want me to go catch the frog so Maddie can kiss it?"

Maddie's mouth fell open with shock.

"Hmm, that's not a bad idea."

"I'm not kissing a frog!" the girl shrieked.

"That's how I found your father," Lily said.

The children fell to giggling when their father made a croaking noise.

"You sound the same when you sing, Pa," Josiah said.

It was Lily's turn to laugh, only she covered her lips with one hand and rested the other on her pregnant belly. Nathan's eyes danced as he watched her. He never tired of those dimples.

"I don't do this for many patients, Maddie, but you're special." Nathan Shaw bent down to kiss the cut on his daughter's knee. "Better now?"

Maddie gave him a smile that was the mirror of her mother's as she wrapped her arms around his neck.

"You best not do that for me," Josiah said.

"Of course not, son. I'll just have you kiss the frog."

LILY EYED A DISTANT THREE-STORY BUILDING. THE MINERAL Springs Hotel was her pride. It was nestled in a pine grove with a bubbling hot spring, and while the hotel wasn't in town, it was close enough to take advantage of the two rail connections. She'd chosen the spot with care. And one day, she'd turn her hotel into a sanatorium for ailing East Coasters.

She already had a doctor at hand.

Katherine Lillian Shaw had been born and raised in Nantucket, and later lived in New Bedford, Massachusetts, where the Quakers believed in social equality and a strong community. Her people had prospered in whaling, then textiles, and running everything from restaurants, hotels, to factories. But New Bedford was established—old brick, old roads, and old money with hotels dating back ages. Land was gold there, and opportunity was expensive.

But as a Choctaw Freedmen, Nathan could settle in the territory, so they'd chased opportunity to his birthplace with the Five Civilized Tribes.

"See, you *can* leave for an afternoon."

"The outside's not up in flames, Nat. But there's no telling the mess I'll find inside."

Lily's gaze might be on her pride, but the hotel wasn't her joy—her joy was with her now. Maddie rode on his shoulders, directing his head like a galloping horse to chase her brother.

"Wasn't I right?" Nathan asked.

"You don't need to be told that, Nat."

"You did marry me for my brains."

Lily glanced at his strutting form. Nathan Shaw had a jaw chiseled from stone and was six feet of muscle with long, powerful legs. He looked more cowboy than doctor. But it was his hands she loved most—strong when they needed to be and always gentle when they could be. His hands were as compassionate as his heart.

"Dr. Shaw!"

It was a call the family knew well. They went to bed every night expecting an urgent knock, a plea for help, a crying mother, or a frantic husband. Hardly a day went by when Dr. Nathan Shaw was not called away for some emergency. Aside from the medicine men and barbers, he was the only doctor in town.

The call came from a lanky boy running towards them. Sometimes it was gunshots, fevers, sick babies or even a cow having trouble birthing. This time it turned out to be a busted ladder and a bent leg from a fall.

Nathan gave his wife an apologetic look as he set Maddie down.

"I'll come, Pa."

Maddie loved working with her father. Lily didn't think it proper, but the seven-year-old had a strong stomach and a curiosity for all things medical that bordered on alarming. Lily had tried to teach her sewing, but the child's efforts with needle and thread looked suspiciously like her father's sutures.

"Not today," Nathan said. "You help your ma with the hotel. Same for you, Joe. She needs help with the lifting." Nathan bent down to kiss his daughter's head, then his wife's cheek. "Time for my hobby, Mrs. Shaw."

Rich or poor, he never turned down a soul in need of doctoring. Fortunately, he'd married a woman with a mind for money and business. Her hotel kept the family fed, while Nathan kept folks from an early grave. And she loved him for it.

"I can always use another chicken," she said.

"Yes, ma'am."

Ten feet away, Nathan snapped his fingers and turned back to his wife. "You're going to love this one. It's perfect... Sherlock Shaw."

"You'd best get, Mr. Shaw."

He flashed a grin before trotting away.

FAMILY MATTERS

1901

SOMEONE WAS BEING RUDE. TOBIAS WHITE WAS BEING SHAKEN awake by a hand. It was cold and dark, and Tobias groaned out a protest.

"Too early for chores," he muttered.

A click of wheels, a rattle of wood, and rocking... Tobias opened his eyes. He thought he'd been having a bad dream— the one where his family was fleeing Ravenwood Manor in the middle of the night. A dream where he'd had to leave his bedroom, the only one he'd ever had to himself, and his friends Jin and Sarah.

Only this wasn't a dream.

"Hurry," Grimm hissed.

His older brother was standing by the door of a boxcar, gesturing him towards the edge. Tobias blinked away cold tears as his mother dragged him to his feet.

The train was still moving. Tobias peeked around the corner of the open door and saw lights in the distance. Why on earth had they bought tickets for Los Angeles, but then hitched

a ride on a boat to Oakland, and had that fellow sneak them
onto a train bound for—

Tobias didn't know where. He never knew. But they'd made
more exchanges like that until he was all turned around—
sleeping in barns, a flea-ridden hotel, and even rough one
night. He was used to having an ocean nearby to find his way.

At any other time, with Jin and Sarah, this might have been
exciting. Instead, he was terrified. He hadn't wanted to leave
San Francisco.

"You first, Maddie," Grimm said.

"Watch your skirts," Lily said.

Tobias watched, open-mouthed, as his boring older sister
sat on the edge of the boxcar and leaped off without hesita-
tion. She landed and rolled onto unforgiving ground.

Grimm tossed out their suitcases, and hopped down. The
train was rolling slow enough that Grimm could jog beside it.
Lily nudged Tobias towards the edge, but Grimm grabbed him
before he could jump.

Getting handed down was boring. He was eight years old.
How come everyone else got to jump?

Even his mother had jumped. She landed hard, though.
And as the train clicked by, Grimm ran over to help her up.
"You all right, Ma?"

"I'm just out of practice," she said, smoothing her skirts.
"And maybe getting old."

Maddie came trotting up with their suitcases, and Tobias
watched the train disappear into the night. The moon was high
and bright, and the air cold enough to make his breath fog.
Distant shadows looked like mountains, but the surrounding
earth was mostly flat, with a beacon of warm light off in the
distance—a city.

"Where are we?" he asked.

"Safe right now," Lily said, taking his hand.

Tobias let her pull him along, no longer caring where they

were going, but brimming with other questions—not the where, but the why.

When the sun peaked over the horizon and thawed his tongue, he asked, "Why are we on the run?"

A year ago, Tobias wouldn't have understood what they were doing, but he was older and wiser—he'd spent enough time with a detective to know they were *shaking a tail*, as Mr. AJ called it.

To his surprise, it was Grimm who answered. He hadn't expected anyone to answer, let alone his near-to-mute older brother.

"Because of me."

"What did you do?" Tobias asked.

Everyone got real quiet, and Tobias had the eerie feeling he was walking with a ghost family.

Grimm had a faraway look in his eyes. "I used to talk a lot."

Tobias snorted. "That's no answer."

"Leave him be," Lily said.

"It ain't no answer, Ma. With as much as I talk, it should be the U.S. Cavalry after me."

No one laughed or agreed—his mother didn't even correct his grammar.

"We'll find a new place to live. We always make do," Maddie said. "Think of it as an adventure like in Treasure Island."

Tobias knew his older sister was attempting to be positive. She had an annoying habit of looking on the bright side of life and trying to make everything 'fun'.

'Just pretend the broom is a cutlass, and every sweep is an attack against a pirate. Or Just think how the quicker you finish your chores, the quicker you can get your schooling done!'

Tobias had never been convinced of that.

"We best be meeting a one-eyed pirate with one leg then,"

Tobias muttered. "And there's no boat. Miss Isobel was going to promote me to second mate. We were all supposed to go sailing as soon as they finished up the case. Now Miss Isobel got shot and we don't even know if she's alive. And you don't even care about her, Ma!"

Lily turned him around by the shoulders and knelt to look him in the eye. Tobias was small, and his mother had strong but gentle hands that refused to be shaken off.

"Tobias, you can't mention the Riots again. Ever. Do you hear me?"

"*What?*"

"Not San Francisco. Not Ravenwood Manor. Not sailing or Jin and Sarah or Mr. Riot or Mrs. Riot. Do you hear me?"

Those gentle hands turned harsh as they tightened on his shoulders.

He looked at Maddie, who seemed to deflate. Even she had run out of chipper ideas.

Tobias met his mother's eyes. "I can't do that, Ma."

"You have to, Tobias. From here on out, we'll go by different names."

"But that's lying. You said we can't lie."

"This is a different kind of lie," Lily said. "Because in a sense, we're becoming different people."

"But *why?*" Tobias demanded, trying to shake off her grip.

"Because if we don't, we'll be killed. Do you understand me?"

His mother's matter-of-fact tone made him shiver. She used that same tone when she sent him to bed with no dinner.

"But Mr. AJ could help us. You *know* he could."

"He can't fix this, Toby," Lily whispered. "We've dug our own graves."

"I sure as heck didn't!" he fumed.

Grimm flinched like someone had struck him.

When Lily released Tobias, he took an angry step back, but

all the fury went out of the boy when his mother braced a hand on her knee and had to push herself up.

Maddie stepped forward to help her stand. For the first time Tobias could remember, he thought his mother looked old. And tired. The dimples on her cheeks looked more like wagon ruts.

"Just pretend this is all an investigation," Maddie said, without enthusiasm. "That you're working for Ravenwood Agency and have to keep quiet about who you are, like Miss Isobel."

"Sure," Tobias said, rolling his eyes.

Lily's only reply was to pick up her suitcase and start walking. But as Tobias dragged his feet alongside Maddie, he started thinking about what she'd said. He would take her advice to heart and treat this as an investigation—of his own family.

4

THE WHOLE TRUTH

HELP US. PLEASE. MEN AFTER MA.

The words were etched on a wall in a child's fort. And now they spun in Atticus Riot's mind. He glanced over to a large bed and its sleeping occupant. A scant month before, his wife had been shot during the gut-wrenching conclusion of a case.

Isobel had skirted death. Barely. She'd charged a man with a gun to save their daughter. The man was dead, Sarah was safe, and Isobel was home from the hospital.

Riot was torn between responsibilities: one to the boy who carved that message into his fort and the other to his young wife.

How could he leave her? Isobel was still too weak to manage the stairs on her own.

Cards flew from one hand to the next, but he barely felt their slim edges. Instead, Riot felt the jagged edges of a child's desperate plea under his fingertips. He couldn't ignore it.

What did he really know about Lily White and her three children? The family had their secrets. But who didn't? He'd suspected they were hiding from someone, but recently Liam

Taft, a suspicious Pinkerton operative, had shed a startling light on their secret: Grimm had a bounty on his head.

Movement brought him out of his thoughts. He watched out of the corner of his eye as a young woman laboriously pushed herself to a sitting position and dropped her feet to the floor.

Riot stopped shuffling his deck. "Do you need something, Bel?"

"I can hear you brooding."

"Cards flutter; they don't brood."

"Same thing where you're concerned."

"I didn't mean to disturb you."

"You're not. The bed is cold, and that fire looks warm."

"Shall I let you battle through or would you like some help?"

Isobel stared at her toes while she considered his proposal. She was pale and weak with pain, her blonde hair rumpled with sleep and glowing molten in the fire's light.

"You know how I like a good fight."

"My creaky middle-aged knees would prefer not to pick you up off the floor."

Isobel Amsel Riot was not one to be coddled. His wife was brilliant, supremely independent, and one of the most capable people he'd ever met. She was also proud, and currently irritated with her body—never mind a bullet had shattered ribs and the resulting infection nearly claimed her life.

Isobel stood and swayed alarmingly on her feet. Riot was at her side in an instant. He touched her elbow, and she turned to him, resting her forehead against his chest.

"I hate this, Riot."

"At least you're alive to complain," he murmured into her hair.

"You're right. And complaining is about as useless as I feel at the moment."

"View it as a chance to work on your patience."

Isobel snorted against his shirtfront. "When hell freezes over."

"And you're not useless, Bel. You're recuperating."

She pulled back to look him in the eye. "Can I ask you something, Riot?"

"That's ominous."

"I want your honest answer."

Riot narrowed his eyes down at her. "I have a feeling I'll regret this."

"Swear it."

"The whole truth, and nothing but the truth," he swore.

"Do I smell?"

Riot shook with silent laughter.

"I'm serious."

He sobered. "You smell like my wife."

"You didn't answer me."

Riot nuzzled the side of her neck. His trim beard was soft, and his lips brushed the pulse under her jaw. She leaned into his arms.

"You smell like a hospital."

"That's a diplomatic way of putting it."

He smiled against her neck. "Would you like a proper bath?"

"I'll even let you hand me into the tub."

"You may regret it when I unwind the strapping."

She shuddered at the thought. "Probably."

And she did regret it.

When Riot unwound the bandages supporting her ribs, she nearly blacked out from the pain. Isobel's knees buckled, and she grabbed the sink for support. Even breathing hurt. But she worked through it by glaring at the woman in the mirror. She was deathly pale and thin, but her right side was bursting with color: angry yellow and black bruises were interrupted by red scar tissue that added a new texture to her flesh.

"I look like a cadaver."

"They don't usually talk."

Her gaze flickered to the slash of white in his raven hair, where a bullet had carved a rut in his skull. "I imagine that hurt far worse than some cracked ribs."

"I'm in more pain right now."

His own pain was bearable; hers was not.

Riot helped her into the bathtub, keeping a hand on the back of her neck until he felt her relax against the porcelain. When she was settled in the steaming water, he retrieved a washbowl and pitcher, and pushed a stool to the bathtub. "Don't even try to argue," he said. "There's a good chance you'll never resurface if you dunk under that water."

"I'm in your hands."

Riot filled the pitcher with hot water, sat on the stool, and set about washing her hair.

"What's troubling you, Riot?" It was more moan than statement as he massaged shampoo into her scalp.

He hesitated.

Isobel knew the White family had left, but she didn't know about the message Tobias had left in his fort. Riot was trying to decide what to do about it.

Until five months ago, Atticus Riot had lived a bachelor's life with no great responsibilities. He'd been free to come and go as he pleased, but now he had a wife and two daughters to consider. Not that he minded; things were just… different.

And there was the catch—Lily and her children were family, too.

"Do you recall when I was recovering from my injuries and you took off after that lecher in Monterey?"

"Yes…" she said slowly.

"And you begged me——"

Isobel arched her neck to meet his gaze upside down. "I did not *beg*."

"You *asked* me to stay behind and rest."

"I was shot in the ribs, not the head. My memory is fine. What is going on?"

Before answering, he said, "You will recall how reasonable I was."

"You were grumpy and ill-tempered."

"But I stayed behind and let you charge after a suspected murderer."

Isobel settled back against the tub with a sigh. "I knew that would come back to haunt me."

Riot told her about the message Tobias had carved into his fort, and what Liam Taft had told Lotario.

"Grimm has a *bounty* on his head?" she asked.

"Apparently."

"What sort of bounty?"

"I don't know," he admitted. "I haven't made inquires. I didn't want to risk drawing attention to the family... But that was before I saw Tobias' message. And neither Sam Batten nor Liam Taft seemed interested in the family."

"When the police searched Ravenwood Manor, Sam Batten sure seemed interested in the Whites, but Grimm had made himself scarce."

"Did Sam speak with Miss Lily?"

"Sam was eyeing her. At the time, I feared he was about to hassle her for the color of her skin. I think Annie thought that too, so she distracted the Pinkerton."

"The White family stayed in the house for weeks after the raid, though."

"Exactly," Isobel said. "So what startled them?"

"I don't know. Tim told me something felt odd about what happened at the racetrack."

Riot felt her frustration, so rather than let her admit she

couldn't remember what he'd told her in the hospital, he ran through the events out loud as if musing to himself.

"Grimm got the drop on Carson and was keeping him in place at gunpoint. Then Carson reached for a gun and Sam shot him between the eyes."

"Sounds plausible," Isobel said. And it did. It was nice and tidy. Except that Grimm, the only witness to the shooting of the suspected leader of a criminal organization, had fled.

Riot said as much.

"What felt odd to Tim?" she asked.

"He said Grimm looked confused."

"Didn't Tim talk with Grimm after?"

Riot shook his head. "When Grimm told him he'd over-heard a telephone conversation about a female detective being shot, Tim went to ring Ravenwood Agency. When he got back, Grimm was gone."

Isobel fell silent in thought as he rinsed her hair. When he was finished, he set the pitcher and washbowl aside, and shifted his stool so he could search her eyes.

They were the color of San Francisco's fog—silver and cool and all-seeing. "We need to help them," she said.

"You need to heal first."

"Ordinarily, I would argue with you."

"Surely not you, Bel?"

A wave of water hit him in the face.

"Feel better?" he asked.

"Slightly."

Riot removed his spectacles to clean the lenses on a towel. "Would it help to splash me some more?"

"Probably not. I'll get your shirt wet."

"It's happened before."

"And we both know what happened after that."

Her suggestive words were like a splash of heat that hit Riot below the belt. How could he forget? His gaze swept down her glistening body, only the heat cooled when his eye caught on the scarring below her breast—not from revulsion, but from worry.

Sensing his thoughts, Isobel reached for his hand. "I'm not as fragile as all that."

Before the shooting, Isobel's grip was like iron; now it was feather-light, and the doctors didn't know if she'd ever regain full use of her right arm and hand.

"You're hardly up for a repeat performance," he said, donning his spectacles.

Isobel grimaced as she searched for a more comfortable position. "You're probably right. I doubt I can even get out of this bathtub."

"I'm hesitant to leave you at all."

"You have to look for them."

"Then stay at Bright Waters while I investigate."

"No."

"Bel—"

"I'm not going back to that hellhole."

"It's a *sanatorium* in Calistoga with round-the-clock nursing care and mineral baths."

"And an alienist who likes to poke around in my head."

"Julius is a friend."

"He still pokes around my head."

"You poke around in people's minds all the time."

"That's different." She tried to remove her hand, but he held onto it.

"Bel… give me an option."

"Sarah and Jin will help me."

"Two children are going to haul you out of the bath?"

"You're not leaving *now*, are you?"

"Not right this second, but there's no telling where the trail will lead."

Isobel considered their options. They'd been paid handsomely for their last case, but that money wouldn't last long, so they couldn't afford a nurse—especially with neither of them working.

"What about your mother?"

"I will drown myself if she moves in here."

"Mr. Hop?" he suggested.

"My parents don't do well without Mr. Hop. Their world falls apart every time he visits his family in Los Angeles."

"Hop has family?"

"Three sons and heaps of grandchildren. They all run businesses down south."

"He has a wife?"

"She died in childbirth a few years before we were born. His wife and my mother were close friends—as close as my father and Hop. It's why Hop frets over her so much."

The 'we' being Isobel and her identical twin brother Lotario, a chameleon who swapped gender like clothes and had three very different personalities and lives: Lotario Amsel, layabout and bachelor; Madame de Winter, famed opera singer; and Paris, an androgynous dancer at a high-class brothel. And those were only the identities that Riot knew about. To save confusion, Isobel simply referred to Lotario as 'my twin' since she had eight other brothers, and sometimes he was her sister.

"Why is Hop still working for your father in Sausalito? Wouldn't he rather be with his sons?" *Working* was a loose term —Marcus Amsel and Mr. Hop mostly spent their time making wine, brewing beer, and distilling Schnaps. Then sampling their efforts.

Isobel absently caressed his knuckles in thought. "I think our family drama amuses him more than his own."

"What about Lotario?"

Isobel gave him a look. "Really? My twin as a caregiver?"

"You're right."

"What about the new cook you hired?" she asked.

Riot shook his head. "Miss Shannon has her hands full."

"I don't have many friends, do I?"

"Margaret?"

"She has her father to care for…"

"Who has a live-in nurse."

"I'd hate to ask her."

"She might like an excuse to get out of the house."

"True, or… I could just not bathe."

The edge of Riot's lip twitched. "You'll stink by the time I return."

Her eyes dimmed. "I thought we swore never to spend another night apart."

Riot half rose to give her a kiss. It was slow and gentle, and held everything he wanted to say. "I'm not leaving yet."

"Good." She smiled against his lips. "After that kiss, I'll definitely need help climbing out of here. A bed warmer would be nice, too."

The water had gone tepid, and she'd lost so much weight over the past month that it left her shivering. "I'll warm you, but nothing more."

"You're not going to break me."

He ignored that. "Shall we wrap your ribs in the tub?"

Isobel knew what he was asking: Did she want to be pulled to a standing position without the strapping or treated like the invalid she currently was. She chose to stand.

It left her trembling and seriously considering a month at Bright Waters, but even the idea of traveling to the sanatorium made her knees go weak. Traveling in her current condition would require a potent dose of morphine—a thought that was rather too tempting at the moment.

To distract herself from Riot binding her ribs, she asked, "What if Grimm is guilty of something?"

He met her gaze in the mirror. "I'll sort it out one way or another."

The steel in his voice made her throat go dry. And there was the catch: they were all guilty of something. Isobel had shot and killed a brother in self-defense. Riot had killed men, too. By law, they were both murderers, but justice… That was a different matter.

Her thoughts turned to an earlier case: John Sheel. The boy had been ten when he'd murdered a younger girl, and eleven when he tried to murder his brother. But it was Isobel's word against his, and his wealthy parents had protected him.

What if Grimm had committed a similar crime against an innocent? Would Lily White protect her son as fiercely as the Sheels had protected theirs? Could Riot turn his back on that sort of criminal?

But Grimm was nothing like John Sheel. He was wise beyond his years with a patience that put Isobel to shame. And he was gentle. She might not know his name, but she'd watched him handle horses.

Guilty or not, whatever the crime, it wasn't without cause.

"He must've been young," Riot said, reading her thoughts. They both knew justice was rarely blind to color.

"Wherever they are, I hope they're safe."

5

PSEUDONYMS

Tobias was no stranger to walking, but they'd jumped the train miles ago. Even more confusing, they'd skirted a distant town and were aimed at a horizon of scrub trees and brush.

The sun rose over snow-capped mountains to the east. The air was cold, his breath misted in front of his lips, and the ground cracked with ice. He wanted to stop, but then he'd freeze—he was sure of it.

"I'm hungry," Tobias complained.

His mother took a folded handkerchief out of her pocket and passed it to him. It was a heel of bread from the day before.

Grimm shot him a glance that said volumes: Don't complain.

"Aren't you hungry, Ma?"

"I'm not growing like you. Not the direction I want, at any rate."

"What about you, Maddie?"

His sister shook her head.

"We have to decide on new names," Lily said.

"How come we're not walking to that town? What's it called?"

"We're near Sacramento."

Finally, Tobias thought. He felt grounded for the first time in days. But hadn't they bought tickets for Los Angeles? He squinted at the mountains, trying to remember the map from school. The Sierras?

"You'll have to tell me something soon," Tobias said, chewing on the hard piece of bread.

"You can give us new names, Toby," Maddie offered.

The boy thought. "So is my name not really Tobias?"

"It is," his mother confirmed.

The boy blew out a breath. There was that, at least. "What about you, Maddie?"

His sister pressed her lips together.

"Is our last name really White?"

No one answered.

"I mean, I know Grimm's name isn't Grimm. What is it?"

Grimm shook his head.

"All right," Maddie said. "I'll pick a new name for you —Percy."

Tobias nearly threw the bread at his sister before catching himself. It was their only food.

"Best get to naming," his mother said.

Tobias chewed and thought as he walked. He'd left a message for Atticus Riot—now he needed to leave a trail for the detective. Why his mother wouldn't ask the Riots for help, he didn't know. Tobias figured everyone needed help from time to time. He'd helped the Riots plenty.

Besides, Mr. AJ was used to trouble—he'd married Isobel.

"All right..." Pirates were too obvious. Isobel always named herself after pirates. He needed something his mother wouldn't recognize, but something Mr. AJ would spot straightaway. "I'm James Brady. You can call me Jim. Grimm will be Harry."

His brother shrugged.

"And Ma... You'll be Alice Brady."

Tobias waited to see if she'd recognize the names: they were all characters from the "Old and Young King Brady, Detective" dime novels. But dime novels weren't something his mother read. The only trouble was... Maddie needed some other name. Denver Doll. But that was from a different dime novel series. He wondered if he should name them all after those novels: Denver Doll, Walt, Yakie, and Chug. He doubted his mother would go for that, so he went with Doll for Maddie.

"That's not a name, Tob—James."

Tobias shrugged. "You said I could name you."

"I hate that name," Maddie said.

"Then name yourself," he shot back.

"It doesn't matter."

Tobias's heart flipped at the despair in his sister's voice. Even more troubling... his mother didn't say a word. Everyone just kept walking.

"So what's our cover?" he asked.

"We're tired, hungry, and we need a warm place to sleep until we get back on our feet," Lily said.

"That's not much of a cover story. How about we were attacked by outlaws and robbed?"

"We still have money."

"Speaking of that... How come we don't get a hotel?" Tobias asked.

"Because I'm saving it for later."

"So we're just walking to the mountains?"

"There's a ranch a few miles from here."

"A *ranch*?" Tobias gawked. "Like with cowboys?"

"No, they raise avocados," Maddie said dryly.

"Would that make them *Avo*boys? Or *Cado*boys?"

No one laughed. Jin and Sarah would've laughed. The thought made him sick—Tobias missed his friends. And he wondered what they were up to. He wondered if they were all in black, crying over a gravesite with their adopted mother buried six feet under.

What would become of Mr. Riot? Would he even see Tobias' message with all the worry or grief over his wife?

"We can't make up a story about being robbed, James," Lily said, trying out his new name. "The law would look into something like that."

"Is that a bad thing?"

"Yes."

"So we're on the run from the law?" Tobias asked.

"Among other things."

Tobias gawked at his mother. "What'd you do?"

"Stop asking questions and running your mouth!" Grimm snapped.

"There ain't no one around!"

"Put everything from the past out of your head."

"I can't empty my head 'less it comes out my mouth!"

Grimm's glare made Tobias shrink. His brother was usually calm—he'd never seen him angry before.

"Then get it all out before we come across someone else," his mother called over her shoulder.

Tobias watched Grimm stalk after their mother, then glanced at his sister. She was on the verge of tears.

"Is it bad, Maddie?"

"It's as bad as it can be."

But that wasn't true. An hour later, they came to a dirt road scarred by wagon ruts. Lily stopped and shared a look with Grimm, who inclined his head. He set down Maddie's suitcase, his mother's, and his own. Tobias had started carrying his own, but his mother had taken pity on him, and shared the load. She set his suitcase down, too.

Tobias flopped on the ground as she began rifling through the cases.

"My legs are done in," he groaned. "Does a stagecoach come by here or something?"

No one answered, so he cracked open an eye. His mother and Grimm were stuffing clothes from the suitcases into a dingy rucksack.

"You know where to go," Lily said to her older son.

"I'll get us there."

"I know you will. Watch yourselves."

Lily reached under her coat and brought out her handbag. She handed Grimm some cash as he shouldered the sack.

"Wait… what's going on?" Maddie asked.

Her mother looked tired. "We're too conspicuous together. We need to split up—"

"*No!*"

"We can't!"

Maddie and Tobias shouted as one.

Lily raised a hand and gave them both 'that' look. "We need to. Tobias will go with his brother, and you'll come with me."

Maddie turned ashen.

"You can't! We can't split up," Tobias shouted, curling his fists.

"There's no other choice." She hugged him tight, kissed the top of his head, and pried him away to wipe the tears rolling down his cheeks. "Listen to your brother and do as you're told. He knows what he's doing. Do you hear?"

"I'm not leaving you!"

Tobias clung to his mother, but a powerful hand gripped his arm and dragged him away as Lily and Maddie started walking in the opposite direction. Tobias screamed at them to

come back. He raged against his brother, punching and kicking, until Grimm hoisted him over a shoulder.

Maddie stopped to look over her shoulder, tears streaming
down her cheeks, but in the end, she followed their mother,
leaving Tobias with a brother he wasn't sure he knew.

6

A SPIRITED MIND

1892

LILY COULD TELL BY THE WAY HER HUSBAND WALKED THROUGH the door that something had happened. His shoulders were slumped and the smile on his face was forced.

With a squeal of delight, Maddie charged at her father. Nathan plucked her from the air, but instead of swinging her around, he hugged her close and buried his nose against her hair. "Love you, baby."

Nathan shared a look with his wife. *Not now*, those eyes said. His arm came out to draw her close.

"It's good to be home with my ladies," he murmured against her temple.

"I'll warm up dinner."

"Just tea."

Lily itched to ask what had happened. Because something had. It radiated from the man. But for now, she let it be. Nathan was walking and talking, and didn't appear to be injured, but something had rattled him enough to steal his appetite.

Nathan went off to sluice himself at the pump. She'd spared no expense putting in a windmill, water tower, and a massive boiler for the hotel, but old habits die hard.

The Shaw family lived in a small house beside the hotel. It doubled as Nathan's surgery, with the family rooms in the back. Nothing large, but it worked. They shared a kitchen with the hotel and there was always water boiling in a kettle.

Lily employed the Roses along with several porters and chambermaids. Mr. Rose was a mixed Cherokee Freedmen and his wife was mixed white and Choctaw—a woman with a quick laugh, and no mind at all for cooking. But she could clean. And her husband, having worked as a cook for cattle drives, was used to cooking efficiently for large numbers. He was also willing to learn and experiment with new recipes.

She found the couple cleaning the kitchen after the afternoon rush, but their usual good-natured banter was replaced with a heavy silence.

"You both look as though someone walked over your grave," she noted, opening a tea tin.

Mr. Rose frowned at the counter before muttering something about checking on the boiler.

Mrs. Rose's face was impassive, her eyes darting to Lily's bulging belly, but before the woman could speak, a lanky boy bolted in—all legs and long arms.

Josiah took one look at his mother and wrapped his arms around her. "You're all right, Ma?" He looked up at her with concern.

"Last I checked. What's happened?"

"Some men turned up at the Turner ranch and held them at gunpoint. They made Mrs. Turner cook, then got themselves all riled up with drink…" Josiah hesitated. "They took her away and beat her something fierce."

Lily put a hand over her pregnant belly. "Oh, Lord." That

explained why Nathan looked sick. It only took one look at Mrs. Rose to know what else the men had done.

"There's U.S. Marshals getting a posse together—"

Lily didn't hear the rest. She abandoned the tea and waddled out the back door to her husband. He was bare-chested, and his suspenders hung around his legs as he scrubbed himself with icy well water.

Now she knew why he hadn't wanted to come any farther into the house. Nathan was trying to scrub away memory.

"Is Mrs. Turner alive?"

Nathan's teeth were clenched as he used a brush to clean his fingernails. "Barely. I couldn't save the baby. Mr. Turner found her hiding in the cornfield bleeding out after they'd—" His gaze flickered behind her to where Josiah stood. "Done what they did."

"Their daughter?"

"They left her alone."

Thank God for small mercies, Lily thought with relief.

"Four men. After they got done with Mrs. Turner, they took Mr. Turner and his son, and amused themselves by making them dance and fight. They eventually got bored and left."

"There's a posse forming at the courthouse," Josiah said again. "I'll saddle the horses so we can ride with them."

"No, son. We'll stay here. The town needs a doctor. Plenty of men can pull a trigger, but few can extract a bullet."

"Then I'm going without you. Every man in town is hunting that gang—Negroes, Indians, and whites."

"Who will take care of your mother if I'm called away?"

"Mr. Rose is here," Josiah seethed.

"You're too young."

"I'm practically a man. I can join if I like."

"*Josiah.*"

The boy stopped short.

"I don't want violence in your future."

Josiah drew himself up with pride. Father and son stared at each other: one young and lanky and the other burdened by a life of violence—Nathan Shaw's muscled torso was puckered with whip scars. Those scars weren't limited to his chest and back.

"What do you know, Pa?" Josiah shot back. "You don't even carry a gun. How can you protect us? If that gang showed up here, we'd be ripe for the picking. *Someone* has to protect this family."

Lily's blood boiled at her son's words. "Don't speak to your father that way, Josiah."

"It's true, Ma. He knows it!"

"Violence makes violence," Nathan said calmly. "Where does it stop, Josiah?"

"With a bullet between the eyes."

Lily couldn't believe her ears. She tensed to grab her son by the ear, but Nathan stopped her with a gesture. Thrashing the boy might make Lily feel better, but it wouldn't add much weight to Nathan's arguments against violence.

They watched their son storm off—hot-headed, spirited, with the stirring sense of manhood in his bones.

Josiah Shaw was in no state to listen to reason.

7

JUST ANOTHER DAY

1901

THE POTATOES WERE BURNT AND THE EGGS WERE overcooked, but they were edible. Sarah poked at the rubber eggs with her fork and tried not to listen to Mrs. Löfgren lecture the new cook about the superiority of a Swedish breakfast.

That was an option, but Sarah wasn't sure if the porridge sitting in a bowl was supposed to taste so sour or not.

Sao Jin sat across the table eating a hard cracker. Mrs. Löfgren, a suntanned stout woman with near to white hair, had tried to make the girl add cheese and mayonnaise to the square of raw wheat. Jin had refused. Mrs. Löfgren took one look at the little Chinese girl and decided not to die on that hill. Literally.

Miss Aisling O'Shannon was another matter. Sarah doubted she was a day older than sixteen. She had curly, copper-colored hair, a storm of freckles across her tawny face, and a four-month-old baby squalling on her hip.

Mrs. Löfgren wasn't helping the new cook's nerves.

"Are you trying to poison the lodgers?" Mrs. Löfgren snapped.

"They want eggs. Not your porridge, ma'am."

"I could bounce your eggs off the walls."

Aisling's face darkened, turning a shade similar to her copper curls and emphasizing every freckle. It looked like a can of freckle paint had exploded on the woman's face.

Woman. Sarah frowned at that thought. Aisling was only three years older than herself. And with an infant.

Sarah was too polite to ask after her background. Even the details of Aisling's arrival at Ravenwood Manor were fuzzy, but that was because Sarah had shot a man. Some details were stark in her mind: the feel of his arm around her neck, his heart beating against her back, the ivory grip of the gun in her palm.

And the blood saturating Isobel's clothing.

Before that day, Sarah would have helped Aisling—the woman couldn't cook to save her life. She flinched at loud noises, and male lodgers made her shrink with fear. But Sarah felt strangely detached from the woman's troubles. From everything of late.

She sighed at her breakfast. She'd learned that poking her nose into things could lead to worse things. And she missed the White family. Instead of laughter and joking, the kitchen was full of chaos and bickering.

"Only a simpleton can't manage an egg. I've shown you how—"

Jin leapt to her feet. "*Stop talking.*" The girl didn't reach Mrs. Löfgren's shoulders, but her growl silenced the woman mid-sentence.

Mrs. Löfgren took a step backwards.

"You cook for your husband. She will cook for others."

Mrs. Löfgren recalled that the scarred girl was only eleven

and rallied. "We pay for room and board—that includes *cooked* food. And this *woman* cannot cook!"

"It is very cooked," Jin pointed out. "You should pay more for how cooked the potatoes are."

A knock at the grocer's door interrupted the standoff. Who would knock on the back door? Before Sarah could stop her, Mrs. Löfgren opened it.

Sarah and Jin tensed when they saw the man in the doorway. He was six feet tall, with sun-weathered skin and eyes like flint. He wore a cocked, wide-brimmed hat, a tan duster, gray vest, and knee-high boots covered in dust.

Those eyes looked straight past Mrs. Löfgren and settled on Aisling.

"Miss White?" he asked.

Aisling hugged her screaming baby closer, and retreated.

"Who are you?" Mrs. Löfgren demanded. The stranger tried to push past the woman, but she held the door firm and planted herself in the opening.

The man tucked back his long coat, revealing a silver star in a circle and a revolver on his hip. "U.S. Marshal Eli Blake. I'm looking for a Negro woman by the name of White, or maybe Shaw." He nodded towards Aisling, whose red hair and light brown skin hinted at mixed blood.

"I don't know a Miss White," she said. "I'm Aisling O'Shannon."

Blake took his time studying the young woman.

Sarah was careful not to glance at her sister, who'd slipped a knife from the counter and moved behind the door. A second stranger stood at the bottom of the steps with his thumbs hooked casually in his belt. Whereas Eli Blake was dusty and travel-worn, this man was impeccably dressed. He had smooth coal-black skin, fine hands, and his boots were polished to a gleam. Two pistol grips poked from beneath his gentleman's overcoat.

"The White family left," Mrs. Löfgren said. "I don't know any Shaw family."

"When?"

"Weeks ago. Mrs. White was the cook here. The owners of the lodging house replaced her with this... *cook*." She made the bitter word sound like *a slur*. "I don't suppose that's illegal in America?"

The man at the bottom step smiled. "Bad cooking should be illegal everywhere, ma'am."

"And you are?"

He raised his hat a fraction. "Deputy U.S. Marshal Angel Davren. I'm sure you won't mind us coming in."

Mrs. Löfgren hesitated, while Sarah shot Jin a look that sent the girl racing silently from the kitchen.

"We do mind," Sarah said, squaring her shoulders.

Blake smiled at her. "And you are?"

Sarah was in no mood for men with pleasant smiles. She'd had enough of them in the past year. "Old enough to know you can't come in without a warrant."

"It just so happens we have one." Blake pulled two slips of paper from an inner pocket. "Did Mrs. *White* have a son?"

"Two," Mrs. Löfgren answered. "Grimm and Tobias."

The woman would blather all their secrets at this rate. Sarah snatched the warrants before Mrs. Löfgren could read them.

Sarah read the heavily creased paper in confusion. "This has nothing to do with them. These warrants are for a Josiah Shaw and Katherine Shaw."

"They conned you, Miss. They're a sly family on the run. The oldest boy is wanted for the murder of a U.S. Marshal."

Sarah blinked. Impossible. Grimm was wanted for *murder*?

"They used to run with a gang of vile outlaws."

Even Aisling's baby quieted as the words thudded into the kitchen.

"Did they now?" a voice said from behind.

Sarah's knees went weak with relief when she turned to find her adopted father standing in the kitchen. Jin stood at his side.

But the tension in the air was lost on Mrs. Löfgren. "That's it!" she exploded. "No more, Mr. Riot. My husband and I are leaving. U.S. Marshals, whores, police, murder charges, and bad cooking." She shook a wooden spoon at him. "I want my rent money back for the month."

Aisling flinched, the baby started screaming again, and Riot stepped past Mrs. Löfgren to study the warrants. He was in shirtsleeves and vest, but he had a holstered revolver nestled against the small of his back.

"I suggest you start packing," he said calmly.

Sarah opened her mouth to protest, only to shut it with a click—another lodger walking out was really the least of their worries.

Mrs. Löfgren stormed out of the kitchen. And Riot took one look at Aisling, and quickly helped her into a chair before plucking the infant from her arms. "You can see we're out of sorts with the family gone."

The Marshals took that as an invitation to enter.

Sarah had known her father for nearly a year now. He was calm and sure, and as quick as a snake. He was also calculating. With a baby in his arms, Atticus Riot was as unthreatening as a man could be. He was making sure not to turn his back on the men so they wouldn't spot his hidden revolver. It served another purpose, too. With the calm he radiated, the baby soon quieted, soothing the men's irritation at the fussy distraction.

"I think you have the wrong family," Riot said. "I can't see the Whites running with a gang, but you can have a look for yourselves. They lived downstairs. Their rooms are still empty."

"Do you run this lodging house?" Blake asked.

Riot offered him a hand. "Atticus Riot."

The two men introduced themselves, then paused when they caught sight of Sao Jin glaring from a corner.

"That's my daughter. Jin, can you lead the way?"

Sarah suspected she'd slid the butcher knife up her loose sleeve. The girl wasn't the trusting type. With good reason.

Before Riot followed, he passed Fiona back to her mother.

"Mr. Riot, I—"

"Nothing to worry about, Miss Aisling," he said, offering the woman a clean handkerchief. He laid a gentle hand on the woman's shoulder, then shared a look with Sarah, who shrugged in return. It was just another day at Ravenwood Manor. Nothing much surprised her anymore—not even the claim that the White family ran with an outlaw gang. Why not?

Sarah followed Riot downstairs to find Jin standing in the middle of a large room they called the dance hall. Although Sarah doubted it had ever been used for entertaining.

The Whites used it as a sort of sitting room. Their comfortable chairs were still in front of the fireplace, and the empty cushions pricked her eyes.

"How long ago did they leave?" Blake asked.

Davren had disappeared down the hallway to search their rooms.

"About four weeks ago. The family left while I was at the hospital with my wife."

"You're a detective, aren't you?" Blake asked.

"I am."

"You didn't know Josiah Shaw had a bounty on his head?"

"I didn't know his name was Josiah Shaw. We called him Grimm."

"Did you do the hiring?"

"I was in Europe for three years. My caretaker for the

manor turned it into a lodging house and hired Mrs. White to run it."

Blake eyed Riot, but even if he'd been lying, Sarah doubted the man could tell—Atticus Riot was a cool hand.

"Who's your caretaker?"

"Tim lives in the carriage house," Riot said. "What gang did you say they ran with?"

"I didn't."

"Is it a secret?"

"The Holden Gang."

Riot's gaze turned inward. He had an uncanny memory and Sarah wagered he was sifting through them like files to pull out an answer. "They operated around Indian Territory, didn't they?"

"They hid there, too."

"I thought the gang was hunted down years ago."

"Some of the members."

"And you think a woman and her boy ran with them?"

"Josiah Shaw murdered my brother in cold blood."

Riot betrayed no surprise. "According to the date on that warrant, Grimm would have been eight or ten."

"You know as well as I do age doesn't matter." Blake nodded towards Sarah. "Considering the Holden Gang's repu-tation, you're fortunate your daughters weren't harmed. Make no mistake, that boy is dangerous."

"People change," Riot said.

"It doesn't bring my brother back."

"So you've been hunting a woman and her son for... eight years?"

"They're cunning."

Riot raised his brows. "Apparently."

"They've had help."

Riot glanced at Marshal Davren as he reappeared from the side hallway. While he blended with the shadows, his white hat fairly glowed in the dim light. He caught his partner's eye and gave a shake of his head.

"How'd you track them here?" Riot asked.

"A Pinkerton recognized the family."

"I'm surprised he didn't apprehend them when he had the chance."

Eli Blake dipped his head in acknowledgement. "Would've saved us some trouble."

"Liam Taft doesn't strike me as a man who'd let a criminal slip through his fingers," Riot said.

His baiting paid off with confirmation. "I never said it was Liam Taft."

Riot could read a man like an open book. The way Eli Blake came back with a defensive reply, along with his sudden suspicion and the ease with which he said the name, confirmed what Riot suspected. "It was Sam Batten, then."

"You worked on a recent case together."

"We did."

"They didn't mention the boy's warrant?"

"Liam mentioned it after the family left. Grimm worked for my agency."

Sarah was surprised he'd shared that much, but with the way Riot was watching the pair, she suspected he was gauging how much they already knew.

Blake didn't look surprised by anything he said.

"Harboring a criminal is against the law," Davren said.

"A known criminal," Riot corrected. "Considering you've been hunting a woman and her boy for eight years, I wager you know just how much they keep to themselves."

"They lived in your house, cooked your food, and worked for you... You didn't look into their past?"

"Everyone has a past. We don't dig too deep here in San Francisco."

Davren studied Sarah. "Did they have any friends? A church?"

"Not that I'm aware," Riot said. "Mrs. White kept the household running smoothly. She was honest, hard-working, and did her job. That's the only thing I cared about."

"Did they take anything when they left?" Blake asked.

"Tim said they borrowed the hack and horse. He found it at a stable by the ferry terminal. They paid for the boarding out of their own wages."

"I'm sure you won't mind if we question your daughters."

"I do mind," Riot said. "But I'll permit it as long as I'm present."

Sarah's heart galloped as she led the way to the upstairs sitting room. She couldn't lie. What if she gave them away? But then she calmed herself.

It didn't matter if she answered the marshals' questions honestly, because the Whites—Shaws, she corrected—really had kept to themselves. And now she knew why.

8

A BAD BROTHER

TOBIAS DANGLED FROM HIS BROTHER'S SHOULDER, FEELING sorry for himself. It was a fitting position to be in—his world had been turned upside down in the space of a week. So he bumped against his brother's back and stared at the dirt road.

What would Jin and Sarah do?

Sarah would likely flutter her lashes and smile, and say something sensible, but Tobias wasn't a white girl from Tennessee, so that wouldn't work for him. And Jin... he was never sure what she'd do. Probably stab someone.

It was up to the Lone Outlaw again—a name he'd given himself when he'd snuck into a lodger's room to investigate. Tobias had been wrong about Harry Hughes authoring a scathing newspaper article on Ravenwood Manor, but he'd discovered a heap of cash in a secret wardrobe compartment.

Not that his discovery had helped anything. But still.

Tobias decided he'd moped enough, so he squirmed off his brother's shoulder. The horizon had changed from a flat expanse flowing into towering mountains to a flat expanse with squat buildings and towering mountains.

"Is that where we're headed?" Tobias asked.

Grimm grunted.

It wasn't much of a town. Tobias studied the dirt road. It was well-trodden by cattle and horse, and marked with wagon ruts. "Is it the ranch?"

"We need work."

"But ma gave you cash. We could take a train, or do like we did before and hitch a ride."

"You know how Mr. Riot had to live in a stable with Jack while he was investigating the Nymphia Hotel?"

Tobias sighed. "We have to make it look real."

"Otherwise, if a colored family with money climbed off a train from San Francisco and took up at a hotel, we'd draw attention and be easier to track."

"So we have money, but we can't use it."

"We'll need it when things get slim."

"Where are we meeting ma and Maddie?"

"Get them out of your head for now."

"What if you get crushed by a cow? Where am I supposed to go?"

Grimm frowned in thought. "Not yet. If something happens, stay put. Ma will know where to find you."

"Who's after us, Grimm?"

"Use my new name."

"Harry." Tobias wrinkled his nose. The new name didn't really roll off the tongue.

"All you need to know right now is that we're brothers looking for work."

"Or I could go to the nearest telegraph office and wire Mr. AJ to tell him you kidnapped me."

Grimm pulled him to a stop. "You do that, and you'll get us all killed. And don't run your mouth like you usually do."

Tobias clenched his fists. "Come on, Grimm. Mr. AJ trusted me with things. I'm reliable. You know it."

"It's not that…" Grimm's eyes dimmed with pain. "I can't tell you."

"But—"

"You don't get it, Tobias!" Grimm exploded.

"Because you're not telling me nothing!"

"You'll hate me."

"I'm close to it right now."

"I don't want to tell you."

"How bad can it be?"

Grimm looked him in the eye, and what Tobias saw in those eyes made him take a step back. "It's worse than you think."

TOBIAS DECIDED THINGS WERE AS BAD AS THEY COULD BE. His opinion didn't change when they arrived at the ranch. A maze of corrals, filthy cowboys, horses and cattle, and bunkhouses with gaps in the walls.

He was cold and shivering, and his legs hurt, but not as much as his heart. Tobias dragged his feet after his brother as he eyed the rough-looking men watching the horses. At least several men had some color to their skin.

The horses weren't anything like Tobias had seen before. These were all muscle and fury, snorting out cold air like puffs of dragon's smoke.

Grimm stopped some ten feet away from a corral. A white man in a bowler nodded to him and walked over. "Are the pair of you lost?"

"No, sir. Me and my brother are looking for work."

The grizzled man gave Grimm an appraising once over. Then his gaze flickered to Tobias, and a bushy brow twitched in amusement. "Do you know your way around cattle?"

"Mostly horses," Grimm said.

"Horses, you say?" The man didn't look impressed.

"Yes, sir."

"Easy enough to test your mettle. I'm known as Finn here."

"I'm Brady. That's my brother Jim."

"His name's really *Harry*," Tobias corrected. "Harry Brady. I'm James Brady. Sometimes they call him King, and I'm Young."

Grimm shot his little brother a warning look.

"You got a first name?" Tobias asked.

"It's Mister to you," Finn said. "What's Jim there do?"

"Mostly runs his mouth," Grimm said.

Finn laughed. "I'll give any fellow a chance as long as he's honest, hardworking, and backs up his talk. Can you bust broncos?"

Grimm looked to where the man pointed—to a round pen with a rider clinging to the back of a bucking horse. "I don't break horses, sir."

"I see."

"But I'll ride her."

Finn raised his brows.

"Brady's practically a horse," Tobias blurted out. "They have an understanding. My brother don't talk much to people, but he talks to horses."

Grimm glared at his brother.

"He's more like a starer," Tobias amended.

"Worked many ranches?" Finn asked.

"Loads," Tobias boasted.

Grimm cut in, "I just need a rope."

"We could use the entertainment." Finn snagged the attention of the others with a sharp whistle. "Got a greenhorn who claims he can bust broncos. Pick one out for the young fellow."

They picked one out all right.

A wild-eyed mare kicking up a storm of frozen earth. Tobias blew into his hands and squeezed between two men to watch the show. They stunk like cow dung and horse sweat, but one of them slapped him on the back.

"Claims he'll charm the horse," Finn said. "So keep quiet."

A ripple of laughter traveled through the men.

Grimm climbed right in with the wild mare. She turned away from him, and he slapped the coiled rope against his thigh, getting her to run. She raced around the pen, and he kept her going with a click of his tongue.

When she slowed and flicked her ears towards him, he stopped. When she turned her gaze on him, he took a step back. The mare took off running, and Grimm clicked her onward, keeping her going.

She stopped and ran twice more, before curiosity compelled her to face him. He took a step back, and she stepped towards him. Then he moved to the side, and she followed for a few paces. But eventually, she looked away, and Grimm got her attention with a smack of the rope against his thigh.

It was a sort of dance between horse and human, and it was repeated twice more, until he held the mare's attention.

Grimm put his back to the horse and walked in a circle. She followed. He stopped, the horse stopped, and he put out a hand. The horse edged forward to sniff it. Grimm walked away. The horse followed, but then stepped to the side and took her eyes off him. He made a loud kissing noise, and got her running again.

Around and around, turning her inwards with a noise, until she stopped and squared off with him. Both eyes were focused, ears attentive, waiting for some cue. Grimm stepped away, and the horse came forward. He rubbed his hand on her forehead and over her nose, speaking softly.

When he'd rubbed his hands over her neck and back, he introduced the coiled rope, touching it to her flesh. And when she jerked in alarm, he drove her to run circles again.

Then came the calm stillness. She got curious, and he repeated the process, until she didn't shy at the touch of the rope.

Grimm unwound a section to lay it over her back. The dance continued until he could toss a section of rope over her back without her even a tensing of muscle.

Next came a rope halter. It barely gave her pause as Grimm slipped it over her ears, whispering soothing words. He rubbed and patted her down, then pressed a hand to her back. Next, he draped an arm and added some of his weight.

When she stood calmly, he backed off, and she followed. Then he lay over her back and let her walk around the pen with his feet dangling off the ground. Grimm slid off and walked away.

The horse followed, watching and waiting for her next cue.

Grimm put his belly on her back again. Then slid a leg over to straddle her. The mare wandered around the pen, and Grimm straightened, turning her with a click or a nudge in the way he wanted her to go.

Finally, horse and rider stopped in front of Finn. By this time, they'd attracted a crowd, who watched in silence.

"Where'd you learn that?" Finn asked.

"It's nothing but respect, sir," Grimm said, leaning down to rub the mare's neck. "I let her tell me what she's comfortable with. Anything will fight when it's cornered, but earn its trust, and a horse will follow you anywhere. I wager she'll permit a saddle in an hour."

Finn gave a low whistle. "If so… She's yours while you work for me. Can Jim do that, too?"

Tobias nearly blurted out that he could sail, track, and pick locks, but one warning glance from his brother made him change his words. "I'm told I catch on quick to most things, sir."

"Fair enough."

They were shown to their bunks, and as they stowed their gear in a locked chest, Tobias leaned in close to whisper, "Where'd you learn all that?"

"There's a lot you don't know about your family."

"Grimm—"

"Don't use that name."

"—I don't care what you did."

"I killed our father."

For once in Tobias' life, he'd run out of words.

9

BURNING WORDS

1892

NATHAN SHAW WAS USED TO NIGHTTIME DISTURBANCES, especially when they came as a knock on his surgery door. With little thought, he climbed out of bed with a murmured reassurance to his wife. A nearby family, the Ryans, were due for a baby. He dressed quickly, grabbed his doctor's bag, and headed to the back door.

The locals knew not to knock at the hotel. They all came around to the doctor's door. But when he wrenched the door open, he froze. It wasn't Mr. Ryan. Instead, a hulking shadow of a man loomed in the doorway.

"You a doctor?"

"I am," Nathan said, shifting his bag closer.

"Come with me."

"You can bring the patient into my office."

"I need you to come with me."

"Let me get my overcoat, sir."

A pistol cocked at the man's hip. "Don't move."

"There's no need for that," Nathan said. "I'm a doctor. I don't have any use for guns."

"All the same…" The man jerked his head towards the stable. Nathan wanted this man as far away from his family as he could get, so he went out into the night.

Only his son came skipping out the back door after him with the overcoat in hand. "Need me to hitch—"

The stranger was quick. Before Nathan could order his son back into the house, the man lunged for Josiah, clamping a hand over his mouth.

"It's just my son, sir," Nathan said in a low, calm voice. "He saddles my horse when I'm called out."

Josiah's eyes were wide and rolling in the dark, and every muscle in Nathan's body tensed to spring at the man, but he forced himself to breathe, to remain calm. Most men weren't vicious animals—only some. Treat a man with respect and they often responded in kind.

"Josiah can walk just fine on his own. He'll go back to the house and head straight to bed."

"This works better." With Josiah firmly in hand, the man strode past the stables towards the stream and trees outside of town.

"Please, let him go. I'll come quietly either way."

"Shut it."

The man looked like he was strong enough to snap Josiah's neck like a chicken.

When they entered the grove of trees with the babbling stream where they'd splashed and relaxed only days before, the man let Josiah go. He scrambled to his father's side, and Nathan put a protective arm around his son.

The man looked Nathan straight in the eye. "Keep quiet and you'll see your home again. Understood?" What he really said was if they cooperated, Josiah wouldn't be harmed.

"Understood," Nathan said. "I don't care who's injured. It's just my job to patch them up."

The man held out his hand. "The coat, boy."

Josiah handed it over. The man was over six feet tall, broad-shouldered, and with a flat forehead, sloped nose, and iron chin. His black hair was shaved on the sides, and he wore a small white arrow in what remained.

Considering his height and the white arrow, Nathan pegged him as a Chickasaw.

The man patted down the coat, feeling the pockets, and then tossed it to Nathan. "Put it on. The boy rides with me."

Three horses and one rider waited under the trees. The rider was a slim, nervous white man with a scruff of beard and a hand that kept straying to his holster grip.

"Told you I'd bring a doctor," the large man said as he swung onto a horse. Before Josiah could dart, he grabbed him by the collar and pulled him into the saddle in front of him.

"No self-taught doctor is going to save him," said the slim man.

"He best try."

With his son at the mercy of these men, Nathan had little choice but to climb into the remaining saddle. "I'm not self-taught," Nathan said. "I earned my doctorate from Howard University."

The large man grunted. "See."

"You think a fancy doctor knows anything about gunshot?" Slim asked.

"First, you say a self-taught one won't do. Now a university trained one won't do. We're not leaving him."

"I didn't say that—"

"You were thinking it."

Slim fell silent. And with his son in the saddle of a dangerous man, Nathan Shaw followed the gunmen into the night.

Josiah's heart thundered in his chest. Were these the same outlaws who'd attacked the Turners? There'd been four men in that gang. Were the other two at the hotel with his mother and sister?

The thought made him sick.

Why wasn't his father doing something? Fighting, struggling, screaming—*anything* other than following like some dimwitted steer.

The big man behind Josiah smelled like horses, pine, and pipe tobacco. He held the reins in front of Josiah, and since he couldn't study the man's face, he studied the man's hands: reddish-brown skin, heavily scarred, mostly around the knuckles, and the tip of his right middle finger was missing.

Josiah could feel the man behind him, along with the weapons digging into his back. He was as solid as a rock, and wore a bandolier of ammunition along with two revolvers and a bowie knife on his hip.

There was a Winchester rifle in the saddle holster.

Josiah eyed the rifle. He could pull it free and toss it to his father, or... Could he throw himself off the saddle and grab the rifle at the same time?

Josiah didn't think so—not with his captor's arm locked around his body. An idea popped into his head like a blaze of fire. "I got to pee," Josiah complained.

"Piss off the saddle, boy," the man grunted.

"I don't want to get any on your leg."

The two outlaws exchanged looks. They were in a gully of sorts, the moon high overhead. The slim man nodded and slipped off the saddle, then cinched the reins over a squat tree limb. He clambered up the side of the ravine and poked his head over the edge.

The big man nudged Josiah, who worked his leg over the

horn, but when he slipped from the saddle, he wrenched the rifle from the holster.

Only Josiah's legs were numb. When he hit the ground, they gave. Josiah rolled, coming up awkwardly with the rifle braced against his shoulder to find that the big man had drawn his revolvers—one pointed at Josiah's head and the other pointed at his father's.

"Got to cock it, boy."

Josiah froze.

"Go on," the big man said.

"Josiah, put the rifle down," his father ordered.

The slim man at the top of the slope wheezed out a laugh. "Ain't that cute. Boy got some spirit in him."

"Cock it," the big man growled.

Nathan's horse danced to the side with its rider's unease, but the big man kept his second revolver trained on the doctor. "Don't do nothing stupid, Doctor. Someone might get hurt."

Nathan tightened his grip on the reins, his eyes pleading with his son.

The rifle shook in Josiah's hands.

"Pull the lever there," the big man instructed.

Josiah worked the lever, chambering a cartridge.

"Good boy. Now point the rifle at your father."

Josiah glared up at the man. "No."

"It's you or him, boy."

Josiah's gaze flickered to his father, then back to the outlaw. He could shoot the man, but could he manage before the man got a shot off with both pistols? Why hadn't he thought this through?

Josiah swallowed. There was only one thing to do—he laid the rifle on the ground and raised his hands. "You'll have to shoot me, then."

"Rare to see loyalty, isn't it, Vito?" the big man asked the slimmer one.

"I would've shot my father."

"You'd shoot your mother, too."

"We're not all blessed with loving kin, Clay." Vito scrambled down the ravine to snatch the rifle from the ground. "Still have to piss, boy?"

Josiah nodded.

Clay jerked his head. "Go."

With shoulders slumped, Josiah turned his back on the men, but he was shaking so badly, he splashed urine all over his boots. His shoulders itched with the feel of a rifle barrel at his back.

Worst of all, he could feel his father's disapproval. When he finished buttoning up his trousers, he turned without looking at his father to take Clay's offered hand. The big man pulled him into the saddle behind him.

"Next time you try anything like that, I'll shoot your father's knees out. He doesn't need them to dig out a bullet."

As the moon rose in the night sky, all Josiah could do was cling to the outlaw in front of him and wonder how far they'd ride before they were both shot.

———

THE OUTLAW CAMP WAS WELL SITUATED IN A MAZE OF RAVINES and canyons and forested gullies. When they came to a shallow canyon cut by a stream that would swell to a river in spring, Vito gave a shrill bird call that was answered with a hoot. A figure detached itself from a dark rock and raised a rifle.

A crude corral had been fashioned at the end of an offshoot. Horses swished their tails inside, ears pricking forward at the riders' approach.

The rock walls rose, uneven and bulging, with a dark overhang at the far end. A cave of sorts. It reminded Josiah of stories his mother told him about Robin Hood and the outlaws of Sherwood Forest.

His father dismounted without permission, but no one pointed a gun at him. Vito handed over his black bag.

"Get down, boy," Clay ordered.

Josiah slipped off the saddle and nearly fell to his knees. His legs shook with fear and fatigue.

Clay tossed the reins to another man, and Josiah limped after the outlaw, trying to work feeling back into his limbs. The night was cold, with frost already sparkling in the moonlight.

Nathan glanced at his son, then firmed his jaw, and strode towards the cave with no hint of saddle fatigue. The entirety of his focus was on his future patient.

It didn't matter to Nathan Shaw—Indian, Negro, white, Mexican, outlaw or lawman—Dr. Shaw treated all sorts of people.

People are people, Nathan often told his son. It doesn't matter if they treat you like an animal. How you treat others is what matters most. No man can take away your humanity, but they can sure cheapen theirs.

Inside the cave, a wool blanket was stretched at an angle, directing the smoke of a campfire towards a crevice in the rock. Beside the campfire, a young man who wasn't much older than Josiah lay drenched in sweat and fighting for each breath.

Nathan dropped to his haunches, startling an old man tending to the younger one. Men reached for weapons, but Clay stopped them with a gesture. He was clearly the leader here—tall and imposing, with a quiet command of the others.

Nathan didn't notice the guns or the tension in the air. "I need more light," he ordered, peeling back blankets and bandages. "A pot of boiled water and clean pans."

"Already done," the old man said, kicking a large pot with his boot.

Lanterns were brought, and Josiah watched as his father

bent over his patient. The young man was long and slim, coiled with muscle, and with skin the color of baked clay. His black hair curled damply on his brow, and a jagged wound ripped through his chest. A second bullet had punched through the meat of his thigh.

Clay crouched, his hat pulled low. "My son. Wyatt."

Nathan locked eyes with their captor. "I'll treat him like my own, sir."

Clay fingered a scar under his jaw, then gave a nod. Nathan got to work.

Josiah didn't have the stomach for doctoring—not like Maddie. His little sister was just plain strange, and fascinated with the inner workings of things. But Josiah was still a better assistant than the other men there—he'd watched his father enough to know what he needed before he asked for it.

Josiah fetched water, handed over tools, and adjusted the light, all with hands as steady as his father's. As Nathan dug out two bullets, Josiah marveled at those hands—despite being large and powerful, his fingers were gentle and his movements precise.

His father always hummed when he worked, or sang under his breath. Nathan couldn't hold a tune to save his life, but he claimed it calmed his nerves; his wife claimed he did it to annoy her.

When his father finally dropped the bloody implements into a bowl of grimy water, he sat back and rolled his shoulders. For what seemed like the first time, Nathan noted his surroundings. He seemed mildly amused to find himself in a cave instead of his surgery.

Josiah cleaned the patient with a carbolic acid dilution, then his father put on a salve that smelled like honey, cloves, and something out of the back end of a cow.

Clay's brows twitched in surprise. Then he nodded, looking pleased with the salve.

Nathan was a Choctaw Freedmen. He'd been born into slavery in the Choctaw Nation, sold more times than he could remember, but after the Civil War, he'd been freed and later adopted into the tribe. He'd picked up a few things from his enslavers.

"I've done what I can. It's all up to him now," Nathan said.

"Who shot him?" Josiah asked.

Clay narrowed his eyes at the question.

"Doctors don't ask questions, son," Nathan said easily. "We just do our best to save lives."

Josiah clenched his jaw at the reply. His father never got involved with anything.

SOME HOURS LATER, WHEN THE SUN WAS CREEPING OVER THE land, Nathan stood to the side with Clay Holden, who was frowning at his sleeping son. "The salve is *alikchi* medicine."

"I learned it as a boy. Just the plants—not the prayers and rituals."

The man's voice was grave, his features expressionless, but there was a hint of amusement dancing in the back of his eyes. "Did the *iyagánasha* visit you as a child?" *Iyagánasha*—the Little People—tricksters and healers who picked children to be medicine men.

"Something like that." A kind old man had once treated his lashes and burns, then showed him how to make medicine of his own. Come to think of it, the fellow *was* short. "I'm sorry to say, but there's nothing more I can do for your son. He's on a bucking horse and he could fall to either side—you could consult a medicine man for his spirit."

"And risk the Light Horse." The Light Horse were the Nation's mounted police force. They were swift and effective regulators of justice. "You're a trained doctor, and still you believe in the rituals and prayers of *alikchi.*"

"There's a lot in the world I can't explain," Nathan said with a rueful smile. "I've seen that salve heal things no modern medicine can. And... I find the smell of burning cedar and sage to be comforting. If anything is going to purify the air of bad energies, it'll be that."

Clay grunted in amusement, then offered a hand along with his Chickasaw name. "*Nashoba itakobi.*"

Nathan took his hand. "Can't imagine you did much to earn Lazy Coyote."

"It took some effort. I owe you a debt."

"Then I ask that you let me and my son go."

Josiah was still mopping the brow of the man's son. He could hear their conversation, but he was trying his best to seem uninterested. These had to be the same men who'd held the Turners at gunpoint and hurt Mrs. Turner, and his father was shaking hands and having a friendly chat with the scoundrels. The thought made his ears burn with anger.

"You're under my protection here," Clay said. "You'll stay and care for my son until he can be moved. Save your debt for another time."

"But people will begin to wonder. It's common enough for me to be gone for a night, but any longer and the town will come looking for me."

Clay glowered in consideration. The two men were of the same height, both powerful, both as steady as they came, with eyes like flint that seemed locked in some weighty matter.

Josiah felt a strong undercurrent of emotion, but he couldn't put a name to it. Later, he'd realize Clay Holden was trying to decide whether to entrust the life of his men and son to a doctor and his word.

His father made it simpler for the outlaw. "Keep me if you must, but let Josiah go back. He'll say I was called away to a nearby ranch to treat a fever. No one will think much of that—not for more than three days or so. Plenty of time for me to tend to your son."

Josiah shot to his feet. "I won't leave without you."

"Son, this isn't the time."

"No, you can't send me away."

Nathan glanced at Clay for permission, then drew Josiah off to the side so they could converse in private.

"You do as I say," Nathan whispered urgently. "Get back to the hotel. Tell your ma what's going on, but *only* her. To everyone else, say I'm out treating a fever at an outlying ranch. You understand?"

"We can't let these men get away, Pa," he hissed. "They're the same who attacked the Turners."

"We don't know that."

"Who else could they be?"

"There are plenty of outlaws in these parts."

"We can't trust him."

Nathan gripped Josiah's shoulder so hard it hurt. "I trust him. And he'll be trusting you and me to not give him away. I don't want you here; I need you to look after your ma. Swear you won't say a word."

Josiah broke free of his father's grip as the words burned into his heart: *I don't want you here.*

JOSIAH AGREED TO LEAVE. HE HAD LITTLE CHOICE IN THE matter. His father had made it clear he didn't want him around.

So Josiah rode away with barely a backward glance at his father. The slim outlaw took him back to a road he knew when the sun was high over the hills, and by the time Josiah dismounted, he was dead on his feet, hungry, and sore in places he didn't know was possible.

Veto leaned down to take the reins. "You got lucky, boy. Clay's not a man to cross."

"There's already a posse after you lot."

"I doubt that."

Angry at himself, with his father, and this whole mess, Josiah glared at the outlaw on horseback. "The whole town knows what you did to the Turners."

Vito tightened his grip on the reins until his knuckles went white. His eyes burned into Josiah's skull and the boy stared right back. He was angry and feeling reckless.

After a long moment, Vito turned his head and spat. "You're a hothead. Tamp it down before you get yourself shot, and keep that mouth of yours shut."

Vito clucked his tongue and rode away, leaving Josiah fuming in a cloud of dust. He glared at the outlaw's back until the dust settled, then trudged back to town. It seemed the entire town was hunting the very outlaws he'd just left.

Josiah muttered a curse and kicked a stone. Their hotel was on the outskirts of town, settled in a peaceful grove with a stream and a hot water spring. A buggy was depositing two guests from the train station—his mother hired a boy to hand out pamphlets to tired travelers in need of refreshment.

Lily Shaw stepped onto the porch with a warm smile to greet her guests, but that smile faltered when she caught sight of her son trudging up the road.

Josiah shook his head and headed for the stable yard while she politely excused herself.

Lily caught him at the water pump. "Where have you been?" She was out of breath from waddling over.

Josiah drank his fill before answering. "With pa."

"And where's your pa?"

"I need food, and I think maybe you should sit down."

His mother was usually a whirlwind of energy. She could

outwork him, outwalk him, and outlast him in everything they did. But lately, he'd noticed she had to brace herself to stand up from a chair, and he'd caught her resting her head on his father's shoulder as he rubbed her lower back. She was due any day now.

Carrying a baby just looked plain miserable. Josiah was glad he wasn't a girl. He held the back door open, then pulled out a chair at the kitchen table for her. It was a testament to her discomfort that she sat heavily in the chair and let him forage for his own food.

Josiah stuffed an entire muffin in his mouth before pouring cold coffee into a cup. "You want tea?" he asked around a mouthful.

"Don't talk with your mouth open. Sit down. You look dead on your feet."

He was too beat to stay on his feet, so he sat and took a swig of coffee, and told her what happened in low tones even though Maddie was at school—where he was supposed to be. What good did school do anyone after learning to read and write? He hated everything about it.

Josiah was glad he'd had his mother sit. By the time he finished relating the details of the night, she looked ashen and was hugging her pregnant stomach.

"Oh, Lord," she breathed.

Josiah leaned close. "We have to tell the sheriff and the Light Horsemen."

Lily shook her head. "No. You and Nathan gave your word. We do as your father said."

"They'll kill him."

"They'll kill him if we talk."

"We can't just let those outlaws escape."

"There's already a posse after them. We're not letting anyone escape. We're keeping your father safe."

"What way did the posse go?"

"Towards the Turner ranch."

"I came into town the opposite way. They're hiding out in the gullies near Five Falls."

Lily shushed him with a harsh word. "You *don't* know where they are. Do you understand?"

"You and pa keep asking me that," he fumed. "Course I understand. I don't have to like it though. I don't trust them."

"Of course you shouldn't, but you gave your word that you wouldn't talk to anyone. And this Holden fellow let you go. It sounds to me, outlaw or not, that a man's word means something to him."

"I doubt that," he muttered. "And I didn't give my word—pa did."

"Then we'll keep his."

"And what if they kill him?" he demanded. "You'll have done nothing to save him."

The moment he asked, Josiah regretted it. He could see the fear in his mother's eyes, in the way she rubbed her stomach, and the quiver in that hand.

Josiah Shaw noticed a lot of things, but his tongue was too quick for his mind, and he often spoke without thinking things through first.

He wanted to unsay it, but it was too late—he'd already driven a blade of guilt into his mother's heart.

"Ma, I didn't mean—"

She used the table to stand. "Wash up, make some eggs, and get some rest."

10

TRAILHEAD

1901

"I don't believe it, Atticus. I don't believe any of it."
Sarah said, following him into the room.

"What's happened now?" Isobel asked from the bed.

Sarah paused inside the doorway. One look at her adopted
mother, and she paled, on the verge of tears. She blamed
herself for the shooting—never mind she'd saved them both.

"For God's sake, Sarah. Stop acting like I'm dead."

Jin stomped inside and threw herself into Ravenwood's
chair. "You *look* dead, *Faan tung*."

"I—" Sarah scrubbed a palm across her eyes.

"Come plump my pillows if it will make you feel better."
Sarah went over to plump the pillows, and Isobel placed a
dramatic hand over her own forehead. "I feel faint. I need a
foot rub, too."

Jin threw a cushion at Isobel. "She will do it."

"Yes, I know," Isobel said, throwing the cushion back with
her left hand. Only the movement made her wince and the
cushion barely cleared the bed.

Jin snorted at her mother.

"If Sarah insists on moping about saving my life, I might as well take advantage of it. It's not like I'll get sympathy from you."

"You do not like sympathy," Jin pointed out.

She ignored that observation, and since Sarah was in no mood for humor, Isobel gestured the girl to sit beside her on the bed. "What did I miss?"

Riot told her about their visit with the U.S. Marshals.

"And I was worried what the Whites—the Shaws—would think of *my* past," Isobel muttered.

"Grimm wouldn't kill someone," Sarah insisted.

"Maybe he had good reason," Isobel said. She could think of a lot of reasons to shoot a man.

"Maybe it was revenge," Jin said. In her mind, that was reason enough. "Or the marshals are lying."

"I don't remember hearing about the Holden Gang—where'd they operate out of?" Isobel asked, looking at her husband.

Riot was sitting in his usual armchair, absently rubbing at the scar along his temple. "Clay 'Lazy Coyote' Holden was the leader—a Chickasaw in Indian Territory. Train robberies, banks, and… other crimes." He avoided looking at his daughters to give his wife a weighty look. "They were a bad sort, but they weren't limited to Indian Territory. The area makes for a convenient place to lie low."

"Hard to imagine Miss Lily running with an outlaw gang," Isobel said. Even her imagination failed to place the graceful and cultured woman living rough with a gang on the run.

"Maybe it was only Grimm," Riot said.

"Their father, maybe?" Jin asked. "What do we know about him?"

"Next to nothing."

"He was a doctor," Isobel said. "So Maddie claimed. She said he died, and seemed uncomfortable about the subject."

"Well, her father died," Sarah defended. "That's bound to make anyone uncomfortable."

"Miss Lily told me she was from Nantucket," Riot added.

"We don't even know if she was married," Isobel mused. "Or if all three children share the same father."

Sarah made a disapproving noise. "That's horrible to say. Of course Miss Lily was married."

"Did she ever mention her husband to you?" Riot asked.

Sarah's mouth worked. "No. Never mind…"

"It's all right, Sarah. What's your reasoning?"

"It's naïve."

"Your impressions matter to us," Riot insisted.

Sarah blushed. With her black curls and freckled skin, the rising pink in her cheeks had a charming affect. "It's only Miss Lily is religious. She was always reading her bible, and even though they didn't attend church, morals mattered to her. I just can't picture her having children out of wedlock. Maybe one… but three?"

"They were hiding from U.S. Marshals," Isobel pointed out. "Miss Lily likely had several stories and identities."

"This isn't right! We can't talk about them like this…" Tears rolled down Sarah's cheeks, and she quickly swiped them away.

"I'm only playing devil's advocate," Isobel explained, placing a hand on the girl's arm. "Your instincts are likely correct."

Isobel shared a look with Riot from across the room.

Before the business with Frederick Starling, who'd held a gun to Sarah's head, the girl had weathered the past year (along with her uncle's murder) admirably. But lately, Sarah's emotions had been swinging from numb silence to anger to tears.

Jin frowned at her silently weeping sister, and Riot got up to hand Sarah a handkerchief. "I'll sort it out, Sarah. I need you to stay with Isobel and help her, all right?"

The girl nodded as she pressed the linen to her face.

"Do either of you recall anything else about the family? Something Tobias or Maddie might have told you?" he asked.

Jin narrowed her eyes. "The first time Grimm spoke in class, it was during Hamlet. He said, 'Revenge is like a poison. It does not leave room to love. It eats a man.' He knew how to fight, too, when he helped me with the men in Chinatown."

The girl shifted at this. She'd stabbed a bully in the foot, but neither of her parents brought that up now.

Isobel added another morsel of knowledge. "Maddie told me their mother was as sick as a dog after Tobias was born, and that she and Grimm were left to care for their baby brother."

"And there was that story about Tobias and the flour," Sarah said, her voice muffled by the handkerchief and tears. "Miss Lily put him inside with the sheep afterwards."

All things considered, they knew very little about the family they'd shared a roof with for the past year. But Miss Lily had wanted it that way and they'd been respectful of her privacy.

Riot didn't mention the name of Miss Lily's business partner and friend—a Miss Vivian Leigh, or her acquaintance with Mrs. Mary Ellen Pleasant. Those were solid leads, and he wasn't about to share that information with his daughters when U.S. Marshals were sniffing about.

By the look in Isobel's eyes, she was thinking the same. "Riot," she said suddenly. "The warrants were issued for a Katherine and Josiah *Shaw*. Assuming those names are real instead of another pseudonym, have you ever questioned Tim about how he came to hire Miss Lily?"

Isobel's suggestive question knocked loose a stubborn penny in his head. He could've slapped himself.

Ravenwood had employed a housekeeper who'd been murdered the same day as her employer. A Mrs. Eleanor Shaw. The seventy-year-old woman was a few shades lighter, but she'd hailed from the East Coast.

"I'm daft," he said.

"Or I'm just incredibly brilliant."

"You are," he agreed. "Shaw is a common name, though."

"Still... We both abhor coincidence."

Riot bent to kiss the quirk on her lips. "Do you need anything before I go?"

"Some new ribs would be lovely."

11

A CROOKED SHADOW

Atticus Riot was being followed. He usually was. His shadow was getting better. When he stopped to clean his spectacles, his shadow anticipated the feint and stepped into a doorway.

He hopped on the Union Street cable car and stood on the running board to watch his shadow dart from cover to leap onto the back.

Riot checked his watch. He had a bit of time, so he decided to put the shadow to the test. He stepped off the running board, strolled down a street, and walked into a general store, where he purchased some mints. Then he strolled out the back, down a lane, and hailed a hack.

He spotted his shadow on a street corner amid a group of newsboys of similar height. The child broke off from the group and hopped on a wagon headed in the same direction.

When the hack stopped for a hay wagon, he stepped down and boarded another cable car. Confident he'd shaken his tail, but sure she'd guess where he was going, he walked the remaining four blocks to Ravenwood Agency to find Sao Jin leaning against a lamppost with her arms crossed.

"When did you spot me?" the girl asked.

"When I left the house."

She fell in step beside him. "You knew I would follow."

"I suspected you might."

Jin sighed, and kicked at a can.

"You're getting better."

"Not good enough."

Riot raised a brow at this. "Are you planning on making a profession of it?"

Jin shrugged. "I am practicing things."

"Don't you have school?"

"Miss Dupree is on holiday."

"Is she?"

Jin looked sharply up at him. "I am sure she told you. She went to visit her family down south where it is warmer."

Riot tapped a finger on his walking stick. "Probably so." With Isobel recovering, the schoolteacher gone, and the household in chaos, he was even more reluctant to leave his responsibilities at home.

"What other things are you practicing while Miss Dupree is gone?"

Instead of answering, Jin waved her cap at the Ravenwood Agency, her ink-black braids slithering down her back. "I do not think the residents of the street like your agency."

Riot eyed the whitewashed brick building. Its windows were tinted, the trim was black, and the name was in gold lettering. The front of the building had been defaced with mud (or worse) and various slurs, incorrectly spelled. There was a smoke stain, too.

"It's not my agency anymore," he said cheerfully. "What do you think of the changes Lotario made?"

"If you stand straight, do not fear a crooked shadow," Jin quoted in Cantonese.

Riot gave a slight nod. "I do wonder if he might have done it on purpose."

"It is bold," she agreed.

Riot opened the door for her, and they stepped inside the agency to find the foyer locked down. Bars had been pulled down to the counter, and the reinforced oak door leading to the back offices was currently being battered by two greasy, red-faced men shouting obscenities.

"Is the agency closed, gentlemen?"

The two spun, cudgels in hand, and glared at the cut of his suit.

"You'll want to be leaving. This agency is closed for business."

"You seem to be locked out, too."

"We don't work here. We're closing it down."

The man slapped his cudgel against a palm. Riot shifted slightly, moving Jin to the side with a hand before she could step beside him in a show of unity.

"And just who sent you?"

"None of your business."

"Perhaps the owner would like a word with your employer."

"This is our turf, and we won't stand for you lot messing about."

"I'll pass that along to Spanish Kitty," Riot said, giving his stick a skilled twirl.

The men sobered. "This ain't her turf," one insisted.

Riot nudged his brim up with the knob of his stick and eyed the pair. "Are you sure about that?"

The pair exchanged glances. Riot appeared relaxed, but he watched their eyes—the eyes were always the first tell, a catalyst for action that few had the discipline to mask.

One man pointed his cudgel at Riot. "There's a bunch of

yellow-bellied bastards up in here. So maybe we'll make an example of you."

The pair took a step forward.

"I'd wager they settled in for a nap while waiting for their enforcers to arrive."

"And just who might that be?"

Riot wagered correctly. He generally did. A hulking shadow filled the doorway—a keg-like man with no neck and bulging muscles that stretched his suspenders. Lotario's bodyguard, Bruno, had several large cousins.

"Meet Mr. Flinch."

Flinch bared his white teeth.

"They were just leaving," Riot explained, shifting his coat to display a pistol grip protruding from his shoulder holster. "With a promise to clean up the graffiti. Isn't that right, gentlemen?"

"I brought the brooms and whitewash," Flinch rumbled.

The pair spat on the polished wood, and rushed out. Flinch watched them go, then looked to Riot. "Does Mr. Lotario want them to clean it up?"

"No, Mr. Flinch, it's all right," drawled a voice from behind the counter. "Splendid timing."

"You mean you didn't ring for help?" Riot asked.

Lotario pushed up the bars, sliding them back into their concealed ceiling slot. "Why bother? It's not like they brought dynamite. Would you and your workers like a drink first, Mr. Flinch?"

Flinch shook his head. "After." He tipped his cap, and walked back outside.

The oak door opened, revealing a young woman with black curls and pink cheeks. "Good morning, Mr. Riot," she said, giving him a charming smile.

He removed his hat. "Miss Reed." Her blue eyes flickered to the glaring child at his side. "This is my daughter Sao Jin."

Daisy blinked and took a second look at the child—over-sized cap, rough peacoat, and trousers. Then another surprise: finely arched brows, monolid, wide-set eyes that shone with a fierce intelligence, and deep knife scars on her cheek and jawline.

Daisy doubted the girl missed anything.

"Good God, you glare like Bel," Lotario noted as they walked into the back offices.

Jin ignored his observation. "Who is Spanish Kitty?"

"Is this really her turf?" Daisy asked.

"One of AJ's admirers," Tim said. The old man was leaning back in a chair, smoking his pipe.

"One?" Garrett asked. "I dread to meet the others."

Jin eyed the new agent as he stood to tip an imaginary hat. Though not at all well-traveled, Jin thought she heard a French accent lacing his words. His voice reminded her of Sarah's, but Jin did not know if he was from Tennessee or some other state where people drawled out their words like slow dripping honey.

"One of a long line of women who'd like to carve out a piece of my flesh," Riot explained dryly. "Were those two friends of yours?"

Lotario waved a languid hand. "Local hoodlums. I was curious to see what they'd do once we locked down the foyer."

"Weren't you worried they'd ransack it?"

"Not especially," Lotario said. "It gives us the appearance of fighting dark forces."

Garrett nudged a newspaper towards Riot, and Jin read the headline over his shoulder: Detective Agency Takes A Stand—Rich or Poor, No Criminal is Spared.

"This also paints a target on your back," Riot pointed out.

"Yes."

Of course, Lotario was aware of that—he was Isobel's twin brother. Both were cunning and fiercely intelligent, though Isobel came across as a razor-sharp blade and Lotario as a carefree layabout. But unlike his sister, Lotario Amsel was an enigma to Riot. The young man was not only an extraordinary actor—he lived the roles he slipped into. Riot could only hope Lotario shared his sister's incorruptible sense of justice.

"I've had to turn away cases."

"We need more agents," Tim grunted.

"Speaking of agents... how is my sister?"

"She looks dead," Jin said bluntly.

"How reassuring."

"I'm afraid I can't return to work yet," Riot said.

"Bel is still recovering—I wouldn't allow you to work."

Riot leveled a steady gaze on his brother-in-law. "I'll be sure to submit a formal request for your approval when I'm ready to return."

"Make sure to dot your i's and splash a little cologne on it," Lotario said, studying his fingernails with an air of indifference.

"Bel's health aside, there's another pressing matter I have to attend to—a pair of U.S. Marshals dropped by the house."

Now that he had their attention, Riot told them about the surprise visit.

It was Garrett who gave a low whistle at the end. "Angel Davren."

"You know him?" Riot asked.

"By reputation," Garrett said. "Him and his partner always get their man—usually sainted."

The first name triggered a memory. "The Angel of Death."

"That's the one."

"And yet a woman and her children have stayed one step ahead of them for eight years," Lotario pointed out.

"They might've been busy hunting the rest of the gang," Tim said. "If I recall, their leader was Clay Holden—a Chickasaw. They hit banks, trains, and raped and murdered their way across a mix of states."

"Which makes it even stranger Sam Batten didn't turn Grimm in right away," Riot noted.

Tim scratched at his bushy white beard. "Everything about that mess with Carson and Batten was odd. Do you think Miss Lily knows where other gang members are holed up?"

"No idea."

"Who issued the warrant?" Tim asked.

"Judge Isaac Charles Parker."

Tim scowled at his boots, Lotario poked at some papers on a desk, and Garrett twirled his mustache.

"Who is that man?" Jin asked.

"He's known as the Hanging Judge," Riot explained.

Jin scowled. "You know the paper is wrong," she insisted. "You cannot trust police or these U.S. Marshals. Why would Miss Lily run with a gang?"

"It might not have been her choice," Daisy said. "Most women don't get much say in matters."

"So we will find them and clear them of the charges."

To Jin, it was straightforward; in reality, it was more complicated than that.

"What were you doing back here while those two hoodlums were banging on your door?" Riot asked Lotario.

It was an abrupt change of subject, but Lotario got his hint. "Playing billiards."

"What is billiards?" Jin asked.

"You don't know?"

The girl shook her head.

"Probably for the best. A lady shouldn't play."

Daisy caught on, too. "Only because I always beat you square."

"You do not," Lotario defended.

"I bet Miss Jin would too."

Lotario glanced at his fingernails. "Doubtful."

Jin frowned at the pair. "You are trying to lure me away from bahba."

"Now she's a perceptive one," Garrett said.

"Like her mother," Riot said. "Jin, I need to speak with Tim."

"And I'm going to beat your uncle senseless," Daisy said, sauntering out of the office.

"While we ruminate over a case," Lotario said.

Garrett stood and straightened his cuffs. "I'll wager on the lady."

Jin watched the trio leave, then turned to her father. "You will not leave without me."

"I'll let you know."

"Promise."

"For today."

Jin stomped from the room to see what could captivate three adults so thoroughly.

Tim fell into a chair at a desk, and took out his tobacco and pipe, while Riot pulled over a second chair and took out his cards.

"Miss Lily told me I might not like what I find if I started poking around their affairs," Riot said. "And even as careful as I am, I could end up leaving a trail for the marshals."

Tim was shaking his head. "You're not going anywhere, AJ. I'll sort it out. You have a family—"

"They're family, too."

"And if you stick your nose in it, you'll have a warrant on your head, too."

"What about your stubborn head?" Riot asked.

"I'm old," Tim snorted. "I can either die in a bed or go out fighting on my feet. You have responsibilities now."

Riot ignored the statement. "How'd you come to hire Miss Lily?"

"She showed up at the house not long after you left. She was looking for Mrs. Shaw. The kids and her looked half-starved and their coats were threadbare. I didn't want to tell her Mrs. Shaw was murdered. But I did. It hit her hard."

Riot frowned at a thought. That was close to four years ago. Tobias must've been four. What had the years before Ravenwood Manor been like for a family on the run? It must have seemed like a haven.

"I knew they'd have a tough time of it in San Francisco, so I asked if they were in need of work. They cleaned up the mess of the murder. Then I got to thinking... I have this big house. So I asked her if she'd keep it for me. Miss Lily came to me later with the idea of running a lodging house. That woman doesn't know the meaning of idle."

"Did she say anything about how she knew Mrs. Shaw?"

Tim sucked on his pipe as he dredged up the memory from near to eight decades of them. "I believe she said Mrs. Shaw was a friend of her husband's."

With the same last name. Only Mrs. Shaw was a seventy-year-old white woman. Riot did not know what Miss Lily's husband looked like, or if the children shared the same father, but it only took a generation or two to change the color of a family's skin. Riot's own half sister was Chinese and white, while he was some mix of white, Spanish, Indian, or any number of combinations.

It was also possible that Miss Lily's explanation was a fabrication. How often had he and Isobel obscured their identities during an investigation?

"Do you have any contacts in Indian Territory?"

Tim shook his head. The pair of them mostly had kept to the west side of the Rockies. "But Garrett might."

"Can we trust him with this?"

Daisy Reed and... Garrett... (Riot didn't even know his full name) were new to the agency. Both hired by the agency's new owner, Lotario Amsel.

"I don't know much about the man," Tim admitted. "But I get the feeling he wouldn't toss in with U.S. Marshals just because they wear a badge."

Riot had to agree.

"I'll have my eyes and ears sniff around a bit. See what we come up with."

Tim had an extensive network of informants. Most of which didn't even realize they were informing. The old man had a way with people.

"I'll send a wire to her business partner." Riot didn't expect much from that end of things. "And question Mrs. Pleasant."

"One thing you might find interesting... Sam Batten is still in the City."

That *was* surprising. "Liam Taft, too?"

Tim shook his head. "He headed back to Oregon with his wife. I don't like it. None of it."

"If the warrant weren't eight years old, I'd say whoever was behind the fake Pinkerton organization drummed up charges to get Grimm out of the way."

"Grimm was a witness to Sam shooting Carson," Tim mused. "It's Sam's word against Grimm's."

"No, it's a white Pinkerton's word against a Negro man," Riot corrected. "We both know how Grimm's testimony would hold up in court."

"Either way, Carson being silenced was convenient."

"One problem at a time," Riot said, more for his own benefit, as he squared his deck.

"They're lining up, aren't they?"

"Don't they always?"

"Makes life interesting."

12

FOUR HORSEMEN

1892

JOSIAH SHAW WATCHED FOUR RIDERS APPROACH. HIS EYES WERE drawn to a white horse carrying a heroic rider. The horse was beautiful. There was no other word for it. It glistened like snow and its body rippled with power and grace.

The rider was also striking. His skin was coal black, and his gaze took in everything. The pearl buttons on his reefer jacket glinted in the sun. He wore a wide-brimmed hat, and his trim legs were encased in tight breeches and riding boots. Two revolvers were strapped to his hips, and a badge was pinned to his chest.

Josiah gawked at the man.

The other three looked to be U.S. Marshals, too. The second man was white, with leathery skin baked from the sun, in a suit and bowler, a round star on his breast; the third had broad features and wore a round hat and duster, and wore his hair in twin black braids; and the fourth man had light brown skin and a pencil mustache, and was wearing a fine coat and a fine vest with a gold watch chain.

They stopped in front of the hotel, and Josiah loped down the steps to greet them. "You looking for a place to bed down? Best grub in town."

"We are," said the fourth man as he checked his watch. "Do you tend the horses?"

"Yes, sir. Good hay, clean stalls. I take real good care of them."

The dapper man on the white horse raised a brow as Josiah gathered the reins from his companions.

The man with the mustache considered him. "Have you laid eyes on a big Chickasaw by the name of Clay Holden? Tall fellow, shorn hair on the sides. He wears a white arrow in it. The tip of his middle finger is missing. He might've been with a twitchy white man who can't grow a beard."

Josiah swallowed at the description. He'd seen those men all right. But he was no liar, so he just shook his head, suppressing a wince. If he didn't say it out loud, would it still be a lie?

"They trouble?" Josiah asked.

"The worst sort," said the white man.

"I'll keep my eyes open."

The white man seemed satisfied with his answer. As they turned to climb the steps into the hotel, Josiah shouted at the men's back. "You make sure and wipe those boots. My ma don't take kindly to mud on her floors."

The white man chuckled, and touched the brim of his hat as they disappeared inside, but only three men had gone inside. When Josiah led the three horses to the stables, he found the marshal inside, brushing down the white horse.

"I can do that for you."

The man shook his head. "Nevis isn't friendly."

"I'm friendly enough for the both of us. I've never met a horse that didn't like me."

"It's your life." The man handed over his brush, and took a step back.

When Josiah approached Nevis, he stomped and snorted, and jerked his head—not in fear, but in warning.

Josiah paid him no mind. "A handsome thing like you must love being brushed." He put out his hand, keeping it straight, instead of sideways, in case the horse tried to bite. It flared its nostrils, but as Josiah spoke softly to the horse, it lowered its nose to sniff his palm.

Josiah got started on the brushing, trying not to beam with the pride he felt at the man's nod of approval. "I don't know that I've ever seen four U.S. Marshals riding together. You joining up with the posse that left?"

"How many rode off?"

"Maybe close to a hundred. Are you after the gang that attacked the Turner Ranch?"

"They're a vicious lot. You watch yourself and your family."

"So how come you didn't join the posse?"

"The posse is out for blood," the man explained. "That many men and horses will ruin any trail to be found. I prefer to work with a small group. Men who can be relied on in a tight spot."

"That makes sense."

"I hear there's a doctor in town."

"My pa. He's away on a call."

"Where?"

"A ranch."

"Which ranch?"

Josiah twitched in surprise. What was he supposed to say? He wasn't supposed to lie—the outlaws had horses in their camp, so maybe it was a ranch, but what name should he give?

"Some fellow's son got shot," Josiah finally said with a

shrug, then changed the subject, hoping to distract the man. "Is someone in need of doctoring?"

The man watched Josiah with a gleam in his eyes. "What's your name, boy?"

"Josiah Shaw."

"Deputy U.S. Marshal Angel Davren." He offered a hand, and Josiah turned to shake it, meeting his eye. He was proud that he was able to return the handshake with a firm one of his own. "It's a real shame about those outlaws lurking around. A man like you can't be too careful with womenfolk to guard."

Josiah felt a heap taller at the words 'a man like you.' With his father gone, he was responsible for his mother and Maddie. "Hard to protect them without a gun. My pa won't let me near them. He says they're only good for one thing."

"He won't even let you have a rifle?" Angel asked.

"We have one for hunting, but I've never shot one."

Angel clucked his tongue. "Every man should know how to shoot a gun. How about I teach you?"

Josiah perked up. His father was gone. There'd be no one to say anything to the contrary (unless his mother looked up from her hotel). "I'm a quick learner, sir."

"I bet you are, Josiah."

"How long will you gentlemen be staying?" Lily asked the three marshals.

Eli Blake rubbed a hand over his chin. "Don't rightly know, ma'am. We're looking for a bath and a shave at the moment."

"And good food," his partner said. He'd introduced himself as Gil Blake, and although he had a tinge of brown to his skin, she thought the shared last name with the sun-baked white man wasn't a coincidence. The two could easily be brothers.

The third marshal with the twin braids had given his name as Jack Ebbs.

Lily smiled. "You'll find it all here."

"I hear there's a doctor in residence," Eli said.

"That'll be my husband. Are you in need of doctoring?"

"Not as yet. Has Mr. Shaw tended any gunshots lately?"

"At least once a week in this territory," she said easily.

"We'd like to speak with your husband."

"He's away on a call."

A porter showed the men to their rooms, and Lily went about her rounds in the dining room, checking on her patrons, but her mind wasn't on the task—her thoughts kept straying back to the lawmen. Four U.S. Marshals under her roof should've been a comfort, especially with a gang of outlaws attacking women. But something about the men raised her hackles.

It didn't help that they were asking after her husband.

———

"HE'S NOT BACK. HE SAID THREE DAYS," JOSIAH HISSED.

Lily straightened from the oven to look at her son. "We have to be patient. He'll come home."

"He could be out there. Shot. Bleeding..."

Lily gave Josiah a look he knew well. It said 'that's enough'. He was on the verge of arguing with her when Mrs. Rose walked in and he received another look he knew well—one that turned his tongue to lead.

Josiah slapped a fist on the counter and shoved open the door, letting it bang shut as he stormed out.

Lily bit her tongue.

"Marshal Blake is asking for you in the dining room," Mrs. Rose said. "They'd like some more coffee."

"Have they given you any trouble?" she asked.

Mrs. Rose shook her head. "Polite, but…"

"There's something there."

Mrs. Rose nodded. "It's a veneer."

"Like a dog on a leash," Lily muttered, cinching her apron over her swollen belly. The last three weeks were always the most difficult in a pregnancy. By the time the water burst and pangs began, she'd welcome the contractions and the messy pain that came with birthing a baby.

Eli Blake had his boots on a table in the hotel's dining room while he smoked a cigar. It was something Lily didn't tolerate, but he was a white U.S. Marshal and she had little choice. His brother Gil sat at the table watching the other patrons. He turned his eye on her when she waddled in, but didn't rise to take the coffeepot from her.

"When is that husband of yours returning, Mrs. Shaw?" Eli asked.

"I suspect soon."

"What's the name of that ranch he was called away to?"

"There's a barber in town if you need any teeth removed. He tends minor injuries, too."

"I prefer a learned doctor."

Lily studied Eli out of the corner of her eye as she refilled their coffees. She hadn't noticed any obvious illness in the man, or injury, aside from a limp, but she decided to play dumb. "Have you tried soaking in the hot spring? Guests come clear from New York to soak in our springs. Most find it rejuvenating."

"I'm sure they do," Eli said.

Gil gave her a smile. "Heaps of things can be rejuvenating."

The brothers laughed, but then Eli sobered and the look he gave Lily turned her blood to ice. "Which is why I find it odd that a man would leave a woman in your condition to run his hotel all by herself."

At his condescending tone, Lily stifled an urge to upend the coffeepot over the man's head. This was *her* hotel. She could run it just fine in her condition. But men like Eli Blake didn't much care for women like her, so she kept her voice sweet and her answer vague. "Other folks need tending, too."

This time of day, the dining room was empty. Most of her guests had moved on with the morning train. Those that remained were soaking in the mineral spring, and her regular diners (she ran the best restaurant in town) weren't due for another two hours. The only other diner there was a semipermanent guest, a painfully shy writer by the name of Mr. Mudd. He was hunched at his table in the corner, writing on a notepad and oblivious to the world around him.

Tomorrow's train would unload a heap of new guests, and she'd welcome the influx of travelers for more than just the income—Lily didn't find these U.S. Marshals comforting in the least.

"Is there any word on the posse that went after those outlaws?" Lily asked.

"No word, but I hope to hear something soon enough."

"I hope they're caught soon. If you gentlemen need anything—" She smoothed her skirts and made to leave, but Gil slammed his boot on a nearby chair, blocking her path. "What ranch was your husband called out to? No one seems to know."

"My husband was at the Turner ranch," she explained. "He was hardly home before he was called away in the middle of the night. I have a hotel to run. I have no time to keep track of my husband."

"How do you know it was a ranch, then?" Gil asked.

Lily raised her brows. "If he was in town, I'd know, sir. He's mostly called away to one ranch or another."

Gil glanced at his brother, then dropped his foot to the

floor, but Lily raised her chin and took the long way to the kitchen door.

Pop!

Josiah's arm jerked from the recoil, but he held his ground and kept the gun from hitting him in the head.

"Nice shot," Angel said. "Get that hammer cocked quick."

Josiah cocked the revolver, aimed, then fired. The edge of the post splintered. Still too far from the tin can.

"You'll get it, son," Angel said. "Relax when you shoot. Don't hold your breath. Focus on the sight, not the target."

The marshal made adjustments to Josiah's stance and repositioned his hands. "Try it now."

This time, the bullet pinged the tin can, knocking it off the post. Josiah gave a whoop of triumph and stood a little straighter under Angel's approving gaze.

"You're a natural. I can't believe your father didn't teach you to shoot. I'm surprised you didn't join the posse."

"I tried," Josiah bit out. "But my pa wouldn't hear it." He cocked the hammer and narrowed his eyes on the next tin can. Anger focused his senses and burned his ears.

Pop, pop, pop, in a quick succession that bounced the can with every trigger pull. "They're never going to catch that gang, anyway."

"You sound certain of that," Angel said.

Josiah pulled the trigger. *Click.* The chambers were empty. *Click, click, click.* The can was no longer there—all Josiah saw was Clay Holden's head. He should've shot him when he'd had the chance. He'd gotten the drop on an outlaw, but he'd hesitated—

Why the devil had he hesitated?

Josiah could have shot Clay, then Vito—the very same men

who'd attacked Mrs. Turner. He could've rescued his father, but he hadn't. And in all likelihood, they'd killed his father and dumped him in a ditch. All because Josiah Shaw hadn't had the guts to shoot a man.

But Josiah still had a choice—he could save his father. This time, he wouldn't hesitate. Clenching his jaw, he looked up at Angel. "Because the posse went off in the wrong direction."

13

A PRIVATE AUDIENCE

1901

SAY ONE THING FOR LOTARIO AMSEL—HE PLANNED FOR THE worst. What his twin sister had in recklessness, he made up for with paranoia. The newly built and designed secret entrance to Ravenwood Agency spit Riot and Jin onto the sidewalk of a different street. The door looked like an entrance to an apartment. And he supposed it was—Lotario had purchased an adjacent building as well.

Riot tried not to think about how the young man had earned his fortune. Or how much he'd invested and was set to lose if the agency failed.

"Why would Lotario place a billiards table in a detective agency?" Jin asked as they strolled towards a cable car connection.

"Lotario isn't exactly…" Riot searched for a word, but like his sister, Lotario Amsel was hard to pin with a single word—the pair were chameleons.

"Practical?" Jin asked.

She'd been reading the dictionary of late and was trying

out larger words, but the girl still had a grudge against contractions.

"I wouldn't say that."

Lotario had a hard grasp on reality.

"More that he likes his fun."

"I do not understand billiards."

"It's a game of skill."

Jin made a frustrated sound. "You hit balls with sticks. There is no skill."

"It's all about aim and trajectory—not unlike shooting a gun."

"Are you a good shot?"

"I hit what I aim at," he said, tapping his spectacles. "As long as I can see it."

Riot hopped onto a cable car headed towards the ferry building, and Jin followed suit. "Have you been keeping an eye out for tails?" he murmured in her ear.

She looked surprised. "Is someone following us?"

"Are they?"

The girl blushed slightly. "I was thinking about billiards."

"If you're going to follow me about, you might as well learn the trade."

Jin perked up at this. "You will teach me?"

"I'm not the Great Detective, but I have some tricks up my sleeve."

"Have you met Sherlock Holmes?"

"I have."

She narrowed her eyes. "You are now 'pulling my leg.' Isobel said he is not real."

"You asked."

"Is he real?"

Riot inclined his head.

Jin frowned, then made a frustrated noise in the back of her throat. "I cannot tell when you are lying."

"I never lie," he drawled. "Have you been watching for followers?"

"Yes."

"How many people are riding this cable car?"

"Eighteen."

"Describe them without looking."

Jin gawked at him for a moment. Then closed her eyes and did as he asked. She got half right.

"How many boarded at the last stop?"

Riot wasn't surprised when the girl answered. Sao Jin had a remarkable memory. Like himself. He corrected what she got wrong, then added details of his own.

She shadowed him as he stepped off the runner, walked across the street to board another cable car, and stepped off a block later.

"There is one drawback to teaching you all this," he said as they walked.

"I will know your tricks."

And he didn't hold back as they made their way to Webster Street. How to spot a tail, how to shake one, and above all, to always be alert and assume someone is following. It was easy to spot an amateur. It was difficult to catch someone who knew what he was about, which was usually the more dangerous kind.

"Above all, trust your instincts," he said at last. "Don't ignore a feeling of being watched."

"I know that feeling," Jin said.

Riot studied his daughter, his heart twisting at a life she'd never get back and the harsh truths she'd learned at an early age.

He'd learned those same truths at her age.

"Do you think we are being followed?" Jin finally asked.

"I think there's a possibility the U.S. Marshals will keep an eye on me and others of the household."

"But you are acting suspicious by shaking your tail."

Riot's lips twitched in a smile. "That's why we're going about it in a casual way."

"Did you spot someone I missed?"

Riot shook his head. "It never hurts to be cautious."

"Where are we going?" Jin asked.

"To speak with someone who knows Miss Lily."

"You mean someone who knows Mrs. Shaw."

"I'm hoping."

They entered an apartment building lobby on Webster. The doorman took Riot's card and rang the apartment. There was a chance they'd be turned away, but if the lady of the house did not wish to speak with him, he doubted she'd be any likelier to under false pretensions.

To his relief, they were granted an audience.

A uniformed boy snapped to attention when Riot stepped into the elevator, but Jin didn't follow. He turned to find her standing stiffly outside, her gaze fixed on the cramped lift and cage door. She looked set to bolt.

The boy at the controls puffed out his chest. "It's an elevator, Miss. They're perfectly safe. I ride it all day long."

"We'll take the stairs," Riot offered, but before he could step outside, Jin darted to his side. She jerked as the cage door banged shut.

"What floor, sir?"

"Fourth."

Nearly a year ago, Riot and Isobel had encountered a girl on the sand dunes, full of rage, pain, and terror. Sao Jin's birth parents had been butchered in front of her, and she'd been taken as a house slave. In the years that followed, and she'd been cut and beaten, and locked into small, dark spaces as punishment.

A year before, the girl would not have permitted Riot to take her hand—she would've lashed out with a blade. But now, having earned her trust, she clung to his hand and pressed against his overcoat. Her palm was cold with sweat, and she was trembling from head to foot.

The elevator stopped, the bellhop wrenched open the cage door, and Jin bolted into the hallway. Riot handed the boy a coin.

"Thank you, sir. See, all safe."

Jin glared at the boy, who quickly stepped back inside his elevator and shut the door.

"I was not scared," she said to Riot.

"Only stuck in the past."

Jin wiped a hand irritably against her trousers. "How do I get unstuck?"

Riot gave her shoulder a gentle squeeze. "If you find out, let me know."

———

THE RESIDENTIAL BUILDING WAS NOT MADE UP OF SINGLE ROOM apartments like the Sapphire House—these were large, multi-room residences with carpeted hallways and electric lights.

A maid in a crisp uniform opened the door. "Mr. Riot," she said. "Mrs. Pleasant will see you."

They were shown into a comfortable sitting room that over-looked a sea of rooftops and streets. It was furnished in a style of two decades before: dark, ornamental furniture covered in luxurious fabrics, and figurines, plants, and knickknacks on every surface.

A cozy fire smoldered in the hearth.

Jin stepped over to study the framed photographs.

Some minutes later, a stately woman hobbled in on the arm of her maid. She had black hair, light brown skin, and despite some ninety years, her eyes were sharp and shone with intelligence. She missed nothing—including the Chinese child in her sitting room.

A tightening of her hand on the cane betrayed her surprise.

Riot offered the woman a slight bow. "Mrs. Pleasant. Thank you for seeing us."

"And just who is 'us'?" she asked.

"Atticus Riot. My daughter Sao Jin."

Mrs. Pleasant remained on her feet to offer Riot a hand. "I knew your partner, Zephaniah Ravenwood."

Riot grasped her hand lightly. "I'm sure he made himself known."

"We didn't see eye to eye."

"I don't know anyone who ever agreed fully with Ravenwood—myself included."

Mrs. Pleasant gave a dry laugh as her maid helped her into a chair. "I'd offer you refreshment, but I'm well past the age of concerning myself with social niceties or the comfort of uninvited guests."

"Then I'll get straight to the point of my visit."

Mrs. Pleasant rested her elbows on the armchair and interlaced her fingers. "You're after my secrets. Your partner always was, too. I never gave him anything."

Riot cocked his head. "This isn't business."

"Not one of your investigations?"

"I think you know what it's about."

"That's presumptuous of you."

"We both have public reputations, Mrs. Pleasant. Some good. Some bad. Most of it is complete fabrication, but there's always a morsel of truth hidden in rumors."

Mrs. Pleasant was no stranger to the cutting tongue of scandal. A rumored millionaire, she'd built and lived in a thirty-room mansion with the family of her business partner, Thomas Bell. But when he died, his wife claimed Mrs. Pleasant had stolen a great deal of money. Ownership of the mansion was transferred to Mrs. Bell, and Mrs. Pleasant was currently mired in a legal crusade to reclaim her fortune, though the legal system didn't much care for the color of her skin.

"And what morsel is truth? That I'm a voodoo priestess cursing folks on Nob Hill? Or that I manipulate poor businessmen into handing me their hard-earned cash?" Mrs. Pleasant asked.

Jin raised her brows at the mention of a voodoo priestess.

"I'm only interested in the rumor that you have a long history of helping women of every color find safety and work in the City."

"And did you bring along a Chinese girl to win my trust?"

"Regardless of any order I give, my daughter generally does what she pleases."

"I would have followed," Jin agreed.

Mrs. Pleasant focused on the child. "Come closer, Miss Jin."

Jin scowled at the woman. "Why?"

Mrs. Pleasant raised her brows. "Because I asked you to."

"That is not a reason."

Jin looked sharply up at Riot when he cleared his throat.

"My eyes aren't what they used to be," Mrs. Pleasant explained. "I'd like to have a look at you."

Jin thought about her reason for a moment, then stepped closer to the old woman. Mrs. Pleasant frowned at the child's scarred face. "You've had a time of it, haven't you?"

Mrs. Pleasant reached for Jin's hand, but the girl pulled away and backed into Riot, who placed his hands on her shoulders in comfort.

"Why did you follow your father, Miss Jin?"

"The Shaw family needs help."

Mrs. Pleasant considered her a moment longer, then

nodded to her maid. When the maid left, she said, "You may both sit."

Riot waited for Jin to choose a chair, then sat down beside her on the settee.

"You're not the first whose come looking for Mrs. Shaw and her kin," Mrs. Pleasant said.

"Have the U.S. Marshals visited yet?"

"Singular," she corrected. "A smooth-tongued man by the name of Angel Davren. I think he intended to butter me up."

"How did he know you were friends with Mrs. Shaw?"

"I don't have friends, Mr. Riot."

"How'd he know to consult you, then?"

"Why did you come to consult me?"

"You advised Mrs. Shaw on a business matter not long ago."

"I also advised her not to trust you."

"Understandable," Riot said. "Considering your own experience."

Mrs. Pleasant raised a brow. "Do you presume to know my business?"

"I've followed the court cases. You're no longer in your mansion, so that part at least must be true."

"Mmm." She folded her hands in her lap and sat back. "What did Mrs. Shaw decide to do with my advice?"

"She chose to trust me."

"That didn't turn out well for her," Mrs. Pleasant noted. "She's on the run and you're here."

"She was on the run before I ever met her."

"And just what is your goal?"

"To help her."

"I think Mrs. Shaw has done just fine on her own. In my experience, well-meaning men with guns tend to complicate things."

"Her son, Tobias, carved a message on a wall in his fort.

He asked for my help. It goes against everything I am to ignore a plea from a child."

"So you claim."

Jin stiffened and clenched her fists on the verge of leaping to his defense, but Riot put a hand on her arm. "I know they took a ferry to Sausalito. Then one to Oakland. I know they bought tickets for Texas, only to board a train for Los Angeles. They're trying to obscure their trail, but sooner or later they'll be caught."

Tim had had a time tracing their movements. But when the family boarded the train to Los Angeles, he'd lost the trail. It was a far stretch between San Francisco and Los Angeles. The Shaws could've disembarked at any number of stations.

"They've managed to keep a step ahead of the authorities for eight years."

"It's true," Riot admitted. "But the world isn't as large as it used to be."

"And you think I know their destination because I advised Mrs. Shaw on a business matter, or would it be my voodoo practicing ways?"

"You're a woman with her ear bent towards justice."

"What makes you think that boy of hers didn't kill a U.S. Marshal as they say?"

"Because Grimm saved me," Jin cut in, surprising both Riot and Mrs. Pleasant. "If he killed someone, it was because he was protecting his family."

"And you claim to be family, Miss Jin?"

"Yes."

The old woman drummed her fingers on the armrest in thought. She was old and bent, and time had whittled her away, but it hadn't diminished her presence. She sat like a queen at court.

After some minutes, Mrs. Pleasant finally inclined her head. "I'm familiar with your reputation, Mr. Riot. If I'm a woman with her ear bent to justice, you're a man who seizes it by the throat. I have one request."

"Yes?"

Mrs. Pleasant nodded to the girl at his side. "I don't involve children in my business. I'll have to ask your daughter to wait outside."

Jin bristled. "I am not a child."

"Child or no, this is my home, and those are my terms. It makes no difference to me if the pair of you choose to leave."

Jin slumped, then stood, and without a backward glance, stomped across the room. But she paused at the door when Mrs. Pleasant called her name.

"Miss Lauren will see to your comfort. You have a hungry look about you. She's a fine cook."

Jin reluctantly managed a curt "Thank you, Mrs. Pleasant" before leaving. When the door shut, Mrs. Pleasant turned to Riot. "That child could do with some manners."

"That child is honest."

Mrs. Pleasant sat back with a nod. "Information doesn't come free, Mr. Riot. I'll tell you what I know in return for a favor. Considering I'm a woman of a certain age, I may never come collecting."

"As long as it doesn't go against my sense of right and wrong."

The old woman chuckled. "That leaves a heap of wiggle room."

"And a less trustworthy man wouldn't have added that stipulation."

From the amusement dancing in her eyes, Riot knew she'd accept his terms. He stood to offer a hand, and she shook it, cementing the deal.

"I can put you on even ground with the U.S. Marshals, Mr. Riot. I see no reason you shouldn't know what they already know…"

14

CURIOUSER AND CURIOUSER

Isobel was frowning at a chessboard. Three of the pieces were still unaccounted for after Riot's arrest and the subsequent police raid some months ago. They'd substituted a thimble for a pawn, a bottle cap for a queen, and a broken seashell for a knight. She now focused on the bottle cap, trying to pick it up, but the required pinching motion proved too taxing for her right hand.

The police had overturned their bedroom with more enthusiasm than method, and what with the investigation and her being shot, she and Riot hadn't put things back together. It was a mess of books and belongings, with pathways to the bed and bathroom.

Sarah had attempted to re-shelve the books, but she kept getting distracted and was currently flipping through pages, lost in words.

Good God, what a mess. Isobel frowned at the room, her thoughts turning to housekeepers and her brief undercover investigation as one. She hoped to never clean another bathroom as long as she lived—it had been nearly the last thing she'd done in life.

Thoughts of housekeeping turned to Mrs. Eleanor Shaw—Ravenwood's late housekeeper, who'd been murdered along with her employer. The manor seemed rather large for a single old woman to be cleaning.

"Sarah," Isobel said suddenly. "Didn't you help Riot pack up Ravenwood's things?"

The girl looked up from a stack of books. "We all did."

"Was there anything of Mrs. Shaw's?"

"Miss Lily didn't leave much."

"Not Miss Lily. I mean the old housekeeper that was here when Riot worked with Ravenwood."

"Oh."

Sarah considered the question. "There were heaps of things. I don't know what belonged to who. But... there was a lady's trunk—a hope chest. Atticus took one look inside and closed the top. He said something about locating family."

"That would likely be it."

"The storage room is locked."

"You can help me downstairs." Could she even manage to pick a lock one-handed?

"Wouldn't it make more sense to use a key?"

"Right. Keys. I don't suppose you know where Riot put the key?"

"Would he remember where he put a key?"

"He likely handed it over to Miss Lily."

"I'll go check her desk."

"Sarah, if I don't get out of this room, I'll go mad."

"You *are* mad."

"I still need to get down there to see the trunk."

By the time Isobel struggled to her feet, Sarah was already gone. She sighed, and being on her feet already, shuffled to the window seat to look down on the yard. Tobias' cobbled together fort drew her eye.

Isobel was rarely home. In fact, she'd spent little actual

time at Ravenwood Manor, but the house felt emptier without Grimm in the stable with the horses, Tim tinkering in his work-shop, and Jin and Tobias getting up to trouble.

She leaned against the window frame and flexed her right hand. Her body would heal, she told herself. Patience. She'd regain her strength, and the pain radiating along her ribs and under her arm to her hand would go away. Eventually. She hoped.

Isobel reached for a book, but her grip slipped and it tumbled to the floor. *Alice in Wonderland*. She'd certainly like to fall down a rabbit hole about now—the morphia the doctors had left for her was calling her closer. The temptation to drift in that dreamlike ocean until she healed was stronger than she'd admit to anyone—especially Riot.

Isobel bent to pick up the book, but a wave of dizziness had her climbing to the floor instead. She rested her back against the bench seat until the world stopped spinning.

Since she was down there anyway, she pulled the book onto her lap and lost herself in a childhood favorite—a story both irritating and fascinating to the twins.

Isobel had detested Alice, while Lotario wanted to be Alice, but they'd both agreed that the Queen was their mother.

Time had given her a new perspective. Perhaps Alice wouldn't be so tedious either.

A banging eventually tore her from the pages. Isobel looked up and blinked owlishly at the tall, sturdy woman bullying a chest through the doorway.

"Are you sure you don't want me to help?" Sarah asked.

"I've carried it this far," the woman huffed.

Margaret Ederle was one of Isobel's only female friends, especially after she'd gone undercover to expose the fiancée of a friend of a friend, with said fiancée ending up dead.

Margaret wore her customary bicycling outfit: shirt, tie, riding bloomers, and boots, with her brown hair up in a practical bun. She was a strong woman who detested the feminine arts and raged against restrictions.

To avoid fines over wearing bloomers, she took her bicycle everywhere.

Margaret thumped the chest down in the middle of an empty spot and straightened, gazing around the room with disapproval. "This is not how I envisioned your bedroom."

"Rude," Isobel said, without looking up from her book.

Margaret marched over to loom. "You look smaller."

"You look taller."

"You're on the floor."

"So I am."

Margaret bent to read the spine. "Curiouser and curiouser!"

"Unfortunately, there's no golden key to the hope chest," Sarah said from the center of the room.

"I'll use a crowbar," Margaret said.

"Or we can find my lock picks," Isobel offered.

"And where would they be?"

Isobel looked around the room.

"Don't start crying," Margaret warned.

"I'm not…"

"You look horrid."

"Thank you," Isobel bit out.

Instead of Isobel, it was Sarah who started crying, and Margaret looked mortified. "I was only joking, Sarah."

"She does look horrid though," the girl said, wiping at her eyes.

"For God's sake, someone help me stand," Isobel said, shoving the book aside.

Margaret practically wrenched Isobel's good shoulder from its socket with the hand she offered. "Sorry," the woman muttered. "I'm not much good at caregiving."

"I'm not much good at getting it."

Or caring for children. A few months ago, Isobel would've fled the room instead of facing a weeping child. But in a moment of madness (at an asylum no less) she'd decided to adopt two orphan girls. Isobel hadn't realized there'd be so much… emotion involved.

Isobel pulled the girl into a hug and knocked loose the rest of her tears. "You're alive. That's all that matters," she whispered. "You saved my life."

"I feel like I should join in the hugging."

"And if Margaret tries to get into this hug, she'll be dead," Isobel said loudly.

Sarah laughed into the lapels of her dressing gown.

"As if…" Margaret snorted. "You look as though a strong breeze would blow you over. We need to get you on an exercise regimen."

"We can start by looking for my lock picks."

"How about we start picking up your room? What did you and Atticus get up to in here—Wait, I don't want to know…"

Sarah groaned in mortification and busied herself with a search for the missing lock picks. Isobel started with the wardrobe, rifling through pockets, and Margaret began rearranging the furniture.

"Margaret, why are you here?"

Margaret glanced over her shoulder. "To visit you."

"Riot rang you?"

Margaret turned to put her hands on her hips. "No one telephoned me. I checked the hospital first. Then the morgue."

"That's horrible to joke about," Sarah said.

"I'm not joking."

"A nurse told you I was dead?" Isobel asked.

"They told me you checked yourself out too early, and you were likely at the morgue. You look like you escaped from there."

"I'm a prisoner in a tower," Isobel said dryly. "No one will let me out of this room."

"Because you can barely walk without collapsing!" Sarah said, throwing up her hands.

Isobel waved away the observation. "A minor hiccup."

"You need a cane," Margaret mused.

"I will not use a cane."

"Stubborn."

"Yes, I am precisely that."

"It's because her mother uses a cane," Sarah called over her shoulder.

"That is not the reason."

Margaret and Sarah shared a knowing look. Isobel ignored it.

"So... why did Sarah have me haul up a hope chest? Is it your dowry? Did the bullet knock you onto the path of proper womanhood? And this is your frilly trousseau."

"It belonged to Zephaniah Ravenwood's murdered housekeeper."

"It's always exciting over here. Why are we breaking into a dead woman's trunk?"

"Because the Whites—we just found out they're really the Shaws—took off and U.S. Marshals came the other day looking for them," Isobel explained.

"Wait... you mean to tell me that the family pulled off the whole fake name thing longer than you?"

Isobel glared.

Margaret gave a low whistle.

"I'm going to kill you."

"You can't catch me. I could crawl and get away, and you'd tumble down the stairs."

"Miss Margaret, it's really not something to joke about," Sarah said.

"Of course it is. Isobel nearly got me ousted from the Falcon's. I can say what I like."

"It wasn't her fault Imogen was going to marry a murderer," Sarah insisted.

"And just maybe it wasn't your fault a murderer shot your mother," Margaret said reasonably.

Sarah's mouth worked. "I got her shot."

"And Isobel caused a schism in the club. By the way, a few members have petitioned for your removal."

"You should let them."

"Who says I'm not the one who filed for it?"

Isobel snorted, then put a hand to her side.

"Here they are! Are these them?" Margaret pulled out a ring of strange looking keys from under a small cabinet.

"How they'd end up under there?" Sarah asked.

Isobel gestured impatiently for the woman to bring them over. She eyed the lock from her chair, then selected the smallest and instructed Sarah to try it. She wasn't as intent on practicing as Jin was, but she knew the basic mechanics of lock picking. The skeleton key worked.

"Nice work, Sarah," Margaret said as she helped Isobel over to the chest. "So why are the marshals after the... Shaws?"

"Grimm is wanted for murder," Isobel said. "Maybe don't repeat that."

"My lips are sealed. Did he do it?"

"Of course he didn't," Sarah said.

"We don't know that..."

"What are we looking for?"

Margaret removed the top shelf of the chest, revealing an array of personal items: crockery and linens, a jewelry box and, finally, at the bottom, an album.

Sarah handed the album to Isobel while they sorted through the other items.

"I don't know what we're looking for," Isobel said, flipping through the pages of mounted momentos and photographs. Her eye caught on one in particular—an older white man standing beside a tall, much younger Negro man. They both beamed with pride. The younger man held a certificate of some sort in his hand, though the words weren't legible in the old photograph.

Isobel slid it from the album and checked the back. Adrian and Nathan Shaw, 1875. Howard University.

Nathan Shaw was a spitting image of Grimm, or rather Grimm of his father.

There were other photographs of interest, too. One with two women and a man. Penciled in were the names of Miss Eleanor Shaw (*Old* Mrs. Shaw, as Riot called her), her brother Adrian Shaw, and his wife Beth.

Isobel lingered over the next: a formal wedding photo of Katherine and Nathan Shaw. She studied the beaming couple, and the carefree bride she knew as Lily White.

And finally, on the last page, a photograph of a severe looking man standing in front of the very house she now sat in —Zephaniah Ravenwood. He was tall, thin, and looked like a bird of prey. Her lips quirked at a second photograph next to it. A twenty-year-old version of her husband sans beard and spectacles, leaning on a railing, his hat cocked at an angle, his hand on a revolver, and a watch chain dangling below his belt that emphasized the fit of his trousers.

"My God," Margaret said. "Is that Atticus?"

Isobel jerked in surprise. Margaret was sitting on the floor beside her, fiddling with a bulky camera.

"It is."

"I'd be instantly suspicious of a fellow who looked like that," Margaret noted.

"With good reason."

"He looks set to charm the camera."

"If looks could kill," she muttered.

"I think this is what you're looking for." Sarah handed over a bundle of newspaper clippings. The accounts made Isobel's blood run cold.

15

THE WAGER

Isobel was lost in a book. She sat in bed with newspapers and journals arranged in front of her and a shawl wrapped around her shoulders. She didn't look up when Riot walked in to hang up his hat and coat.

He paused to study the orderly room. "I hope you didn't do all this."

Isobel jerked in surprise. "Riot." She looked around the room, expecting to find someone else, and seemed mildly surprised by its orderly state. "I didn't hear you come in."

"Something more enticing has your interest. I should be jealous. Is he tall, dark and handsome?"

"I'm reading Ravenwood's journals."

"I can't compete with that man's mind," he said with a sigh.

"Mmm." She closed the journal but kept a finger in place as he leaned in to kiss her lips. "But you make up for it with charm." An impish look flashed across her gray eyes as she slid a photograph from a journal. "And I found this."

Riot adjusted his spectacles to peer at the photo, then laughed in a silent convulsion of mirth. He sat on the edge of the bed, studying the photograph. "This must've been twenty years ago. I'd forgotten about it."

Isobel leaned against his shoulder to study the photograph. "A picture truly is worth a thousand words—it captures you in one. You look like you're making love to the camera."

He glanced at her. "Old Mrs. Shaw took this photograph."

"I said the camera, not the photographer. Are those the same Levis you were wearing as William Kyd?"

"They'd be twenty years old."

"Same fit," she noted, plucking the photograph from his hand. "Regardless, this is going into a frame on my bedside table."

"Why do I feel as if I'm about to be blackmailed?"

"Oh, come now, Riot, I'd hardly keep such a valuable piece of blackmail in an easy to reach location—I'd keep it in a hidden compartment in the fireplace mantel."

"If the house is on fire, I hope you wake me instead of grabbing my photograph. What else have you discovered?" he asked, reaching across her to grab the photo album so she wouldn't have to wrestle it one-handed.

Isobel flipped to the last page. "You should be jealous of Ravenwood—he had a certain something about him, didn't he?"

"Like Lucifer himself," Riot muttered, easing the photograph from its tabs. The date penciled in on the back was shortly after Ravenwood purchased the manor. "This was a few years before I met him."

"I take it Mrs. Shaw was the resident photographer?"

"A hobby of hers."

"I'd say it was more than a hobby—these are quite good."

Riot lingered over the photograph of Nathan Shaw.

"You don't look at all surprised," she said. "What did you learn from Mrs. Pleasant?"

"Ladies first," he said.

"Oh no, Riot. If I'm to sit out this investigation, you owe me my little victories."

But Riot didn't answer straightaway. When he stood to add more coal to the fire, she suspected he was putting a safe distance between them to say the next. "I'm not sure I should tell you."

"Riot," she warned.

"U.S. Marshals are hunting Miss Lily and her family. I don't want to give them reason to come sniffing around here."

"They've already been here."

"And when I take off, they may come again. You could be charged with aiding a wanted criminal."

"We're not harboring them."

"But we were, after a fashion."

Isobel sank against the pillows. "If the marshals come to interrogate me, I'll play the swooning lady of the house."

"With your reputation?"

"That's low, Riot."

"Or a compliment. Depends on your viewpoint."

"Sometimes I hate that you know me so well."

He flashed a grin across the room, but that smile disappeared when she tapped the journal resting against her breast. "I propose a small wager."

"Did Ravenwood look into the murder for Mrs. Shaw?"

Isobel fluttered her lashes.

"That would've saved me from owing Mrs. Pleasant a favor," Riot said, stabbing at the coals.

"You may have learned something useful, too."

Riot replaced the fire poker, then shed his clothes down to shirtsleeves and trousers before pulling a chair to the bedside. He set the photo album beside her and flipped through to a group photograph.

"I don't know how Mrs. Shaw came to work for Ravenwood, but this is her, and these…"

"Are her brother and his wife? And this has to be Nathan Shaw."

"Grimm looks just like him, doesn't he?"

"A spitting image, as they say."

"I wager Mrs. Pleasant didn't reveal all her secrets, but she put me on even footing with the marshals," Riot explained, turning the page to Miss Lily's husband. "Nat, as he was known, was born into slavery. He was torn from his mother at a young age, sold over and again, and was eventually bought by a Choctaw plantation owner fighting for the Confederacy."

Riot carefully removed the photograph from the album and turned it over, frowning at the date. "Mrs. Pleasant said his enslaver dragged him along to war. Based on this photograph, I can't imagine he was more than thirteen at the time."

Isobel shuddered at the thought. So much brutality, so much death—what horrors had that boy experienced? It made her despair for humanity.

"As part of the U.S. treaty with the Choctaw Nation in 1866, slaves were freed and granted limited citizenship. Nat drifted for a few years until he happened on a white man who'd been shot in an attempted robbery. Not only did he tend to the man, but he tended to his injured dog, too. Carried the dog on his shoulders for miles so the man could ride easier. The white man was a Mr. Adrian Shaw—an engineer, among other things.

"Nat got Mr. Shaw safely back to his lodgings, cared for him, then the man offered him employment. Only it turned into a little more than that—the Shaws treated Nat like a son. Instead of taking the last name of one of his owners, as was common, he took Adrian's last name.

"Nathan was a bright, curious young man, and the Shaws saw to his schooling. When he came of age, they sent him off to live with Mr. Shaw's sister in Washington, D.C."

"Ravenwood's housekeeper, the budding photographer?"

"I believe so."

"Riot, has it occurred to you that Ravenwood's house-keeper may have been more than an employee?"

Riot blinked at her. "If she was, I don't want to know."

"I don't necessarily mean Ravenwood's lover—"

Riot winced at the thought. "Is there something in those journals?"

"You really should read his journals."

He ignored the suggestion. "At any rate, Nathan attended Howard University, became a doctor, and sometime after met his future wife."

Isobel turned the pages to their wedding photo. "Katherine Lillian Shaw. He must've been about thirty here and she looks around twenty."

"They settled in New Bedford, Massachusetts, where Miss Lily was living. She came from money and a long line of businessmen. They lived there for a time, and were both active in philanthropy and fighting for equality. Eventually, Nathan and Lily uprooted, and opened a hotel in Indian Territory, along two railway connections.

"The Mineral Springs Hotel."

"You already knew all this."

"Not all," she admitted. "You've confirmed some deductions. It explains why Miss Lily had this lodging house running like a well-oiled machine."

"Her hotel was thriving."

"Earning a reputation as a sanatorium with fine cooking—a place to recuperate and rest."

"Precisely. But what happened next is mired in rumor."

"With some fact." Isobel shuffled through a stack of journals and newspapers until she found the most recent clippings Mrs. Shaw had saved.

Riot picked them up to read. "The facts being that U.S. Marshals were present when the hotel burned."

"And two bodies were inside: U.S. Marshal Gil Blake and a Mr. Rose, who worked for the Shaws."

When Riot had finished with the articles, he rubbed his beard in thought, studying a rough newspaper sketch of a hotel on fire.

"Does it match up with what Mrs. Pleasant told you?" Isobel asked.

"It's all rumor," he said.

"Miss Lily never confided in her?"

"No."

"And you believe her?"

"I do," Riot said. "She said Miss Lily wouldn't speak of it."

The three articles of the account all said the same: Dr. Nathan Shaw was aiding the Holden Gang. When U.S. Marshals questioned him about the gang's location, he refused to tell them. They threatened arrest, and Grimm shot Marshal Gil Blake in cold blood. A Mr. Rose was caught in the crossfire, a bullet knocked loose a lantern and the hotel caught fire. In the confusion, the family fled to join up with the Holden Gang.

"But there's one thing that doesn't add up." Isobel pointed at a single sentence in Ravenwood's journals. "A Mrs. Rose, who worked at the hotel, claimed she only heard three gunshots."

"A very precise crossfire. Three bullets. Two dead men. It hardly sounds like Dr. Shaw and Grimm were covering their backs as they fled."

"I suppose this Mrs. Rose could be hard of hearing."

"Did Ravenwood discover what happened to Nathan Shaw? The articles only say he's at large."

Isobel shook her head. "The trail went cold."

"Or... Ravenwood dropped his enquiries at Mrs. Shaw's request."

"Because it would draw attention to a family on the run."

"Which is exactly our current issue," Riot said, studying the beaming couple in the wedding photograph. Nathan Shaw had gone to university to become a doctor, and had a family. It was hard to imagine a man involving his family in a shootout, but if his son's life was in danger, or (Riot hated to think it) the boy had been involved with the gang, how far would a parent go to protect their child?

"Did Mrs. Pleasant tell you where they're headed?"

"She claimed she didn't know."

"You think she was lying?"

Riot cocked his head. "Do you know… that woman has the straightest poker face I've ever encountered."

That was saying a lot. Atticus Riot had an uncanny sense for people—he generally read them like an open book.

"I think it was the strict truth."

"But she had an idea…"

Riot's lip quirked. "Why do you have the look of a woman about to win a wager?"

"We didn't set terms."

Riot leaned in close to whisper in her ear. "That's because I distracted you on purpose."

"So you claim."

"What are your terms?"

When Isobel met his eyes, her amusement vanished. Instead of making an outrageous wager, she laid her head on his shoulder. "Just come home."

16

OUT OF MIND

Grace Madeline Shaw was accustomed to hard work. She'd always made a game of it or imagined herself in a horribly tragic novel like Jane Eyre.

She'd chosen a new name for herself after parting ways with her brothers. Maddie was not about to live for who knew how many years with the name Doll Brady. Her mother had chosen another name, too.

So to the world, they were now Kate and Jane Rogers. And as Maddie poured a basket of soiled linen into a vat, she decided Tobias would never be allowed to pick aliases again.

Laundry work was grueling—an endless process of soaking, scrubbing, scalding, rinsing, wringing, mangling, starching, and ironing.

The soaps and cleansers left her hands dry, and the paler skin of her palms blue. Sour milk for iron rust stains. Chloride of lime for wine stains. Oxalic acid or buttermilk for ink stains. Ammonia, turpentine, sal soda... the list went on.

Maddie wanted to be a doctor, not a laundress. She reminded herself that this was temporary. But then, so was life. She might never realize her dream of being a doctor—not that any of the women here had a dream of working in a laundry.

While she worked, she watched the others. They were splintered into friend groups, mostly divided by race. So far, none of the women had been rude to Maddie or her mother, but the women made no attempt to befriend them, which suited them just fine. The fewer people who noticed them, the better.

The manager—an energetic man who barked orders from his office doorway—was a whole different sort of trouble. He'd already hinted to Maddie that there were ways to make her work easier by relieving the constant stress he was under.

Maddie watched as he caught a woman's eye and motioned her over with a jerk of his pointy chin. She set down her basket of dripping linens and sauntered into the man's office. The woman would get a full day's wage and go home early.

The man made Maddie's skin crawl.

"Remind me again why we didn't take work in a kitchen?" Maddie muttered.

Lily was working beside her. "Because my cooking attracts too much attention."

"You could just cook mediocre meals."

"I can't cook a bad meal to save my life," Lily whispered.

Maddie snorted. "Pride comes before a fall."

"If that man looks at you one more time, he'll find himself falling into a vat of boiling water. Make sure you aren't caught alone with him."

Despite the steaming water, Maddie shivered.

"This is temporary," Lily reminded. "We'll move on in a week or so when the snow thaws."

Maddie's thoughts turned to her brothers as she stirred the vat of clothing. "Do you think they're all right?"

"Harry will make do," Lily said, eyeing the manager's office.

Maddie made a face. "That's a horrible name."

Lily ignored the comment. "They're probably safer than we are."

"With Toby's mouth?"

Lily hissed a sharp rebuke.

"Sorry," Maddie said. "I'm out of practice. We had it good for so long."

Her mother fished out some dripping bed linens from the vat with a paddle and dumped them in a basket. She hoisted the basket and took it over to a machine to wring out the excess water before heading to the drying yard.

Maddie soon followed with her own load. When they were alone pinning up clothes, Maddie edged closer to her mother. "I don't really remember that night, Ma."

The transformation from focused worker to stunned deer was instant. Maddie might as well have just punched her in the gut. Her mother was frozen with something close to terror in her face.

"I mean, I remember... some," Maddie hastened to explain. "But I never understood just what happened. The *why* of it."

"Don't think about it." Her mother's voice usually warmed Maddie from the inside. But not now. The warmth had turned to ice, and her smooth voice was hoarse with grit.

Maddie had been told "not to think on it" ever since that night, and for eight years she'd not once pressed her mother, but she was fifteen years old and had spent the past year growing into herself.

Maddie Shaw was no longer the shy, quiet girl who did as she was told. She had a mind of her own.

"Do you know why those marshals came to our hotel?"

"Quiet."

The look on her mother's face would've turned her tongue to lead a year ago—now it just made her more determined.

She blamed Isobel for that. "You never talk about it," Maddie pressed. "You never talk about *him*. You won't let us talk about pa."

Maddie regretted the words the instant they were out. Something horrible happened. Lily put a hand to her mouth, looking like she might be sick; she seemed to fold in on herself, her gaze growing distant and... empty.

Maddie grabbed her mother's arm. But Lily jerked free and kept working with numb efficiency. And later, when Lily burned her hand in the scalding water, she didn't even flinch.

It was well past sunset when they finally dragged themselves to a cold lodging house, where they rented a single room with a cot.

Lily didn't eat that night. She curled on her side and faced the wall, and Maddie soon joined her, snuggling against her back for shared warmth.

"Ma?" she whispered. "I'm sorry."

Lily moved her head a fraction. "I should be stronger."

"We can't be any stronger than we are," Maddie whispered, burying her nose against her mother's back.

Her mother said nothing more, but Maddie knew it was because she couldn't—the words were washed away by silent weeping. And as Maddie wrapped her arms around her mother, she wondered if her mother ever asked herself the *why* of it, because Maddie knew that Grimm wasn't the only one who'd gone mute after that night.

17

THAT NIGHT

1892

LILY BREATHED WITH RELIEF WHEN HER HUSBAND WALKED INTO the mudroom. He was tired, dusty, and strained around the eyes, but he was home. She rushed into his arms.

"I'm a mess."

"I don't care," she whispered. He smelled of sweat and campfire, but it was him underneath it all.

"Did Josiah get home safe?"

"Yes." She felt a shudder of relief travel through his body.

"Everything's all right now," he whispered in her ear.

"They just let you go?" she asked.

"Their leader gave his word. He's a fair man." Nathan leaned back to search her face. "There's those dimples of yours."

"Only for your eyes."

"Pa!" Maddie squealed. Blurry eyed with sleep, she rushed her father, and Nathan plucked her off the ground to make kissy noises against her neck and cheek. She shrieked and laughed.

"What were you fixing?" she demanded. "Water in the lungs? A cut with rot? A broken femur?" She rattled off a list of possibilities until he cut her short.

"Whoa there, now. Slow it down, girl."

"You smell."

"Now you do, too."

Maddie squirmed out of his arms, and Lily laughed, a sound of pure joy.

Nathan smiled like a lovestruck young man. "I'll get washed up and take myself to the spring for a long soak, then I'll tell you all about it." He was opening the door as he talked. "Where's Jo—"

Nathan cut off when he spotted his son standing a few feet from the back step with two men behind him. One was pale and weathered, and the other was dark and polished, blending with the night. Both wore shiny badges.

The white man had a hand on Josiah's shoulder. "I wouldn't bother cleaning up, Dr. Shaw."

———

NATHAN GAVE A SHARP GESTURE BEHIND HIS BACK TO HIS WIFE, who gripped Maddie by the shoulders and backed out of the mudroom.

"This is Mr. Angel and Mr. Eli," Josiah explained. "They just want to talk with you."

Nathan smiled and stepped outside. "I'll be pleased to oblige. You go inside now, Joe."

Eli tightened his grip on the boy's shoulder. "Josiah's been so helpful. I wouldn't want to cheat him out of this conversation."

"Surely we can come in out of the chill, Dr. Shaw?" Angel asked.

Lily jerked in surprise as two more men marched from the

hotel kitchen into their private room. Deputy Marshals Jack Ebbs and Gil Blake.

"The two of you have no right—"

Jack Ebbs grabbed her by the neck and shoved her into a chair. At Maddie's scream, Nathan rushed into the sitting room to stand between his wife and daughter and the marshals.

Josiah tried to break free, but Eli's grip was like a vise. Angel stepped inside and removed his white hat offering a pleasant smile. "It's real kind of you folks to be hospitable."

Nathan took in the four men standing in their little family room, and finally looked to his son, firmly in the grip of a U.S. Marshal. Realization was only dawning in his son's eyes—the child-like trust was burning away into unrealized horror.

Nathan spread his hands as the marshals closed the doors to both the outside and the hotel kitchen. "Look, sirs, we don't want trouble."

Angel inclined his head towards Josiah. "Your boy here says you're aiding and abetting criminals."

Lily made a strangled sound. She was struggling to sit upright in the chair, a protective hand over her pregnant belly.

"No—I didn't say that!" Josiah argued.

"Calm down now," Nathan said. "I'm happy to speak with you gentlemen outside. This business doesn't involve my family."

"Oh, but it does," Eli said.

Nathan moved Maddie behind him, and Lily grabbed her daughter's hand, drawing her beside the chair.

Josiah jerked free of Eli's grip and went to stand beside Angel, looking up with hope and admiration. "I didn't say that, Mr. Angel. You remember—a fellow came and held a gun to us. Just tell them, Pa."

The look of disappointment in Nathan Shaw's eyes burned a hole in his son. "A man is only as good as his word," he said hoarsely.

"Not if he's dead," Gil pointed out.

The door from the kitchen flew open, and Mr. Rose stood framed in the doorway with a rifle braced against a shoulder.

Everything happened at once: Jack Ebbs drew and fired, Mr. Rose squeezed the trigger, and Josiah didn't stop to think—he ripped Angel's revolver from the holster, and fired.

Mr. Rose dropped, his rifle shot went wide, pegging Ebbs' shoulder, and Josiah's shot hit Gil Blake in the gut.

Nathan rushed forward, but Jack Ebbs recovered, pistol whipping the back of Nathan's head to bring him to his knees. Angel wrenched the revolver from Josiah and the handle came down hard against his cheek.

Josiah staggered to the floor.

Maddie was screaming, and Lily threw herself at Ebbs as he beat Nathan with the pistol. The man bellowed when she dug her fingers into his injured shoulder and shoved her away. She hit the wall with a thud and gasp, hugging her stomach as she slid to the floor.

Eli grabbed Maddie by the neck and put a gun to her temple. "How about we all calm down?"

Blood streamed from Nathan's face as he put up his hands, but Jack Ebbs drove his fist into the man's face until he was staring at the ground.

"*Jesus*," Eli said. "What a heap of shit. You just shot my brother, boy."

"He's quick," Angel noted, eyeing the gutshot marshal writhing on the ground. "Got to give him that."

Josiah looked across the floor, past his bleeding father, to the man he'd shot, gasping and groaning and clutching at his gut. Then to Mr. Rose, dead on the floor.

"I can help him," Nathan said, coughing out a mouthful of blood.

Eli shoved Maddie at Angel, then grabbed Josiah by the collar, dragging him across the floor to the dying man.

"Leave my family out of this!" Nathan begged. "Just let me tend to him."

"Too late for that, Dr. Shaw. I think Josiah here should watch and learn about consequences. You ever shot a man before, boy?" Eli whispered in his ear.

Josiah gave a shake of his head—he couldn't take his eyes off the dying marshal.

"Eli," Gil pleaded.

Eli looked at Angel, who gave a shake of his head. Angel turned to leave, his gun pressed to Maddie's temple, and Jack Ebbs grabbed Nathan by the collar. "Unless you want to see the color of your daughter's brains, I'd come quiet like," Angel said.

Josiah stared at his friend in shock. "You…"

"He had you fooled, didn't he?" Eli chuckled. He patted his dying brother on the cheek, then stood, looking to Lily, who was trying to struggle to her feet.

"Go help your mother, boy."

Josiah shot to his mother's side, helping her to stand, as Eli Blake picked up an oil lamp and chucked it into the kitchen. It must've hit some cooking alcohol, or oil, because the flames grew angry.

He smashed a second lamp, knocking it beneath the curtains. They caught like tinder. Josiah felt his mother convulse as if she'd been struck, but he kept her from tripping over her skirts, and dragged her from the burning room.

———

THE TOWN'S FIRE BELL WAS RINGING IN THE DISTANCE. JOSIAH looked over his shoulder to the glow on the black horizon; Gil Blake's screams still rang in his ears. He felt nothing—only disbelief and a vague hope this was a nightmare. Any second he would wake up, and his parents would be there with their arms around him.

Then he looked at his mother riding a horse of her own. Her eyes focused on Angel Davren's back, who had a casual arm draped around Maddie's body as she rode in front of him.

Josiah had a horse of his own, but they'd made his father walk at gunpoint. Jack Ebbs held his mother's reins, and Eli Blake had a Winchester across his saddle, ready to shoot father or son at the first sign of trouble.

Eli looked at Josiah, his eyes burning with the heat of the fire and smoke, but most of all... accusation. *Look what you made me do, boy.*

Lily shared a look with her husband, and in a flash of moonlight, Josiah saw fear in his father's eyes. And apology.

When they were far enough from town, Eli held up his hand and drew up on his reins. "Now then, Dr. Shaw. I'll make this easy for you. We're after the Holden Gang. In particular, Clay Holden. Your boy here told us you tended his son's injuries. That's aiding and abetting wanted men."

"He didn't join up with the gang," Josiah burst out.

"But that's what it comes down to, doesn't it?"

Nathan's hands were tied behind his back, but he stood straight and proud. "I was at a ranch..."

When Eli cocked his revolver, Lily spurred her horse forward with a surge to put herself between the marshal and his target—Josiah.

"Six of one, half dozen of another," Eli said. "It don't matter which one of you I shoot."

"It *doesn't* matter which one of you I shoot," Maddie growled out the correction.

Eli snorted out a laugh.

Lily caught her daughter's eye and gave a shake of the head, but seven-year-old Maddie looked set to bite the arm wrapped around her.

"Let my family go and I'll take you wherever you like," Nathan said.

"See now," Eli said with a cluck of his tongue. "I bet you said the same to Clay. You likely gave your word, too. And he believed you. The difference between me and Clay is that he has a soft spot for women and children. I don't, especially for a brat who shot my brother."

Eli fired at the ground under Lily's horse. It reared, but she didn't have the reins, so it was all she could do to clutch the horn and stay in the saddle with her pregnant belly.

Maddie struggled against Angel's hold, and Jack Ebbs gave a sharp tug on the reins, until the horse pounded to the ground, throwing Lily forward against the saddle horn. She hunched over the horse's neck with a groan.

"You seem set to kill us anyway," Nathan said.

"Only thing I care about is Holden and his gang. You can do what you like when I find him."

Josiah didn't believe a word of it.

"Do I have your word on it?" Nathan asked.

"You have my word," Eli said.

Nathan nodded. "Fair enough. I'll do my best to find their camp, but I can't guarantee they didn't move on after sending me away."

"That's won't be an issue," Angel purred. "We have a tracker."

———

LATE IN THE NIGHT, FOUR RIDERS JOINED THE GROUP WITHOUT a word. These new men set Josiah's skin to crawling worse than Eli Blake and Angel Davren. He didn't like the way they eyed his mother and sister. Unshaven, smelling of sweat and dust, they'd been on the road for a while, but there was something else—a casual air about them that was nothing like the controlled intensity of Clay Holden.

The journey was a surreal one, and Josiah was hit with a sense of déjà vu, only this time things were far worse. His mother and Maddie were here, and these men made his skin crawl. They'd shot down Mr. Rose and set fire to the hotel. And he'd killed Eli's brother.

How many people had been burned alive in the hotel?

Nathan had been given a mount of his own, though his hands were tied to the horn. Time flew with the horses' hooves, and all too soon they were back in the gorge, with the stream running through a maze of rocks and gullies.

Angel held up his hand, calling for a halt, and Eli cocked his gun, holding it casually across his lap so it was aimed at Lily. "In case any of you think of screaming."

Nathan swallowed. "Their camp is down in the canyon, at the end of a branch. There's a cave and a stream."

Eli and Angel shared a look, and Josiah wondered just who was in charge. "How bad were the boy's injuries?" Angel asked.

"Gunshot. I did all I could. His fever broke before I left, but I told them not to move him."

Eli turned and spat. "What do you think, Angel?"

"We'll scout first." Angel dismounted, leaving Maddie on the horse and handing its reins to Eli, then he motioned to Jack Ebbs and one of the new arrivals—a white man who looked like a grizzly bear. The large man grabbed Nathan off the saddle and shoved him to the front of the group.

That left Eli and the three newcomers. One man smiled at Lily with a look that made Josiah shiver.

"Guess you were right, Eli," one man said.

"It was Angel's idea. He knows how Clay thinks. *You* lot nearly ruined it."

The three men snickered. "Just some fun."

"*Fun?*" Eli glared. "You riled up the whole goddamned area!"

"Angel told us to create a diversion," a scruffy man shot back. "So we did, then we left a trail. They're all looking towards the Red River."

"Might've served our purposes," Eli muttered.

"And blown off some steam. Speaking of… What do we have here?" The scruffy man grabbed Lily by the chin and wrenched her face towards his so he might get a better look in the moonlight.

"Don't touch my ma!" Josiah growled.

Lily caught his eyes, and tried to shake her head, but the man's grip was like iron.

"This here is Dr. Shaw's family. We're keeping them as collateral until we sort this business out. The boy here just shot Gil in cold blood, so watch him. He's quick."

The three looked at Josiah. "Did he now?"

"Mmhmm. Gunned down a U.S. Marshal, then tried to destroy the evidence by burning the body."

"I didn't!" Josiah raged, but what could he do in the face of an accusation from a man wearing a U.S. Marshal's badge?

Sitting atop the horse, a hundred possibilities sped through his mind. He wanted to act. He wanted his mother and sister away from these men, but he was on a horse, with no gun, without the reins, and his father was off with the scouting men.

Now that they'd led them to the Holden Gang, what if these marshals shot his father? Or all of them?

Waiting for the scouts to return was the longest hour of Josiah Shaw's life—up to that point.

It was chilly out; the air misted from his lips, and his mother was shivering and trying not to show it.

So was he, for that matter.

The night was bathed in moonlight, making it bright enough to see. A quick burst of noise and dim shapes moved in the night. At first he dared hope it was Clay and his gang— why, he didn't know. They were outlaws. So why did Josiah fear these lawmen and their posse more than a violent gang?

The signal stirred the others into action. Eli clucked his horse forward, and Josiah's reins were tugged along with the others down the winding gorge.

The camp was deserted.

As the horses stamped and huffed, and bent to drink, Nathan limped forward to help his wife down from the saddle, but the cock of a hammer brought him up short. He raised his hands. "Do you think she's in any condition to run anywhere?"

"It's all right, Jack. We'll have to wait until light. Get your family get into the cave. 'Cept this one." Eli gave Maddie's cheek a pat.

Nathan gripped Lily's shoulder in warning as she tensed to rip her little girl from the man's hands. "She's liable to panic if she stays with you," he said in a low voice. "There's no way out of that cave, and I doubt you want a child urinating on your saddle."

Angel inclined his head, and after Eli gave an indifferent shrug, Nathan gathered his family into the cave. It was pitch dark inside and the moon without seemed bright and glowing in comparison.

One man leaned a casual shoulder against the opening, but the flare of a match gave a brief glimpse of his watchful eyes.

Nathan helped his wife sit, and she gathered Maddie close. The little girl clung to her, shivering in the cold.

Josiah stood frozen. This was his fault. All of it.

"Come here, son," Nathan whispered.

Josiah didn't move.

Nathan gripped his shoulders. "They already suspected

where I was," he said in a low voice. "They knew Clay's son was shot. They knew he'd get a doctor."

"But I…"

"You did what you thought best." He squeezed his shoulders. "That's all anyone can ever do."

"Will they let us go now?" Josiah asked hopefully.

Nathan pressed his lips together. Josiah could smell the drying blood on his face and had the impression more than sight of the swollen lip and cheek on his father's face.

"I don't know," Nathan admitted.

"But they're lawmen. How can they be like this?"

"A badge makes a man right, but it doesn't make him good."

Nathan sat beside his wife on a log. He reached into his medical bag and palmed something, then handed it to Lily with a whisper in her ear.

She grimaced, but tucked the item away, and leaned into his chest as he pressed his lips against her temple.

"What are we going to do?" Josiah whispered.

Nathan glanced at the cave entrance again. Once the family had settled, their smoking guard turned his back on the cave to watch the outside world. Snatches of murmured conversation drifted into the cave, but Josiah couldn't make out any words, could only see that Eli and Angel had their heads bent together.

Nathan gripped the back of his children's necks, and pulled them both close until their foreheads touched. "You listen to me. There's a crevice in the back of the cave that you both can fit through. You'll need to help your sister up, Josiah."

"I can't leave—"

"The two of you are our only chance," Nathan said urgently. "Do you understand? I'm putting you in danger; not taking you out of it."

It was a lie. More or less. But Josiah wouldn't realize that until it was too late. The children nodded.

Sparing a final glance at their bored guard, Nathan ushered his family to the back of the cave. He crouched and traced quick marks in the dirt.

"Maddie, I need you to remember these marks."

"I can't see them, pa," she whispered.

"I know. Close your eyes and picture them as I trace them with your hand. Make a picture in your mind. Just like I taught you in surgery."

He did so with Maddie, then Josiah.

"It's a map," he whispered. "The two of you are going to get help. You climb up and out of this crevice, and walk towards the mountain in the distance. You'll come to a river and follow it into another set of gullies. Got it?"

Maddie clung to her mother, making a soft mewling sound of despair. "Answer your father," Lily said firmly. "You'll remember the map?"

Maddie moved her head against her mother's skirts.

"Now do as you're told." Lily kissed her head and helped her daughter climb into the crevice. "Josiah will be right behind you."

"I can't leave you…"

Nathan grabbed his neck and pressed his forehead to his. "You have to find Holden, because you're the only one that can tell him your mother is in the mine shaft. Do you understand me?"

Lily made a strangled noise. Not for herself, but for what she knew her husband meant to do.

"What—" The words stuck in Josiah's throat, a slow dawn of horrible realization turning his bones to dust.

"Help your sister. She can't climb out alone," Nathan whispered. "You know your mother can't fit up that crevice. I'm counting on you, son. I know you can do this."

Josiah nodded.

"Don't you ever forget, no matter what happens, that I love you. *Go* on now and protect your sister."

The desperation in his father's voice left no room for questioning. Heart racing, body numb, Josiah squeezed himself into a chimney-like crevice and climbed after his sister.

18

DOVES

1901

Maddie's back hurt, her arms quivered, and the stench of chemicals seared her nostrils. But she was resilient.

The hardest thing was her mother's silence. Lily had fallen into a dark hole and turned to work for comfort. Her tears hadn't dried up; she was stuck in a dark well nearly drowning in them. There was just nowhere for the tears to go.

Maddie missed her father. What she remembered of him— snatches of laughter and warmth, of kindness and compassion. The feel of his broad shoulders under her as he galloped after Josiah and made her squeal until she thought she'd burst with joy.

And her mother's smile, too.

Nathan Shaw had been a fire on a cold night, and warmth radiated from Lily's eyes when he was around. Maddie hadn't seen that in a long time.

Those men had stamped out their lives with no more care than a man putting out a campfire.

So when another man in power called Maddie into his office one cold day, she was resigned to his leering.

The manager, a Mr. Abberton, sat behind his desk, entering figures into a book. He stopped to stare at her over the rims of his spectacles.

Despite her working rags, a loose blouse and stained skirt, the man still leered at her. Maddie might be nearly sixteen years old, but she had the curves of a woman, and the bright, intelligent eyes of her father. And although she'd tried her best to conceal her education, her proper tones occasionally slipped through.

An impulse to gouge the man's eyes out nearly overtook her, but she recalled her father—the way he hummed and sang off key when he was in surgery, his gentle hands, and easy smile. She thought of Dr. Wise, too—of his patience and respect, and his endless well of compassion despite the injustices he faced every day. And Atticus Riot—as dangerous and honorable as they came.

All good men. Nothing like the man currently undressing her with his eyes.

Abberton set down his pencil, and picked up a cigar. "You're a hard worker, Miss Jane."

Maddie dipped her head in a kind of awkward curtsy. She might be innocent, but she wasn't naïve. '*Be ye therefore wise as serpents and harmless as doves.*' There was a protection in that guise. One she'd worn like a second skin since That Night.

"Thank you, Mr. Abberton. Me and ma are happy for the work, but I should be gettin' back to it. We've got a big order from a big house."

Abberton clipped the cigar and put a match to the end. When it was drawing to his satisfaction, he gave her a smile that she supposed was meant to be friendly. "You've been getting all the large orders. Working like a dog. Wouldn't you like some easier work?"

"Me and ma don't mind," she said brightly.

Most girls would ask, 'What work is that?' But Maddie knew better.

"You could have yourself a lie down," he purred, climbing to his feet and nodding towards a second door.

"And leave my ma to do all the work? I can't do that, Mr. Abberton."

"I'm partial to the way you work, Miss Jane." He smoothed his thinning hair and moved to the other side of the desk to lean against it. With the way his legs stretched out and his body was positioned, his pelvis was thrust forward.

"That's real kind of you. I'll be gettin' back now, sir." The moment she touched the doorknob, Mr. Abberton stepped forward and slapped a hand against the door. She was sure he stank by the yellowed patches of dried sweat at his armpits, but couldn't smell much aside from laundry chemicals.

Maddie looked him straight in the eye. "Do you know, Mr. Abberton, that a man's testicles are held in a paper-thin sack of flesh that's only attached by a flimsy cord that can be yanked out of his body and severed with a flick of a sharp nail? I'd really rather not use you for practice."

Mr. Abberton blinked down at the girl who'd transformed from dove to snake in a few icy words that made his anatomy shrink back in terror.

His face turned red as he vomited several choice slurs at her, but Maddie contented herself with mentally walking through the surgical steps of an orchiectomy.

The door behind her wrenched open to reveal her mother. She looked from Maddie to Abberton, and put on a mask of polite inquiry. "Mr. Abberton, there's a stubborn stain on one of the men's shirts, I—"

"Get out," he snapped. "Both of you. You're fired, and don't expect no pay for the week."

Lily pulled Maddie behind her to look the man square in

the eye. Maddie gave an internal groan—she knew that look in her mother's eye.

"We earned that pay. You'll give us what's owed."

"That bitch of yours threatened me."

"And I'll whisper the word 'union' into these women's ears right after I go to the newspapers with an exposé on lecherous laundry managers."

The threat sparked rage. A fist came up and Lily absorbed it—physical pain was nothing compared to the pain of a tortured mind. She snatched the cigar from his other hand and went for his eye.

"ARE YOU ALL RIGHT, MA?"

To Maddie's surprise, her mother started laughing. It wasn't comforting, not entirely, but it was something—even near madness was better than numb silence.

"I've had worse. I survived childbirth three times."

"Your eye is already swelling. We need to find you some ice."

"I have another plan."

One of the first lessons they'd learned from a life on the run is never keep your possessions where you bed down, unless you're in that bed, but when Lily turned in the opposite direction of their meager belongings, Maddie cocked her head in puzzlement. "We're not skipping town?"

"Not yet," Lily said.

"But, Ma, he's bound to get the police. They'll be looking for us."

"Which is why we need to give them a trail to follow before the gears of justice get rolling."

They went to the train station instead and bought cheap tickets for Sacramento's main station and its multitude of weblike connections. Maddie summoned tears and rumpled her collar, and Lily made sure to wince and show off the bruised and swollen side of her face.

They waited until their train came, handed off their tickets and climbed into the carriage, then got right back off and disappeared into a crowd of arrivals and a cloud of train smoke.

Maddie swapped her coat with her mother's and turned it inside out, then unwound the scarf around her hair to hand it to her mother, who wore it like a shawl.

It'd been years since she'd done this sort of appearance change, but it came back like an old habit. It was easy to become someone new when your life was on the line.

Mother and daughter kept to back roads as they walked to the room of an old woman who kept herself from starving by sewing by candlelight despite her near-to-blind eyes. The old woman had been grateful for the coins they paid her to watch their things. Even more grateful for the money they paid for a few of her possessions.

Some quick adjustments, another change, and ten minutes later, an old bent woman in a mourning veil, white gloves, and cane came hobbling out on the arm of her young Negro nurse.

When the two women walked into a respectable hotel and a cultured, upper-class voice emerged from beneath the veil along with a generous tip, no one suspected it was a mother and daughter formerly employed at a laundry.

19

TREMORS

ATTICUS RIOT SHUFFLED CARDS AS THE TRAIN CARRIAGE rattled its way towards Sacramento. Lost in thought, he barely noticed the women who shared his first-class carriage, or their multiple attempts to entice him into conversation.

The trail was a month cold—eight years, really—but he'd worked with less before. The newspaper clippings, Mrs. Pleasant's revelations, and Ravenwood's journals painted a dark picture of the Shaw's family history.

These were far deeper waters than a simple murder.

The official report filed by Eli Blake claimed they'd been hunting Nathan Shaw for his involvement with the Holden Gang, and they were waiting at a hotel for him. When he snuck in late one night to visit his family, the marshals tried to arrest him. Josiah Shaw opened fire. Mr. Rose and Gil Blake were killed, and the hotel caught on fire. Nathan Shaw had used his wife and daughter as shields, while his boy kept a gun aimed at the lawmen. The family rode away into the night to rejoin the Holden Gang, who were wanted for rape, murder, and robbery.

But Garrett had put him in touch with a reporter friend in

Tulsa who had a different tale. The townsfolk all disagreed with the official report—Dr. Nathan Shaw was an upstanding citizen. A good man.

Good men went bad all the time, but bad men could also turn to good. The fact that old Mrs. Shaw kept the newspaper clippings about the young man her family had taken in and mentored told Riot she'd never made peace with the official account.

But Ravenwood's journals muddied the waters—Josiah Shaw had been spotted riding with the Holden Gang after the events of that night. According to reports, he'd played an active role in later robberies. There was also a list of likely places where the family might seek refuge—sympathetic acquaintances and distant friends.

Old Mrs. Shaw had probably helped with that list, but it was eight years old.

Riot was missing a piece of the puzzle—and that piece lay with the Shaw family.

It was Tim who picked up the first sign of a trail. It came from a man at a racetrack named Skunk.

"I hear they got themselves a horse charmer in Davisville, just outside of Sacramento."

Tim blew a line of smoke from his lips. "What's the fellow do, give 'em roses?"

"They say he talks horse."

Tim's ears were pricked, but he kept his reaction in check. It never did to show too much interest. People remembered that, then they'd decide their story was worth repeating.

Instead, Tim smoothed his bushy white beard out to the tips. When he let go, it sprang back to its cottony fullness. "What do you reckon horses talk about?" he asked.

Skunk considered this question with more thought than it warranted. "What their lives was like before."

"Before what?"

"Before they got themselves saddled with our smelly hides."

"You can't smell yourself, Skunk."

The man wheezed. "That's because I'm blessed. Not a bad thing in this line of work."

This line of work being horses. But it wasn't the horses that stank, it was the bunkhouses, boots, and bedrolls.

"I don't believe it. No man can talk with a horse."

"I got it from a friend here who works with a purveyor. He looks for them wild runners. A ranch up that way catches some fine mustangs."

"And I take it your friend got this from a friend who knows some fellow at a ranch?"

"Got it in one."

"What's this charmer's name?"

Tim was shocked when Skunk answered. Generally, rumors didn't come with names. "Harry Brady. Young colored fellow —said he was darker than me."

Tim choked on a mouthful of smoke, and had to slap his chest to get his lung working again. Harry Brady. He knew that name. If only he could place it…

"My friend Jim was wondering if I could talk with horses on account of my skin color."

"Well, can you?"

Skunk chuckled. "You're daft, old man."

"I was dafter young."

"Well, you know I can only talk with skunks. That's not very useful."

Tim flashed his gold teeth. "Maybe they'll start racing 'em."

"Now there's an idea."

Tim let Skunk run with that thought. And they did—Mr. Skunk could be the one to round up the creatures and Tim the one to work out the particulars of a track. Although the two disagreed on some details, they both agreed that people would empty their billfolds to wager on a race.

Much cheered by Skunk's information, Tim had returned to Ravenwood Manor to relate the rumor. Riot packed a bag, left his injured wife, and boarded a train in the guise of a gentleman. And Tim was back near the horse car chatting up the porters.

Riot squared his deck, and plucked out the queen of hearts. His thoughts inevitably returned to Isobel.

"Be careful," she'd whispered the night before. He held her in his arms, her head nestled under his chin as he traced the ridges of her spine.

"You know I won't," he murmured.

"You could lie about it."

"I don't lie."

"I hate that I love you so much," she admitted.

"You know what they say… absence makes the heart grow fonder."

"I'll be bursting with it by the time you return."

A sudden worry clutched his heart. "You'll ring Margaret or Lotario if you need anything?"

They'd arranged for Margaret to check in and stay overnight when possible, but the thought of Isobel alone, with only the children and lodgers, made him uneasy. It wasn't just her injuries. They both had enemies in San Francisco, and she was near to helpless just now.

"If you swear to keep Tim close."

"I'd rather he stay and watch my family."

"We'll be fine, Riot. You need someone at your back. I'll feel better if it's Tim."

She didn't say it, but she was thinking it—that he was probably safer with Tim at his back than with her. The old man was made of grit and shoe leather.

"I could ask Meekins and Payne to stay in the carriage house."

Mr. Meekins and Mr. Payne were two ex-convicts that Riot had sent to San Quentin. They were reformed, somewhat, and they made a skilled pair of bodyguards for the manor.

"It'll look suspicious if you and Tim disappear and we get our two toughs to guard the place. They don't exactly blend in with the neighborhood."

"Still, you know where to reach them."

The plan was for Riot and Tim to slip out on a case. They did it often enough.

Isobel had kissed his throat about that time. The feel of her lips chased away worry, but when her hands started exploring his body, he gave a groan of protest.

"As if I'd let you leave without a proper goodbye," she whispered in his ear.

"You're in no condition to—"

"Have you forgotten the first night we spent together?"

"You've apparently forgotten. It was daytime."

"I had a bullet hole in my leg. You had broken fingers and bruised ribs. We managed then, and we'll manage now."

It was tempting, but he feared he'd hurt her.

Isobel was slim and fit, and she'd climbed masts and drainpipes with the ease of an acrobat. But in the last month, after the shooting, she'd lost an alarming amount of weight and her body felt hollow.

Isobel slid a hand under his undershirt, then tried to push him onto his back. He arched a brow at her. And when he didn't budge, she muttered an oath. With a sigh of frustration, she eased out of his arms and gingerly rolled onto her back.

Riot propped his head on a hand to gaze down at her. "Are you trying to have your way with me?"

"I'm trying to entice you to have your way with *me*."

"I'm enticed. But worried. I'm afraid I'll hear a crack of bone at some point."

"Possible, but worth it."

"No, it wouldn't be worth it. I'd never forgive myself for causing you more harm."

"Don't get protective with me."

"You were *shot*." It was nearly a growl.

Isobel ignored that detail to reach under the covers with her good hand. "I understand if I'm no longer appealing… Just say it."

"That's unfair."

"I have no qualms against cheating, Mr. Riot. I never hesitate to go below the belt."

"You're a cruel woman."

"Just horrid."

He'd protested. She'd persisted. And since his heart wasn't really in it, she'd convinced him with greater powers of persuasion. They'd made slow, gentle love, and remained tangled long after their hearts had slowed.

"Sir… sir?"

Riot came back to himself and the train carriage. The train had reached the station and his fellow passengers were rising to leave, gathering their things. He tucked away his cards and sprang to his feet to open the door for them.

Oakland to Sacramento was only a few hours by train, so Riot had left without a valise. Instead, he'd stuffed spare clothing in his saddlebags, which were with Jack in the horse car.

He offered a hand to help the first woman navigate the train steps, then her doe-eyed daughter, who either had something caught in her lashes or was attempting to flirt. He smiled, tucked her arm through his, and escorted mother and daughter to a line of waiting hacks, conversing and keeping an eye out for any tails.

The last thing the Shaws needed was Riot putting the marshals on their trail by trying to help them. There were eyes and ears everywhere, and an army of private detectives for hire in the largest city on the west coast.

He handed the women into the first carriage, accepted their calling cards, and excused himself without offering one of his own. He waved the next carriage on, then climbed into the third, and gave an address. But Riot never reached his destination.

Three blocks from the capitol building, he climbed out onto a main street and lost himself in a swirl of tule fog and traffic, his stick clicking in rhythm with his steps. He eventually ducked into a coffeehouse, and shed his overcoat to take a table in back with a view of the murky street.

Half an hour later, Riot tossed a coin into the saucer and tucked his newspaper under an arm. Another block, and he hailed a cab. Once inside, he made quick adjustments to his cuffs, reversed his waistcoat, and removed his stiff formal collar.

The cab deposited him near the train yards, and he stopped to pat a pinto horse standing outside of a saloon. "Did you enjoy your train ride, Jack?"

The horse snorted, nibbling at his lapels, his nostrils flaring as he sniffed a familiar scent. Tim soon emerged from the saloon, and Riot handed him the newspaper. "Page five."

Tim read as Riot slipped his walking stick into the saddle holster before checking the saddle girth and straps. Jack liked to hold his breath when the cinch was tightened. He thought he was being funny.

Tim sucked irritably on a gold tooth. "Hot damn."

Riot grunted in agreement. The petty crimes on page five had a sketch of a mother and daughter wanted for assaulting a laundry manager with a cigar. Kate and Jane Rogers.

The two bedraggled faces that stared from the ink had a

hopeless look about them. Maddie's hair was a frizz, her eyes puffy from crying, and Miss Lily's eye was swollen shut. The artist had given the women an air of low intelligence.

"At least it doesn't look much like them," Tim said, squinting at the sketches. "Assault my ass. Look at that shiner."

Riot clenched his jaw. It wasn't a stretch to imagine what really happened—he only hoped a black eye was their only injury.

Sensing his anger, Jack stomped a hoof and stood alert, eyeing the surrounding street for what had gotten Riot on edge.

Tim slapped the paper against his palm in thought. "This was a petty crime… and it's still in the papers."

Riot shared a look with the old man. They'd both been at this business long enough to spot the signs—someone wanted that article to keep circulating. The U.S. Marshals had a larger network of eyes and ears, along with the Pinkertons on the railroads willing to cooperate with government officials. It was safe to assume that the marshals were on their trail and had heard about the assault.

"There's this, too." Tim pulled out a folded up piece of paper from his inner pocket. It was a wanted poster. The face that stared back looked violent and sinister, and the description said that Josiah 'Grimm' Shaw might be traveling with two women and a small boy.

"Was this sketch of Maddie and Miss Lily posted at the station?"

"Not that I saw, but I didn't get behind the ticket window. Just saw this one on a wall." Sometimes stationmasters kept sketches of suspects where only they could see.

"Should we risk questioning the manager at the laundry?" Tim asked with a gleam of his eye.

"We'll go to the ranch first. They might not have seen this poster yet."

"Guess we don't have to be too worried about leading the marshals to the Shaws. Seems like they have leads enough."

Riot swung into the saddle and considered what he knew of the family. "They've stayed one step ahead of the law for eight years now... They could be leaving a trail of false leads on purpose."

Tim wheezed out a chuckle. "Always knew there was something more to that woman."

"Let's hope Tobias keeps leaving us breadcrumbs."

SACRAMENTO WAS SITUATED IN A VALLEY ALONG A RIVER AND wetlands. The state capitol was prone to flooding and in cooler months to tule fog—a thick, cold fog that clung to the ground. Visibility was low, but the road was clear as they rode west towards Davisville.

Eager to be on the move, Riot gave Jack free rein, and Sugar followed at a more dignified pace. After two miles, Riot reined in Jack, who made a show of being irritated but was likely grateful, since he wandered to a stop by some grass to nibble on.

It was close to dusk by the time they arrived at the King Ranch. It was a sprawling ranch of cattle and horse, and a man rode out to greet them at the gate.

"Can I help you, gentlemen?"

"I'm in the market for fresh racing stock," Riot said. "The last one I bought developed behavior issues from being caught and broken. I hear you have a charmer here."

The man took in Riot's fine clothes and kit, then offered a hand. "Name's Finn. I'm the foreman. We had a charmer, but he's moved on. We still have the horses he trained, though."

Riot arched a brow. "Did he turn out to be a fraud?"

"No, he's the real thing. He had these mustangs taking a

saddle within a day. Strangest thing I ever saw—the boy's got a gift."

"He give a direction?" Tim asked, who'd been introduced as a trainer. "I'd be keen to hire him at the tracks."

Finn snorted. "You and everyone else."

They spent some time perusing the horse stock—Tim playing the scout and retired jockey, assessing health, agility, and speed with a professional eye that was not at all an act.

And Riot played the wealthy amateur, walking over to the round pen while Tim conversed with Finn. Riot leaned against the fence with other men watching a rider cling to a wild mustang for dear life.

The horse won and the rider went flying. The cowboy scrambled away and crawled between fence slats as the wild horse bucked and kicked in a rage.

"I take it the charmer didn't pass on his methods," Riot said to the man by his side. He had the narrow hips and the gut of a man who spent his life in the saddle.

"There's a reason we do it like we do," the ranch hand said defensively. "It takes a real man to break broncos. It's been done like that since man rode horse, and there's a reason for it."

"What's that reason?" Riot asked.

"The horse has to know whose boss. Put it in its place once and it'll stay there when it gets a mind to do something else."

Clearly the man had never encountered a horse like Jack, Riot thought wryly. Instead, he voiced his agreement. "Nothing quite like staking a man against beast to ride the wild right out of it."

The man eyed Riot sideways. "You know something about breaking broncos, sir?"

"In my youth. My back's not much good for it anymore."

The ranch hand grunted, then turned to spit, part agreement and part distaste for something as little as a bad back keeping a man from work.

"You didn't care for the charmer, then?"

"Quiet fellow. Real dark, too. You'd think he'd of spooked the horses, but they always took right to him. He had a way about him, but I wouldn't trust one of his horses—they were fine with Brady, not so good with others."

"So you wouldn't buy one?"

"Oh, with proper training, they'll be fine."

"Good riddance, then?"

"Nah, we all liked that brother of his. Had a mouth on him, though. Ran it nonstop."

"Didn't that get irritating?"

The ranch hand laughed. "Not this kid. At first, sure, but he wasn't half bad... real entertaining. Good sport even when he broke his arm."

Riot stifled his alarm at that last. Instead, he said, "The young heal quick."

"Little bastard tried to get out of work."

"Did he climb on a bronc?"

"Well, not willingly, precisely. But most of us got a taste of it at his age. More like an initiation."

Riot wanted to press the man, but too much interest in an eight-year-old boy who was supposed to be a complete stranger would rouse suspicions.

"No idea where the charmer went? I was hoping to observe his methods."

"One morning they were just gone. Took a horse and saddle, too, though Finn says he earned it and it was part of his pay."

The ranch hand muttered an insult under his breath. Clearly, he thought it undeserved.

"Did the boy say anything about where they were headed?"

"You know... some other fellows were asking about the pair. U.S. Marshals, in fact. You a lawman?"

Riot adjusted his spectacles. "Once upon a time. Doesn't pay well enough."

Unfortunately, his ploy didn't work. The man closed up and moved away, and his attempts to converse with the others were met with a cold shoulder.

They might not have had much love for Grimm's horse charming methods, but they were a loyal bunch.

20

NEGOTIATIONS

"We're gonna die out here."

"We're not going to die."

"Freeze, at the very least," Tobias insisted.

"It's not that cold."

"They're gonna find me one day all frozen and twisted up in the snow with this look on my face." Tobias leaned over the saddle and, despite himself, Grimm twisted around to look at his little brother. He had his tongue lolling to the side and his eyes were crossed.

"I'm sure a wolf will bite your face off before they find you."

Tobias' eyes widened. "You're cheery."

Grimm turned back around.

"Look, I didn't give us away," Tobias whined. "Even when I got my arm broke." His arm was in a splint and sling. Thankfully, it'd been a clean break.

"I told you not to get on that horse."

"The fellows said it'd be fine. You're just sore they didn't like you. They liked me just fine."

Being liked was apparently more important to his little brother than a broken arm.

"I don't know why we left."

Grimm unbuttoned his coat and worked a gloved hand through the opening to fish out a piece of paper. He handed it back to his brother, who tugged off his mitten with his teeth before taking it.

Grimm listened to paper rustling.

"Hah! You look like an outlaw."

"I am," Grimm said, grimly.

"It doesn't look like you. The fellow on this paper looks like a cool hand—like a dime novel gunslinger. You just look…" Tobias searched for a word to describe his brother. "Constipated."

"Tobias," Grimm warned. "I'll make you walk."

"You rather I said you look like a fellow who can't shit?"

Grimm looked heavenward. Why on earth was he stuck with Tobias? He'd rather have taken Maddie when they split ways. Instead, he'd been stuck with the loudest mouth brother the world ever knew—and antagonizing to boot.

"You're trying to provoke me," Grimm noted.

"Ma would've washed my mouth out with soap," Tobias grumbled.

And then only the sound of clopping hooves broke the silence that stretched between brothers. Tobias had never been away from their mother, and just when he'd been getting the hang of things as a ranch hand and making friends, they'd packed up and moved again.

Grimm was used to a drifter's life, but Tobias was too young to remember those early years. He'd spent the last three years at Ravenwood Manor, and to Tobias that was home.

It seemed a lifetime ago since Finn had awakened Grimm in the dead of night, but Grimm had already lived many lifetimes in his short one. Finn had been severe when he'd drawn Grimm outside and handed him the wanted poster.

"Look," the ranch boss had whispered. "One of the fellows came in from a supply run and gave me this. It was down at the grocers."

Grimm said nothing. Only waited to see what he'd do.

"Don't you have anything to say for yourself?" Finn asked.

"It's me."

"What the hell did you do?"

Grimm was tempted to put his hands on his head and just turn around and wait for someone to put a rope around his neck. It'd be the easier way. He was tired of hiding, tired of running, and riddled with guilt for dragging his innocent little brother into his mess.

But what, exactly, was *this* mess?

The hurt, hate, and guilt had turned into numb pain. And acceptance. It was the acceptance most of all that annoyed him.

Why the hell should any of them accept what those men had done to their family? Badge or no—they'd had no right to take his family and burn the hotel to the ground.

Time had given Grimm perspective, and the chance to accept what he'd done. He was willing to hang for it, but after spending time with Atticus Riot and working for the detective agency, the fog surrounding that night had begun to lift. Snippets of conversations returned and nuances that he hadn't understood as a child came into the light.

Grimm had been thinking hard on that night of late, and he was beginning to wonder why U.S. Marshals had dragged a woman and children into the night and set fire to their home.

Two answers came to mind: to obscure the trail and use his mother and sister as hostages. The marshals never intended to arrest the Holden Gang. They'd been after something more.

But what? And why, after all these years, were Eli and Angel still on the hunt?

So instead of giving up, he'd looked Finn square in the eye. "U.S. Marshals came for my family because my father helped a man's son. They threatened my mother, they shot our uncle, and they had nothing good in mind. I was ten, and I shot one of them."

It was out. He'd said it for the first time in his life. Why had he blamed himself all these years? Because the alternative was just as terrifying—that there was no law but the law of might.

Finn's mouth firmed up, and a fire lit his eyes. "Goddamned lawmen ain't nothing but bullies with badges."

"Not all of them," Grimm corrected. "But these were. Whatever you want to do is fine… But my little brother wasn't even born yet, and they'll drag him to the gallows, too. I only ask you to give him a chance to leave."

Finn stared hard into his eyes for a long minute. Finally he reached a decision and thrust the poster into Grimm's hand. "Far as I'm concerned, none of us recognized you. I think the boys will agree. You've done good work here. Take the horse you trained on that first day—she's yours. And take a spare bridle and saddle from the supply shed. But come morning, Brady, you best be gone."

"Thank you, sir."

He could leave Tobias here and sort things out, but something told Grimm that Angel and Eli wouldn't leave the boy out of this affair.

So he woke up his little brother, got him dressed and bundled, and hoisted him on a horse half asleep. Unfortunately, Tobias was awake now.

"So now you're wanted. With a picture. I'm not sure Sarah would like this sketch of you. Her sketches are loads better, you know. But don't tell her I said that. She'll blush and start getting all giggly and girlish. I mean, you know what I mean?"

Tobias was babbling into the night. Probably because he'd done his best to keep quiet while they'd been working at the ranch. With limited success.

"If I was good at something, I'd say 'Thank you, I know.' Such as talking… I'm good at that. Everyone knows it. But you can compliment me for it all you like. Say, you think there's a wanted poster for me? How come I'm not on this?" the boy grumbled.

Grimm eyed the distant glow of Sacramento, with an idea beginning to form. He told himself that the idea stemmed from wanting to safeguard his brother, but really… he didn't think he could stand weeks of listening to Tobias go on.

It was really the only way. Grimm doubted Tobias would survive the journey otherwise.

"You want to keep warm?"

"I do. It's freezing out here."

"When we get to the city, you're going to buy a ticket and take the train somewhere."

"Ma told us to stay together."

"Things change."

"I'd rather stay with you."

"I don't think you want to go where I'm going, but we'll end up in the same place."

Tobias fell quiet.

"You'll meet up with ma and Maddie before me. You'll be more comfortable."

"No."

"Tobias…"

"My name is James," Tobias corrected.

"It's going to get colder."

"We stick together."

"I can't be worrying about you."

"How long will you be gone?"

"As long as it takes."

"You gonna tell me what happened?"

"If you get on a train, I will."

"You're gonna tell me now, Grimm. So I know who's after us. If I learned one thing from that fancy poet and his stories, it's that you got to say things, or people end up dead. Like that Romeo fellow. If he'd just sat down and had a talk with his girl, everyone would've lived."

Grimm frowned. He hated it when Tobias had a point. Of course, with as much as he ran his mouth, he was bound to hit on something of substance at some point.

21

THE DAMNED

1892

THE SPACE BETWEEN ROCKS WAS TIGHT, BUT NOT IMPOSSIBLE for Josiah Shaw. His sister was having an easier time, except she kept slipping. He braced his back against the stone with his feet in front of him and used his hands to push his little sister upwards towards a thin slice of moonlight.

"I can't, Joe. I'm slipping," Maddie whimpered.

He shushed her. "Keep quiet," he hissed.

His father hadn't told them to keep quiet, but he knew they had to—some instinct inside screamed for silence.

Protect your sister.

I love you.

Protect your sister.

Find Holden.

His father's words beat like thunder against his eardrums.

Josiah squeezed upwards, trying not to think about the growing distance below, nor the crush of stone against his body. If he slipped...

He shoved it out of his mind and pushed Maddie's foot

upwards. He could feel her legs shaking with fear as he guided her foot to a hold.

When she seemed to have the rock under her, he let go to search for his next handhold. It was tedious and worrying, and the darkness and cold made it seem like a lifetime.

Rock scraped against his back and knees with every inching movement upwards. And then a voice came like a crack of terror: *Shaw!*

It echoed and bounced and clutched at Josiah's throat. Maddie slipped, and he braced himself hard as she came crashing down on his head. He clenched his teeth and strained to keep them both from falling down the crevice.

"Where's Shaw!" Eli demanded.

"Go, Maddie, just go," Josiah hissed.

Her feet were on his shoulders and he pushed with his own, scraping his back along the stone to push her upwards. Again. Inch by inch.

"You know something, Shaw."

"I told you they probably moved after I left," came their father's calm voice.

Maddie's weight left his shoulders as she finally found purchase of her own and, to his relief, began steadily climbing. Fear likely drove her, and knowing Josiah wouldn't let her fall.

"Clay moved after you sent your boy back, didn't he? And he took you along."

It was just as his father had said: they'd figure it out.

"Clay's son couldn't be moved—"

A muted echo of flesh on flesh turned Josiah's fear to ash in his gut.

"You think we don't know what a cold fire looks like? That damn fire is four days old!"

"Clay didn't want to be spotted. They snuffed it out," Nathan explained.

Josiah marveled at that voice. Even now, faced with an

angry group of men and their fists, his father was as calm and reasonable as could be. How could Josiah ever have taken him for a coward?

"Grab his little girl."

That order lit a fire under Josiah's feet. He climbed for all he was worth, trying to escape the greater implications of those words. He hoped Maddie hadn't heard it.

She stopped, the moonlight was blacked out by her body, but it seemed lighter in the passage, then he heard her soft grunting and her feet disappeared over an edge.

They were free, on solid ground and open wilderness. He grabbed his sister's hand and took a moment to get his bearings.

"What about ma?" Maddie asked, peering down the crack.

Josiah tugged her away. "Pa is keeping her safe," he lied.

You find Holden. You tell him your mother is in the mine shaft here.

Josiah swallowed. How long would it take to reach Clay Holden's new camp? Would the outlaw gang still be there?

He froze suddenly. "I can't remember the map," he whispered in horror.

"I remember," Maddie said, tugging him forward. "Head towards those mountains and follow the river to another set of gullies."

His sister had a way of remembering things. She made little rhymes and songs to remember everything from a person's name to medical terminology.

Josiah never understood it, because it seemed to him that remembering the rhymes took more effort than memorizing the word.

They slipped through the forest and underbrush until the voices fell away and the ground opened up into a sprawling meadow.

"We have to run, Maddie. We have to find Clay."

She was shivering and running would keep her warm, but

most of all Josiah knew he had to bring back help. He tugged her into a trot, but her legs were shorter and she wasn't as fast as Josiah. Still, they ran across the meadow and a good distance farther until she stumbled to a stop, hands on her knees, the night air puffing from her lips.

A tremor in the earth alerted him to trouble. Josiah knelt and placed a hand on the ground, straining his ears past his sister's gulping breaths.

Horses.

"We got to go, Maddie."

"Can't we walk?"

"Come on, quick, climb up on my back."

She did without complaint and clung to his back as he moved as quickly as he could over the rough terrain. It wasn't long before they heard the rhythm of galloping horses.

"Maybe it's pa?" Maddie whispered in his ear.

Josiah was too tired to reply. He only shook his head and focused on the moonlit ground as he tried to think what to do.

Without a word, Maddie squirmed off his back to run at his side as the sounds of hooves grew louder. He glanced over his shoulder, across the wide flat plain, and spotted the silhouette of four riders. The group fanned out to search.

He pulled his sister down into a creek bed. "They don't know where we are," he whispered.

"But they're following us."

He shook his head. "They split up. They haven't seen us."

Maddie stared at her big brother, eyes wide, waiting for direction from the wiser ten-year-old. Only he didn't know what to do.

Protect your sister.

Josiah did not want to be a man anymore. He wanted to weep with fear.

"This is a creek, right?" she asked between chattering teeth. "Don't they go to rivers?"

Josiah frowned at the bubbling water. For all he knew, its course could turn back the way they'd come. He risked a peek over the bank. One rider was headed their way. At least they couldn't track in the dark. He hoped, at any rate.

"We'll follow it downstream for a ways. Keep low, though. We'll look for a spot to climb out into some trees or something."

He felt rather than saw her slight nod. Grabbing her hand, they moved downstream, picking their way past slippery rocks and avoiding any sandy bank or muddy patches that would leave an obvious footprint.

They moved quickly, the trickling water masking their foot-steps and occasional splashes. Somewhere off in the distance, a pack of coyotes yipped and barked.

A heavy splash froze the children. Josiah glanced over his shoulder to spot a large, dark shadow in the creek bed upstream. A horse and rider.

Josiah nudged Maddie and put a finger to his lips, then slithered over to a tangled mess of roots and bushes. But when he turned to help his sister into the hiding place, he spotted her frozen in place and clinging to a boulder.

He started to call her name, but caught himself. The rider was slowly picking his way along the bank, with an eye to the ground.

Grimm picked up a pebble and flicked it at his sister, but she didn't move. At a distance, she might look like a rock, but up close…

Josiah's heart galloped. He tensed to dart from his hiding place, but stopped himself. Acting without thinking had gotten them all here, but thinking wasn't getting him anywhere either.

He only hoped to God the man would turn back around.

Seconds crawled into eternity, and the blood beating against his eardrums was as loud as a waterfall. Josiah couldn't leave things to chance—every instinct told him to act.

With glacial care, he picked up a heavy stone, then slipped further back to edge up the bank and out of the water. A rain of drops splattered into the earth, but the night was alive with yips and owl hoots, croaking frogs, and flapping bats.

The rider stopped in front of the cluster of rocks where Maddie huddled. He huffed out a laugh and dug around in his pocket. The flare of a match illuminated his grizzled face for a moment, then smoke wafted into the air. He nudged his horse forward, then dismounted with a splash.

"It's a good thing the boss wants you alive."

Maddie whimpered.

"Oh, come now, girlie, I don't bite," the man purred.

Maddie sprang towards the bank, startling the horse. It reared, and the man turned to keep it from bolting, trying to keep control of his mount. The front hooves kicked in the night, water splashed and churned, and the man tugged on the reins.

Protect your sister.

Josiah surged to his feet and took a running leap off the bank with a rock poised in his hand. The man turned, reaching for his gun, but caught the stone on his face. He staggered back. The horse came down, a hoof smacking against the man's head.

Horse and rider went down. The horse bolted, the rider didn't move. Josiah dove for the dragging reins. He bumped over rocks and stones and skidded through the water as the horse sought escape.

The horse reared, lifting Josiah out of the water as he clutched the reins for dear life. "Easy now, easy boy," he soothed. With each splash landing, Josiah inched up the reins until he could grab hold of the bridle. "You're fine. It's just some noise. Just sniff my hand here…"

When the horse was calm enough to keep all four hooves on the ground, Josiah led it back to its former rider. The man stared sightlessly at the moon with a concave skull as the stream washed away his blood.

"Maddie?" he hissed.

The little girl rushed from the tangle of roots and threw her arms around him. "I couldn't move. I'm sorry!"

The horse danced back, and Josiah kept one arm around his sister, and the other soothing the horse. "It's all right," he said to both. "But we got to get moving. You get up on this horse."

He helped her mount, but didn't pass up the reins. Instead, he kept them firmly in hand and bent to inspect the dead man. It was one of the four men who'd only just joined the marshals.

He felt no remorse. Just a cold emptiness. Not even a ripple of emotion as he unbuckled the man's belt and holster, and slung it over a shoulder before rooting around his jacket.

Josiah took the man's billfold.

He'd murdered two men now. It made no difference he was a thief, too. Josiah Shaw figured he was already good and damned.

───────

"THEY SEE US!" MADDIE SCREECHED.

The night stretched to eternity. Josiah wished it would end. He wanted to wake up and find out this was all a bad dream. That he hadn't told Angel Davren where his father had gone. That he'd kept his mouth shut and stayed true to his word.

He wished he hadn't shot a man.

But most of all, he wanted badly not to be clinging to a horse with his sister's arms around his waist and men with guns at their back.

Josiah risked a glance over his shoulder. Three dark shapes were gaining ground, but the moon only offered enough light to make the earth look treacherous. He didn't dare urge the horse into a run—they'd be sure to hit a gopher hole.

"We're nearly to the river. I can hear it."

"They'll catch us," Maddie said.

She was right.

Josiah clenched his jaw and urged his horse into a gallop. The horse had better eyes than he did, so he gave it the freedom to pick its own path. Time stretched and slowed all at once. The ground flew under their feet, and the wind bit into his cheeks. The crisp smell of the wild night and horse sweat filled his senses and his ears picked out the distant yip of coyotes and mournful owls. His sister was wet and shivering at his back, her weight like a bird's ready to fly off the saddle at the first jolt.

With one hand he held the reins, and with the other he held Maddie's hands to keep her in place, bending over the horn and moving with the horse's gait.

The sound of flowing water soon drowned out his frantic breaths. And then they were there, a fast flowing expanse of silver with jutting boulders and white churning water.

"Josiah!" Maddie's scream was lost to the river as Josiah urged their horse forward into the icy spring water.

Up to its knees, past the belly, until the water bumped and flowed around Josiah's boots. The horse moved on and then dipped down into the water.

Maddie gasped.

"Hold on!" Josiah yelled.

But the order was unnecessary—she had a death grip on his waist. Their father had taught them to swim in creeks and streams over the summers, but this was different—the river was fast flowing and deep, and bone-chillingly cold.

The horse swam as it was swept downriver and the water tugged and pulled at Josiah's body. He gripped the horn and the horse's sides with his thighs, but the saddle had gone slippery and the horse's back was at an angle.

His feet slipped free of the stirrups, then his legs were pulled with the current. Maddie screamed, and he grabbed her arm, holding on tight to the horn with his other hand as they were dragged through the water. Josiah closed his eyes and silently urged the horse onward.

He felt the first touch of a hoof on sand, and when the horse began to level out, he floated back onto the saddle, and pulled Maddie up behind him. The horse broke free with a cascade of water and it huffed its way onto solid ground.

Josiah bent over the horse's neck. "Thank you, boy," he whispered, rubbing its dripping hair and patting the quivering muscles. "We got to keep going. You'll warm up if you walk."

The horse gave a snort, but followed his suggestion, and they were soon trotting downriver.

"You think they're gone?" Maddie chattered.

Josiah didn't reply. He didn't have the energy to lie to his sister—she'd know he was lying, anyway.

The three riders were experienced lawmen, or outlaws, or whatever they were—this wasn't the first time they'd run down a horse and rider.

It wasn't long before the first crack of a gunshot split the night. "You stop right there or we'll go back and take it out on your ma!"

Josiah hesitated for a moment. But these men were crooked and everything that came out of their mouth was vile. He urged the horse to a gallop until the roar of a waterfall drowned out the pursuing hooves and hooting men.

He gave the waterfall a wide berth, searching for an easier route, but the boulders were steep and wide and the men were on their tail. They skidded down a hill, dirt and pebbles spilling around the horse's hooves as Josiah leaned back in the saddle, hoping the horse knew what it was about.

It hit the bank with a splash, and another gunshot barked from above. "Next shot is taking out your horse!"

Josiah looked back to find a man taking careful aim. With a speed that surprised him, he drew his stolen revolver and fired first. His aim was off and it didn't come close to the man, but it startled him enough to take a step back.

A deep pool churned at the waterfall's base before surging down a wide ravine, but there was a fork in the ravine, where a shallow stream joined the greater flow.

Josiah slid off the saddle behind a large boulder. "You remember the way?" he asked.

"I do."

"I'm going to lead them away. Follow the map down that creek and find Holden."

"But—"

Josiah slapped the horse's rump to get it moving and was relieved to see Maddie scramble for the reins. She rode their horses all the time, but she'd never had to manage alone.

Josiah ducked behind a nearby boulder and crouched, squinting into the night, his stomach churning with revulsion. He did not want to kill another man.

Protect your sister.

If these men made it back... they'd tell Eli and Angel where the camp was. If Clay Holden was even still here. Josiah tried not to dwell on that possibility as first one rider, then another skidded down the steep slope. He could take them out here, but he'd never practiced hitting anything at this distance.

Better to wait.

Josiah put his back against the hard stone. It'd lost its warmth from the heat of the day and was cold with night and the river's ice. His feet were wet and numb in their boots, and he was shaking with fear.

When he could hear their murmured voices, he risked a peek around the boulder. The riders had dismounted, and were leading their horses by the reins, guns in hand. The third man had a rifle.

He tensed to spring from cover, to buy his sister time to find help, but a chorus of yipping coyotes echoed in the ravine. Trickster and a creator, savior and a villain—a coyote was many things.

Tonight they were saviors.

A silent arrow pierced one man's back, and one yip turned into a bark as a bullet ripped through another's throat. Screams and yells, thunder and sparks of lead biting rock.

Josiah squeezed his eyes shut and gripped his revolver with both hands. It felt like an hour had passed before the world fell silent. He swallowed and cracked open an eye. The revolver in his hand quivered.

A shadow moved up top, and another slipped from a crevice in the rocks. Slim Vito sauntered into view and stood grinning down at the boy.

"I knew you couldn't keep your mouth shut."

Josiah took a shuddering breath. "My sister—"

Vito jerked his head down the ravine. "Put that away, boy. Are there anymore after you?"

Josiah carefully uncocked the revolver and slipped it back into the holster. "U.S. Marshals took us. They burned our hotel. I shot one of them." His voice sounded cracked and worn as an old man's. "My parents need help. My ma—"

Slim Vito yanked him to his feet. "What the hell do you take us for—lawmen? Come on, get moving." Vito gave him a little shove.

"You have to help us!"

"We just did." Vito turned to whistle at the second shadow with a bow, then gathered up the horses and led them down along the shallow creek bed.

The camp was as well hidden as the last. Clay Holden had a way of finding hideouts that were as scenic as they were secret. The tall man with the shaved hair on the sides crouched in front of Maddie, who'd been given a blanket. She was sitting on a rock, sobbing.

Josiah rushed at the man, reaching for his pistol, but then caught himself as he noticed the comforting hand on his sister's shoulder.

Clay turned his head and cocked an eye at the boy.

"This quick little devil claims he shot a U.S. Marshal," Vito crowed.

The rest of the camp was a chaos of activity as they rolled up gear and saddled horses. They were getting ready to move again.

"You have to help them," Maddie cried.

Clay stood to scowl down at the pair. "What happened?"

Josiah told him. Everything. Even the shameful part he'd played. When he fell silent, Clay shared a look with Vito.

The slim outlaw shrugged. "Not our concern."

"You got us involved in this mess!" Josiah raged. "My ma's in the mine shaft. She's with child and my pa never told them anything. He sent us here to warn you—to give you time to escape."

Maddie grabbed Clay's scarred hand and looked up at him with pleading eyes. "You have to help them, sir. *Please*."

Vito made a sucking noise before turning to spit. "Ah, shit."

22

HARD TRUTHS

1901

Tobias gawked at his brother. "But... *Why*?"

For the first time, Tobias heard his brother laugh—it bordered on madness and was so unnerving that Tobias took a step back, nearly tripping into the campfire before catching himself.

Grimm wiped his eyes. Then, feeling suddenly exhausted by the telling, he dropped his head in his hands and rubbed his neck.

"What happened to ma and..." Tobias hesitated. He'd never uttered the word 'father' in his life. No one ever mentioned the man. "My father?"

Grimm shook his head without looking up from the ground. He sat cross-legged and hunched over, resisting the urge to rock back and forth. "I didn't understand it then, and I still don't—Angel Davren, Gil Blake, and those other men were Negros and Indians. I'm not sure Eli was even their leader. He seemed to look to Angel for answers."

Tobias considered something for a moment as he poked at the campfire. "I didn't know we could be U.S. Marshals."

Grimm raised his head enough to eye his little brother. Despite everything, Tobias had a cheerful bounce about him. "*Deputy* U.S. Marshals."

Tobias scratched his head. "Isn't that what Mrs. Pleasant did?"

"She wasn't a U.S. Marshal."

"I mean, you said that Angel fellow seemed like the leader... like a mastermind. Looking back and all, I was just thinking how useful it is having a white girl around. I use Sarah all the time when I got an idea for something I can't do. And I heard ma talking with Mr. AJ... Mrs Pleasant used a white fellow to conduct business. That's sort of the arrangement ma had with Mr. AJ. He has no mind for business, but ma does. Easier to do things in his name, since he's white—or can pass for it, anyway."

Grimm gave a grudging nod. "A U.S. Marshal can deputize anyone he likes. I think."

"Can girls be marshals?"

"No."

Tobias snapped his fingers. "Darn. I'd get Sarah to become one so she could deputize me."

Grimm sighed at his brother's heroic ideals. He saw too much of himself in his little brother. And he didn't want him to experience the same pain he had. If only the path to wisdom wasn't so brutal.

"Who the hell cares who was in charge," Grimm said, staring into the flames. "They were all working together, and all of them had a hand in killing our father."

"You said you killed our father," Tobias shot back.

"I basically did. I was a loudmouth like you."

"You didn't kill him, Grimm. You made a mistake. I make plenty of those."

"You can't afford to make any more."

Tobias looked guilty.

"What did you do?" Grimm demanded.

Tobias blinked a pair of all too innocent eyes. "Nothing."

"Tobias White."

"Not my name."

Grimm growled.

"What happened next?" Tobias asked.

"What'd you do?"

Tobias huffed at him. "Nothing. I just… carved a message for Mr. AJ."

"You did what?"

"No one's gonna find it but Jin. It's on a wall in my fort."

"What'd you say?"

"I asked him to help us."

Grimm muttered an oath.

"Why don't you want his help?"

"It's not that," Grimm said. "It's… I don't want to mess up another person's life. Look what I did to yours."

"I'm happy with it," Tobias said with a shrug. "Overall. I mean, you're a pain sometimes, and Maddie's a tattletale, but—"

"You know what I mean. You don't even know your own father."

That hit home. Hard. Tobias went quiet. After a time he shifted, because knowing his brother, he might just stop speaking for another eight years. "I kind of figured he would be like you," he whispered.

Grimm's eyes welled with tears, and before he could stop them, they fell, dripping slowly to the earth. God, he missed his father.

"What happened next?"

Grimm wiped his eyes and gave a shake of his head. "Ma never said."

"How'd... pa die?"

Another shake of the head. "He never came back."

A HOLLOW SHELL

A LONELY WAIL JERKED MADDIE OUT OF A DEEP SLEEP. SHE took in the dim fire smoldering in an ornate hearth, the plush bedcover, the thick curtains…

We're in a hotel, she told herself. Then why had she heard the howl of a wolf?

The answer came a second later when a shadow on the floor took shape. Her mother sat on the floor by the bed, clutching her head.

Maddie tossed aside her cover, and rushed to her mother's side. "Ma, what happened? Are you all right?"

Her training and instincts took over, and without waiting for an answer, Maddie pressed her hand to her mother's brow to check for fever. It was cold with sweat. She checked her pulse. Racing. Then straightened a little to gaze at the tangled mess of sheets.

Maddie concluded her mother had had a nightmare. She rose and poured water from the pitcher into a glass and handed it to her mother.

"Drink this."

Lily did as ordered, and Maddie retrieved a blanket to

wrap around her shoulders, then helped her mother stand and drew her over to the fire. She added coal and poked it to life, listening to her mother's harsh breathing.

"I shouldn't have sent your brothers off alone," Lily whispered.

"Grimm will take care of him." Maddie didn't bother using their new names. Not here. She was sick of changing identities. There were some days after That Night that she didn't know who she was anymore. Times when she could recall the oddest details with acute precision, spinning round and round in her mind's eye, but still unable to see the whole picture of That Night.

After Josiah sent her down that ravine, she'd clung to the horse, shivering with cold and numb with terror, following the mental map her father had drawn. Only she'd never reached the end on her own.

A large wraith had detached itself from the night. It moved like ink, with a predatory gait that made her horse tense to bolt, but the wraith grabbed her horse's bridle and spoke soft words to girl and beast.

"Easy now," the man said. "The coyotes out there are friends. You're both safe here."

Maddie didn't know who the man was, she didn't know if he was one of the men after them… not really. But something about this wraith had put her at ease. Or perhaps it'd been desperation at finding an adult out in the wilderness who wasn't shooting at her with guns.

Gunshots cracked in the canyon and Maddie screamed, tensing to turn her horse around and race back to her brother. But the man made a sharp sound, and fluid shadows moved silently over the earth.

The man swung up into the saddle behind her, and spurred the horse forward, until they'd reached a campfire. He dismounted, nodded to another man to take the reins, and plucked her from the saddle.

She was crying, choking on her fear in silence, having no idea if this man was friend or foe. He'd set her down by the fire and wrapped her in a coarse blanket, then stood to issue orders.

The big man sat on his haunches to look her in the eye. "I'm Clay Holden," he said, studying her in the firelight. "You look familiar, Miss. Is your name Maddie Shaw?"

"My brother—" She choked to a stop.

"We have guards out there. They'll bring him back."

He handed her a waterskin and rested a hand on her shoulder as she drank. "Where's your father?"

But the moment he asked, she started crying again. She couldn't get her breath, couldn't get warm, couldn't form a thought. All she wanted was her family back.

"What happened?" the man asked again.

Maddie didn't really know. She was trying to put words to things she didn't understand. Mainly, she just wanted her family back. What if Josiah left her all alone with this man?

But then Josiah appeared—full of rage, making demands, and bristling with threat. He told Clay everything that had happened.

Maddie felt tension between the men, a silent conversation she couldn't fathom, but one thing became clear in her mind— they weren't racing after her parents. So she'd taken the man's large hand—scarred and calloused like a stone—and looked into his eyes with a plea.

"You have to help them, sir. *Please.*"

The man's flint-like eyes softened, and he gave her hand a gentle squeeze.

Clay Holden had brought back their mother. And a baby brother. But not their father.

The days after were a dream of moving and traveling from

one camp to the next, always under cover of night, with a squalling infant that wouldn't keep quiet.

Clay Holden hadn't raised his voice once. Not to her mother nor to the loud infant that could give them all away. Lily took the infant to her breast when needed, held it when required, but it all seemed sort of mechanical, like one of those dime machines that made the figurines dance.

And every time Maddie had asked after her father, her mother only leaked tears—the silent kind that bleed from a person's soul—until Clay had taken them aside to let her and Josiah know their father was dead.

After a while, Maddie was sure she didn't want to know what happened in that cave. One look at her mother told her all she needed to know.

It came as a surprise when her mother finally broke her silence. "They killed him," Lily whispered, her voice raw.

"Did they hurt you, Ma?"

"They tore out my heart."

Lily stared at the fire with a haunted look in her eyes.

Maddie watched her for a time. They'd been on the run for eight years. For most of those years, they had Clay watching out for them. Josiah had run with the gang. But the marshals eventually caught up with them, killing them off one by one. In the end, Clay Holden disappeared. Not hanged—just vanished, like her father.

Something felt wrong about the whole business, and while her mother would soldier on, unwilling to bring anyone else into this deadly affair, Maddie was seeing the truth of the matter: this was beyond them. Gentlemanly outlaws, wicked lawmen, and a horde of secrets.

Maddie knew what she needed to do—and she wasn't about to tell her mother.

"I'll go out first thing for the shopping we'll need."

Lily stirred, giving her head a shake. "I don't want you going alone."

"I'll be in the maid's outfit we nicked from the laundry. No one will suspect a thing. I don't look anything like that horrid sketch." And despite herself, she started laughing. "Can you imagine the fun Tobias would have poking fun at me over that?"

The edge of Lily's lip twitched as she wiped her eyes on a handkerchief. A single dimple showed on her cheek. "We'll clip the article and save it for him."

"Don't you dare, Ma. That's cruel and you know it."

"It doesn't look anything like you, baby."

"It just goes to show what an actress I am."

Lily sat back with a sigh and tightened the blanket around her shoulders. "All the times we bit our tongues when Isobel was playing at her guises."

Maddie grinned. "If she'd only known what we were up to."

"She's probably angry that we pulled it off longer than she did."

Maddie snorted into her hand, but quickly sobered. "I miss them."

"They're safe. That's what matters."

"We don't know that."

"The paper—"

"Said she was shot. I haven't seen anything about her recovery. Maybe we could telephone—"

"No." The clipped word was absolute, but Maddie was nearly sixteen, and she had a mind of her own.

Lily seemed to realize it too, because she leaned forward to lay a hand over her daughter's. "Maddie, we can't involve the Riots in this—we'll get them hanged."

"You don't know that."

"Those men have badges and the law behind them."

"They broke the law and you know it."

"So did we. So did Josiah."

"Father was held at gunpoint and forced to help Clay's son."

"He knew where their camp was and he didn't…"

"No, stop claiming we're outlaws!" Maddie growled. "We were wronged, Ma. Every step of the way, we were wronged."

"The Law doesn't care about that."

"It should!"

"I agree."

"Mr. AJ will too."

"And we'll get him shot. Those men will go after Jin and Sarah to get to us. Do you understand just how ruthless they are?"

She had a point. And Maddie let herself seem convinced. It wasn't that Maddie was a wonderful actress; it was more that her mother wanted to believe she was convinced, so Maddie just went along with it.

It was true, the Riots would be getting themselves into a viper's nest of trouble, but they did that on their own. And Maddie was tired of running—tired of watching her mother and brother shoulder the burden of surviving.

It was time she did something to help.

24

WE'RE ALL MAD

A BABY WAS CRYING. SCREAMING, REALLY. WHEN ISOBEL reached the last step, she slumped against the railing to catch her breath.

She'd made it downstairs without falling. Small victories. Only now her knees shook so badly she was forced to sit on the last step before they gave out completely.

Isobel slumped against the railing and listened to the cries of the infant. A part of her wanted to cry, too. She felt as helpless (or was the creature furious?) as the baby sounded.

She was furious at her helplessness, and it left a bitter taste in her mouth. She was not one to sit down and wait, and leave others to a task—that her partner and husband had left her behind stung even worse.

Not that she blamed Riot—there was no one else to blame but herself and the limitations of her cursed body. Isobel wanted to be at his side, or racing ahead. Instead, she was left wondering if she could climb back to her feet.

With the help of the railing she managed, and shuffled off towards the kitchen. The pain was one thing, but her weakness was a surprise—she'd lost a great deal of weight and muscle in the hospital, and her body felt like it'd been replaced with hollow bird bones.

Would she ever recover? She'd forgotten what strength felt like—of climbing a mast with laughable ease. Her memories seemed to belong to another person. She'd taken her abilities for granted. No longer.

"Consider me humbled," she muttered, catching herself on a wall.

Isobel found the wailing infant sitting in a high chair with armrests that encircled the sides and front to keep it from tumbling out. She hesitated in the doorway. Shouldn't its mother have come for it by now? She listened for hurrying footsteps, but the infant's screams of outrage beat against her eardrums.

"Hello?" she called.

When no one answered, she shuffled past the headache-inducing imp to check the coffee percolator. It was down to cold sludge. Isobel eyed the wet grinds in the basket on the counter and weighed how much trouble brewing a new pot would be against drinking what was left.

A wave of dizziness interrupted her dilemma, and she caught herself on the countertop. Before it overtook her, she fell into a chair and gripped an armrest to steady the world.

"God, I hate this," she growled.

The crying stopped. She cracked open an eye to find the infant staring at her and coating its pudgy fist with slobber. It was a chubby little thing with large blue eyes and a fuzz of copper hair.

"That's better," she told it. "Where is your… minder?"

The baby gummed its fist, then its eyes and nose crinkled and it started up again like a crackling telephone line.

Isobel put a finger to her lips. "Shh."

For a blissful second, she thought she'd startled the creature to silence, but it only lasted a moment. It began crying with renewed enthusiasm.

Isobel planted her good elbow on the table and rested her head in a hand. Her right arm was in a sling. She wasn't supposed to be out of bed. Sarah and Jin had taken the horses out for exercise and Margaret was out burning off excess energy on her bicycle with the pair. She was fairly sure the bicyclist would triumph over the horses—Margaret Ederle lived her life on a bicycle and had the calves to match.

The thought inspired her. Ever competitive, Isobel used the table to stand, and wandered over to the cabinets to search for a coffee tin. Despite living in Ravenwood Manor for several months, this was Miss Lily's domain and even now, with the family gone, Isobel felt like an intruder.

As the infant screamed, she glanced over her shoulder in consideration. Perhaps she should rouse Miss Annie Dupree? The woman had been a governess, after all. No, she reminded herself, Annie had taken a holiday. She suspected she'd gone on a trip with one of her paying gentlemen.

Isobel walked over to the infant, bent to peer into its gaping mouth, then searched the kitchen until she found a bottle of brandy. She poured herself a glass, drank half, then took the glass over to the table, dipped a finger into the alcohol, and rubbed it over the infant's red gums.

The infant snatched her finger and gummed it. "I thought that might be the issue." She took her finger back and came back with more brandy. "You should know my mother disapproves of giving brandy to infants."

Marcus Amsel had used the remedy for his eleven children and his mob of grandchildren. Isobel could never keep her nieces and nephews straight, but they were all hale and hearty. Her father claimed using brandy to relieve teething was a scientific fact by now.

The blissful silence was interrupted by rhythmic thumping

against a wall. Isobel frowned at the drool-coated creature. "What is that?"

The infant gurgled in reply. She started to take away her finger, but the infant gathered itself to wail anew. She picked up a rattle from the table, dipped it into the brandy, and handed it over.

The creature was appeased.

Isobel pushed herself up from the table and opened the mudroom door. A redheaded woman sat against the back door leading into the yard. She was hugging her knees, her face buried in her skirts, and her body knocked against the wood with a slow rocking motion.

"Did someone hurt you?" Isobel demanded.

The woman didn't respond.

Isobel checked the mudroom window. No one stood on the back porch. The yard appeared empty, and the carriage house was silent. She turned back to the woman. "What happened?"

No response.

Isobel lowered herself to the floor, but instead of the slow descent she'd intended, it turned into more of a controlled fall. She landed with a jolt of pain.

Only after she was firmly on the floor did it occur to her that a fellow lodger might have put this woman into a state of shock. In which case, she'd just placed herself in a position of vulnerability. Or maybe the woman was about to fly into a violent rage. This was the woman who'd smashed a vase over another woman's head—what if she was mad and prone to violent outbursts, and it hadn't been just to save Riot's life?

When the redhead beside her didn't attack her with a jar of preserves, Isobel dredged up her name. "Aisling."

No response. Her eyes were out of focus and far away as she rocked gently back and forth. "Your baby needs you."

When Isobel ventured a calming touch, the woman

flinched away, so she rested her head on a wall to wait for the woman's panic and terror to subside.

"*I'm mad. You're mad. We're all mad here,*" Isobel quoted under her breath. "*Drowning in our own tears.*"

"*How do you know I'm mad?*" Aisling whispered.

Isobel smiled at the continuation of *Alice in Wonderland.* "*You must be or you wouldn't have come here.*"

"I didn't have much choice," Aisling said with a shudder.

"You're not a prisoner."

"It's not that…" Aisling seemed to shake off whatever had hold of her mind. She climbed to her feet and lurched into the kitchen to pick up the infant.

Isobel narrowed her eyes. When the woman had climbed to her feet, she'd glimpsed an inch of bare wrist. There were bruises around her wrist. Isobel rested her head against the wall and watched as the young woman slumped in a chair to comfort her baby. She looked as exhausted as Isobel felt.

"Her teeth are coming in…" Feeling Isobel's gaze on her, Aisling looked up, surprised to find her still in the mudroom. "Sorry, I don't know your name, ma'am. Are you one of the lodgers? Do you need breakfast?" And finally… "Are you all right?"

"I may be able to manage coffee on my own," Isobel admitted. "But I'm not entirely sure I can get off this floor."

Aisling's eyes widened. "Oh, God—You're Mrs. Riot, aren't you?" It was near to a squeak. "I'm sorry, it won't happen—"

"Call me Isobel," she cut in. "I'm not the lady of the house. We all just live here."

Aisling had turned slightly to the side, as if shielding her baby in a gesture of protection. She was a nervous thing, but then Isobel probably would be too if she'd bashed the madam of a whorehouse over the head and fled a cruel pimp.

"You saved my husband's life," Isobel reminded her. "You have my gratitude."

"He was kind to me."

"Irritating, isn't it?"

Aisling grinned. "I hardly knew what to do."

"So you bashed a woman over the head who fired a shotgun at him. Seems reasonable. I don't suppose you can manage coffee and the baby? I'm not much good for anything of late."

"Of course." Aisling set her baby into a basket on the floor and set about making coffee, only to look back in puzzlement. "Would you like some help standing?"

"I don't normally like help, but I don't have much choice at the moment."

Aisling got the water boiling in the percolator and came over to offer a hand. When she'd pulled Isobel to her feet, she helped her to a chair.

"Being shot is dreadful," Isobel said. "I really could do without the lesson in humility."

"I don't like anyone to see me like—" Aisling faltered, looking to the mudroom. "*That.*"

"I have an Alienist friend who—"

"No." Aisling turned abruptly. "I'm fine. It's nothing. I just… my heart races and I can't see straight."

Isobel studied the woman's back and decided that pressing her was not wise at the moment. She'd only just met her and she had her own issues to deal with—to say nothing of her daughters' emotional states.

Isobel wished Annie Dupree were there. Aisling O'Shannon had worked as a prostitute—or possibly been forced into the trade. The older woman might be able to help her.

"Did it happen before you came here? Or is it just… the

unfamiliar surroundings?" She'd been about to say the change of profession.

Aisling gave her a shy glance. "I can't ever remember feeling so safe."

"No one's going to take that away from you, Miss Aisling."

"I wish I could believe it."

Isobel didn't miss the furtive glance towards the mudroom door. "Did someone come by just now?"

Aisling's eyes widened a fraction. "No... no, it's only I can't really cook. I shouldn't have this job."

Isobel could not read people as well as Riot, but even she could tell the woman was lying. Something *had* triggered her episode—but Isobel sensed pressing the matter would make the woman retreat.

"You're in good company then," Isobel said.

"But you weren't hired as a cook."

"You can always improve—as long as you don't poison us."

Aisling laughed, a sound that edged madness.

25

UMBRELLA DEFENSE

AISLING DROPPED A TEACUP WHEN A RACKET OF NOISE SOUNDED from the yard. Pottery splintered on the tile, but the woman barely noticed as she rushed to the kitchen window. Her shoulders slumped in relief.

The infant was wailing again.

A moment later, Jin's voice rang in the courtyard. "You cheated! The horse would not move."

"That's because she's old," Sarah said.

"Oh, don't be sore, Jin," Margaret said. "You can ride the bicycle next time."

"I cannot ride it yet."

"You need to practice. That's all. I'll look for a smaller one for you."

Isobel could practically hear the returning growl.

"I'm so sorry," Aisling said, frantically cleaning up the shards. She cut her finger on a sliver and hissed in frustration.

Isobel closed her eyes. She was tired. Drained of the energy needed to sort this woman and her troubles out. She rallied, somewhat.

"Aisling, I'm not about to send you away. No one is. But

you need to tell me who came to the door." The steel was gone from her voice, but her observation hit home.

Aisling froze, looking up at her. "How... how did you know?"

"I notice things." Isobel nodded to the wailing infant. "Your baby needs you—sit down and rest."

"Let me just…"

"*Sit down.*"

The young woman picked up her baby and sat, looking stunned. Before Isobel could pursue her line of inquiry, someone stomped into the mudroom and strode into the kitchen.

Margaret paused at the crunching sound under her boots. "Did I break something again?" She was coated in sweat, her shirt and riding bloomers dusty, and her hair was trying to escape its confines.

"Yes."

Margaret glared at her. "You aren't supposed to be out of your room."

"I'm a rebel."

Margaret muttered something rude and retrieved a broom to clean up the broken teacup. "You're worse than my father at taking his medicine and following instructions."

"Did you think I'd be a complacent invalid?"

"I'm tempted to slip some laudanum into your tea."

"I'd trounce you."

"You wouldn't stand a chance against me."

"Not presently."

"Not *ever*." Margaret gave her broom a skillful twirl before bending to sweep the teacup shards into a pan. "I've been training with the Umbrella Defense Academy."

"You don't carry an umbrella."

"It's more than that—fencing, cane fighting, and something called jujitsu."

"You mean like 'bartitsu' from the Sherlock Holmes story?"

"It's not that. It's Umbrella Defense."

Aisling had unbuttoned her blouse and exposed a breast for her infant, who latched on with a slurping and snuffling sound that made Isobel shudder. At least it had stopped crying.

"I'm sorry she was hungry. Should I—"

"Stop apologizing," Isobel said.

Margaret sighed. "Don't mind her... Isobel is positively inhuman. She's just been confronted with the undeniable fact that she was nursed by her beloved mother."

"Hop would claim I suckled on the teat of a malevolent fox spirit."

"You wish."

At this last, Aisling smiled and seemed to relax at their good-natured ribbing. It was finally something familiar.

The door gave way to Jin's forceful push. "It does not like me," she argued with her sister.

"Of course Mrs. May doesn't like you. You treat her like a tool. She's a living, breathing animal, Jin. You can't just expect a horse to do what you want."

"I am not asking the horse to dance. It knows what it is supposed to do. It is as bad as the cat."

"Watson is perfectly well-behaved—" Sarah cut off when she saw her adopted mother at the table. "Why are you downstairs?"

"Because I'm worse than a cat."

Jin snorted in agreement.

"And I wanted coffee."

"Oh, goodness," Aisling said, rising abruptly. She pried the infant from her breast, and plopped it into Jin's arm, who settled it easily against her shoulder.

Isobel narrowed her eyes at the infant snuffling at the side of the girl's neck. Jin patted its back without thought and cocked her head at Isobel's astonishment.

The child glared. "What?"

"You're holding a baby."

"Yes."

"It's not crying."

Jin shrugged. "I was a house slave. The household had babies. I had to carry one on my back while I did the house-cleaning."

All the women in the kitchen stopped to stare at the little girl.

Jin scowled. "The baby was in a sling on my back. I did not tie it there. He was big and fat and heavy."

"And you've been a huge help to me, Jin," Aisling said. "Fiona just loves you."

"I suppose."

"I don't know what I'd have done without Sarah and Jin here," Aisling said to Isobel. "They're a pair of angels."

Jin made a face at Isobel behind the woman's back that made Margaret erupt with laughter.

"So, did you ask her?" Sarah asked when the woman recovered.

"I was getting to it when you two hellions came stomping in," Margaret said.

"Ask me what?"

Sarah pulled out a chair and sat next to her. "Margaret is training with an Umbrella Defense Academy. Jin and I want to take lessons."

Jin plopped down in a chair with the infant in her arms. "They will not let me take the class."

"Have you asked?"

"The clubhouse where they meet has a 'No Chinese' sign."

"But it's not the club's policy," Margaret explained. "It's just the gymnasium they rent, and, I should add, that the gymnasium barely tolerates them."

"So we're thinking—"

"You were thinking," Jin told her sister.

"That we could ask them to give classes here—downstairs in the hall." It was called the dance hall, but Isobel doubted Zephaniah Ravenwood had ever thrown a ball at his manor house.

The baby let out a belch and Jin shifted it, so she cradled it in her arms. Pudgy fists wrapped around her braid and pulled the end into its gummy mouth. To Isobel's surprise, Jin didn't even make a face.

She'd never get the child's limits.

"We cannot use the dance hall," Jin insisted. "The Whites—Shaws will return. It is their sitting room."

"It's only temporary," Sarah said. "And we could use the extra money."

"Actually, it might be permanent—if we ask them. I'm not sure they'll be able to rent the gymnasium again," Margaret said, as she set two mugs on the table. "Anyone else for coffee?"

"Thank you, but it makes Fiona restless when I drink it," Aisling said.

Isobel cocked her head at the woman. "Can a mother poison her child with breast milk?"

Aisling's lips parted in shock.

"I don't think she means on *purpose*," Sarah said quickly. "Just if it can pass from mother to child—like if the mother was poisoned. *Unknowingly*. Right, Isobel?"

Isobel blinked at her daughter, then noticed everyone was staring at her (save for the infant). It took a moment to realize why. "Yes. Of course I meant that."

"I… don't know. I mean, I suppose since everything I eat seems to affect her."

Isobel set that aside for further study.

Aisling frowned at the coffee she'd just poured. "Was there a reason for your question?"

"No."

"You'll get used to it," Margaret assured, taking her own cup before sliding one to Isobel. "Can you manage to drink on your own, or would you like me to hold the cup to your lips?"

Isobel shot her a glare.

"So can we?" Sarah pressed.

"It is the Shaw's room," Jin argued.

"Maddie would like the lessons, too—when she gets back."

Isobel took a sip of coffee, wondering how she'd gone from roaming Europe and catching murderers to handling domestic crises for a house full of women. This must be how a madam felt.

———

A KNOCK AT THE FRONT DOOR INTERRUPTED THE ARGUING girls. Before Isobel could make her snail-like way to answer it, Margaret marched out of the kitchen.

Aisling picked up a rolling pin and clutched it with a white-knuckled grip. A minute later, Margaret returned with Dr. Ewan Wise on her heels. He offered the women a bow before turning his bespectacled gaze on his patient.

"Yes, I know. I escaped my room."

"Did you fall down the stairs?"

"I did not," Isobel said with pride.

"Good," he said cheerfully. "You can show me how well you walk up them."

"Only if someone carries my coffee."

"You should only be drinking the tea I left for you."

Isobel grumbled as he helped her to her feet, then took his offered arm. When they were halfway up the stairwell, he said in a low voice, "I received a most interesting letter from my niece."

"Oh?"

Isobel was more focused on climbing one step at a time than his family affairs.

"I do not have a niece named Mary Bennet in Sacramento," he confided.

That got her attention. Isobel stopped to stare at the doctor. The edge of his mustache twitched. "And how is she?"

"On the surface, it's… a quaint letter. But I thought you might be able to glean more from it."

The challenge of a puzzle charged her mind and made her forget her infirmities. She managed the stairway without stumbling and didn't even stop to rest at the top, but made for her bedroom with the doctor on her heels.

Dr. Wise stopped at the doorway.

"Come in."

He gave another bow, and entered, then reached under his coat to hand over a letter. Isobel sat in Ravenwood's armchair to study the thick envelope, while Dr. Wise studied the medicines on her bedside table.

The envelope was thick, expensive, and had a Sacramento stamp from two weeks earlier. It was written in a flowery hand from a Miss Mary Bennet.

"I apologize for its late arrival," Dr. Wise said, picking up a vial to study the contents. "I've been racing from one house call to the next, along with running my clinic—I've barely had time to sleep, let alone check my mail. My wife, understandably, thought this a puzzling but trivial piece of mail."

"I'm sure Maddie's abrupt departure didn't help things."

"My wife and I miss her," Wise admitted. "Miss Maddie is a most promising young woman. Bright, observant, and a quick learner, along with dexterous fingers. And cheerful as well, no matter what she's confronted with. She'll make a fine doctor. Do you know why the family left so abruptly? It isn't like her."

The letter inside was written on expensive paper with a

Western Hotel letterhead. It reeked of perfume. At first glance, it appeared nothing more than a rambling letter from a niece to her uncle commenting on a train journey, the architecture of California's capital city, and the book she was reading: *Pride and Prejudice*.

"I suppose it won't hurt me telling you… but not now. Ah, you two, get in here—fetch me *Pride and Prejudice*."

Dr. Wise was at her side, reading over her shoulder. "Is it something, then? I thought it was sent to the wrong address, but it used my name and has details about my family. And I thought it more than coincidence that it mentioned Atticus' favorite book."

Jin leaned over the armrest to read the letter while Sarah retrieved the book.

"Did either of you play at ciphers with Maddie or Tobias?" Isobel asked her daughters.

"We left coded messages around the house for each other," Sarah said.

"What type of coded messages?"

"Every third word, every fifth, the first letter of every sentence…" Sarah shrugged. "We made a game of trying to decipher them."

Dr. Wise nudged Watson aside on the opposite armchair and sat down with a grateful sigh. He removed his spectacles to clean, and the motion reminded her so much of Riot that her heart lurched. By God, her husband had only been gone a week, and she was already missing him.

Isobel focused on the letter, trying a few ciphers out, using *Pride and Prejudice* as the key.

"Grimm is wanted for murder," Jin was explaining to the doctor. He stiffened in surprise. "They are being hunted by U.S. Marshals."

"Maddie and Tobias, too?" he asked.

"I don't think so," Sarah said.

"I did not like those men. I do not think Maddie and Tobias would be safe with them."

Sarah didn't argue. Instead, she frowned at the ordinary letter and the flowing handwriting sweeping across its page. "How come she didn't use the back? I suppose hotel paper is free?"

"Lemon juice," Jin said at the exact moment Isobel came to the same conclusion. "We were playing with hidden ink." Without being asked, Jin lit a candle and brought it over. Isobel held the paper some distance away until brown lettering began to appear on the back.

Isobel turned the paper away from Jin's eyes. "It's better if you don't know what it says."

"That is not fair. I thought of it."

"Jin, I agree with you about those marshals. The less you all know, the better."

Jin crossed her arms, defiant as ever. "We know about the letter."

Dr. Wise interlaced his fingers. "I would like to know what it says."

"I don't want to involve—"

"I run a clinic on the edge of Chinatown that receives threats from the criminal tongs and bullying from white policemen daily."

"Curiosity kills the cat," Sarah said.

Dr. Wise poked at the cat on his lap. "So do wagons, dogs, and too much food."

"Watson is big-boned," Isobel said primly. "And fine… I'll read it. It's not like I can stop you three from snatching it from the fire."

"You are not taking your medicines."

Isobel ignored the doctor, and read.

If you're reading this, then you probably know more about our situation. We're from Indian Territory—at least I was raised there…

What followed was a summary of events. Nathan Shaw being taken off at gunpoint by Clay Holden. The arrival of the U.S. Marshals. And what Maddie could remember of the night their world was turned upside down.

Ma and I are staying at the Western Hotel in Sacramento, but we're moving on—I'll try to leave a message at the desk. We split with Grimm and Tobias. Ma doesn't know I'm writing to you. She thinks those marshals are still hunting us, but she's… not herself. I don't know what to think anymore. That whole business with the fake Pinkerton's badge has me thinking—were they even U.S. Marshals? How can lawmen threaten women and children and burn down a hotel with a dying man inside? Grimm did shoot that man—but the marshals were holding us at gunpoint. They'd hit a pregnant woman and threatened children. Things don't add up in my mind and ma won't involve anyone else in our affairs because of the danger. Truth be told, I'm not sure she's thinking straight. She's been running so long… I don't know who else to turn to.

We're running without a moon.

"I would not be surprised if they were official U.S. Marshals," Wise said when she finished reading. He was fully alert now, a look of profound concern and unease on his face.

The Rock Springs Massacre was not far from memory. Where was the law when mobs of white miners scalped, mutilated, decapitated, dismembered and burned Chinese miners alive?

Ewan Wise had about as much faith in lawmen as he did for the criminal tongs.

"Jin, hand me a notepad and pen, please. I need you to dispatch two telegrams, then take a note directly to Ravenwood Agency. Hand it to Lotario and no one else."

Sarah was dabbing at her eyes while she leaned on the armrest, and Isobel put a hand over hers. "We'll sort this out. I only wish they'd told us before those *lawmen* caught their trail again."

"It's not just that... Atticus is in danger, too."

"Isn't he always?" Isobel kept her voice light—the last thing the child needed was to know just how worried she was. "Look on the bright side, Sarah. If something happens to your father, you'll still have me."

Jin's snort echoed in the room.

WRITERLY TROUBLES

GARRETT HUNG UP THE RECEIVER AND LEANED BACK IN HIS chair to prop a boot on his desk.

"Did you wager on a banker?" Daisy asked.

Matthew Smith glanced up from his own desk, spotted the woman in the office doorway, and quickly rose to his feet.

"Matt, stop it. You'll tire yourself out every time I walk in here."

"It's habit."

Daisy smiled at the ex-policeman. She knew she shouldn't, but she couldn't help it—it was an honest reaction to an honest man.

Matthew blushed, cleared his throat, and sat back down to focus on his reports, though he found it hard going with Daisy Reed standing nearby.

"Do you know," Garrett mused. "I'm finding this detective business more satisfying than gambling."

"Heavens, no."

"Better than sex?" Lotario asked over Daisy's shoulder. She drove her elbow gently against his ribs.

Matthew turned beet red.

"You're supposed to be an example of morality for the rest of us, Lotario."

He gave a sigh. "Guiding my wayward employees is a yoke of responsibility that's heavy indeed."

"We're all doomed."

"And I thought Isobel was bad," Matthew muttered.

Lotario laughed, rich and musical and full of mirth. "Don't tell her I have her trumped in misbehaving—she'll try harder. And we wouldn't want that, now that she's a respectable married woman."

Daisy shivered. "She's terrifying."

"I'll let her know. She'll be honored."

"Don't you dare."

"Gambling and horizontal refreshment aside," Garrett said, tearing a page from a notepad and holding it up like a prize trophy. "Do you want to know what's better than both?"

Lotario walked over to perch on the man's desk. "Do tell."

"Jasper, Serge Tremble, and Chandler Pascall."

Lotario cocked his head as if trying to dislodge a thought.

"I was following up with one of my contacts in Indian Territory. He put me onto a fellow who was staying at the Mineral Springs Hotel the night it burned down—a fellow by the name of Gary Mudd."

"What a dreadful name," Daisy said.

"Which is why he uses several *nom de plumes* for writing."

Garrett waved the paper under Lotario's nose before the man snatched it from his hand. "That's why the names sounded familiar. He writes lurid little novels under the name Serge Tremble."

"So you pair have a lot in common," Daisy noted.

"Shush, woman," Lotario said. "No one is supposed to know about my budding literary career."

"I know about it already," Garrett said, twirling an end of his mustache. "I'm your editor."

"Matthew doesn't."

"Well, now he does."

"I'm sure I don't want to know," Matthew sighed.

Lotario favored the handsome detective with a smile. "I'll let you borrow one of my novels."

"No, thank you."

"You best leave Matthew alone," Daisy said. "He'll take off and hire on with the Pinkertons, then tell them all your dirty little secrets."

"He wouldn't. Would you?"

Matthew shot Lotario a look of forbearance. "I'm trying to develop selective hearing around you, *sir*."

Daisy laughed, which made Matthew relax and stare at her with mooncalf blue eyes.

"We all do that with Lotario."

"Thank you."

Not for the first time, Matthew puzzled over Daisy's and Lotario's relationship. At first, he'd thought they were a couple, since they flirted and Daisy thought nothing of reaching up to straighten his tie or of leaning in close when Lotario casually slipped an arm around her shoulders.

Matthew could understand that—Lotario was handsome and charming, if fussy. What woman wouldn't be attracted to him?

But Daisy also showed the same familiarity with Garrett, and Lotario wasn't at all jealous of the man. And (Matthew's mind shied away at this) Lotario seemed to flirt with Garrett, too, at times.

Matthew did not want to know about all the laws being broken in this agency. If he didn't know better... But, no. Best to focus on his work.

"Mr. Mudd is a member of the Fuzzy Bunch," Lotario mused.

"And currently lives in Carville."

"Shall we?"

Garrett folded his arms behind his head and closed his eyes. "I think I deserve a siesta."

"Hardly a siesta in this weather," Daisy noted.

"True," Garrett admitted. "But given Mr. Mudd's literary exploits, he may be more amenable to the gentler sex."

"I'll get a coat."

Matthew rose to his feet. "He doesn't sound like a respectable man. I'll question him, or at least escort you."

"That's sweet of you, Matthew, but I can take care of myself," Daisy said. "Besides, Lotario is coming with me."

Lotario sighed. "All work and no play makes me a dull boy."

"Mr. Mudd is a writer. I'm sure he has a cabinet of alcohol."

That cheered him. But as they were gathering their hat and coats, the secret door banged open and Sao Jin appeared in the hallway. Her face was flushed with exertion as she hurried over to the clock to check the time. The scarred little girl gave a satisfied huff of triumph.

"Did you win a race?" Lotario asked of his niece.

"Yes. With myself." She fished out a folded piece of paper and handed it to him, sparing a glare for Daisy, who took a step back.

Lotario read the note from his sister. "Hmm."

"What is it?" Daisy asked.

"The Shaws are not merely wanted—they're likely the only living witnesses to a crime."

───────

"I've always found Carville slightly morbid," Daisy admitted. She clutched her hat to her head as Lotario offered his hand to help her from the cable car runner. The wind was spitting sand in their faces, and blowing his hair every which way.

"And why is that?" he asked.

"It's where horsecars come to die."

Lotario glanced sideways at her. "That was dreadful."

"I know," she said cheerfully. "Would you live here?"

"Never. I hate sand. It gets everywhere." As if to emphasize his point, he peeled a strand of his golden hair out of his mouth and tasted the grit of it between his lips. "I'm surprised Bel doesn't have a bolt-hole out here, though."

Isobel loved everything that was the ocean—she loved the salt and the sand, the grit and the wind. The smell of brine and the biting chill. Lotario preferred to be wrapped in a blanket by a fire.

He flipped up his coat collar as they slipped over the sand to the resting place of dozens of old horse cars, cable cars, and rail cars.

The ocean's roar made him shudder—he'd spent far too many days trapped with his sister in storms. And it was more than that—Lotario Amsel had been abducted by a handsome devil and left to die in a sea cave, with the white water churning around his body and climbing towards his mouth.

Before that he'd tolerated the sea because it made his sister happy; now he feared it. Every time he looked at the endless expanse, he saw betrayal. But that was the way of the ocean—it turned on you in a heartbeat.

Four sets of white-capped, turbulent waves stretched to a gray horizon as they pounded towards the shore. There were no beachgoers today.

"Good God, is that the lifesaving longboat?"

Lotario squinted into the spray. "I believe so. Either some poor bugger's been caught in a wave or they're conducting drills."

Daisy grimaced. "They're mad, is what they are."

Lotario couldn't agree more. "Bel has been known to swim out beyond the breakers if the tide is right."

"Why am I not surprised?" Daisy said with a shiver. "She's as terrifying as this ocean here."

"Mhmm, she keeps the sharks away."

Daisy snorted and tugged her coat firmly around her, but it did nothing against San Francisco's chilling bite. The air cut right down to the bone—summer or winter, the ocean along this shoreline never paid seasons much mind.

Lotario slipped his arm through hers. "Surely you're not afraid of her? It's not as if she's going to attack you. Well, so long as you don't provoke her."

"It's not that. I feel like she's peeling my scalp back and peering into my innermost thoughts."

"Oh. That."

"Is she a mind reader?"

"Not to boast—"

"Because you're humility incarnate."

"—but I am as observant as my sister."

Daisy patted the hand on her forearm. "Yes, Lotario, but you're too lazy to be bothered half the time."

He could not disagree.

"So where does this Mr. Mudd live? Surely not in the lair?"

"I'm not sure." Lotario eyed the Fuzzy Bunches 'lair,' as they called it.

The *La Boheme* was a three-story affair of converted horse-cars and add-ons, complete with a water tower and windmill. It made quite the clubhouse.

Since it was before noon and a weekday, Lotario didn't bother going to the clubhouse. Everyone was sure to be in a drunken stupor from the night before, and it would do no good to rouse a hungover artist too early.

Instead, they stopped by Mrs. Gunn's Home Cooking and ordered two coffees. "I can't believe I'm up this early."

"Responsibility *is* dreadful," Daisy agreed, then smiled at Mrs. Gunn—a stout woman who looked carved by gale force winds.

Mrs. Gunn knew everyone in the area, and Daisy easily shifted her personality to win the woman over with a down-to-earth conversation that made her seem like a pretty young girl who wasn't afraid to get her hands dirty. She had no trouble getting Mr. Mudd's location from the woman.

"You have a remarkable way with people," Lotario noted as they finished their coffee and strolled towards the outskirts of Carville, where the abandoned horsecars were some of the oldest and most decrepit. Most were half buried in sand.

"Adapt to survive."

"It's not that," Lotario insisted. "You genuinely care about people. You leave them feeling better about themselves for having met you. I don't know how you manage it."

"It's the only way I can keep going," she admitted.

"I prefer indifference."

"No, you don't."

"If you say so."

And then they were forced to brace themselves against ocean gusts and sweeping sand as they struggled closer to the outlying dwellings.

Mr. Mudd's horsecar conversion was a rotting rectangle with sand up to its shutters. Lotario squinted at the shack through the gritty haze.

"Perhaps we should've brought Matthew along for protection," Lotario shouted into the wind.

"I'll protect you from murderous writers."

They ducked behind the horsecar to get out of the wind and into a sphere of eerie silence. Lotario shook the sand from his hat and dusted off his shoulders while Daisy tried to put her hair back in order.

She raised a brow in question.

"Windblown suits you," he said.

"Same to you."

Lotario flipped his hair with a flashing grin, then rapped on the door with his gentleman's stick. There was no answer save for the howling wind.

"Well, that's anticlimactic," Daisy pouted.

Lotario tried again. "Perhaps he's out… or dead drunk."

"He is a writer."

"So which is it?"

"They tend to be home*bodies*." She waited for her pun to hit home, and with a roll of his eyes, Lotario tried the door-knob. It opened.

"Hello?" he called, sticking his head inside the long shack, or at least that was his intent—one whiff of the interior had him reeling back in revulsion.

Daisy made a noise and pressed a scented handkerchief to her nose. "My God, what is that smell?"

"A drunk author?"

"It smells like something's rotting…"

"Perhaps it's the horse that belonged to this car."

Lotario pressed a handkerchief to his nose and mouth, and used his cane to push open the door. It swung open, revealing a lightless interior. "Ladies first," he said.

Daisy slapped him on the shoulder. "Go on, you twit."

"I'm paying you."

"You're the fearless leader."

Lotario grumbled as he stepped into the horsecar, and slipped. He grabbed for a table, knocked over a lamp, and caught himself on a settee. What he saw made his breakfast come up.

Lotario stumbled outside to retch.

"Lotario…" Daisy gathered his hair back. "There's blood on your shoes."

He spit into the sand and tried not to look at the gore coating his handcrafted Italian leather shoes.

"Have a look for yourself."

"I think I'll pass. I don't suppose it's a rotting horse?"

"No…" He was an odd shade of green, and he seized her hand and drew her away. "His throat is slit."

She glanced back at the horsecar. "Shouldn't we… you know… investigate?"

"Be my guest."

Daisy wrinkled her nose. "You're the detective. I'm a clerk."

"I'm a *theoretical* detective. Preferably one in an armchair."

"You wanted to come."

"You lured me here with the promise of alcohol."

"I'm sure there's alcohol in there."

"And a bloated man. He's dead, by the way."

"I gathered that. Are you all right? You're shivering."

"I could use a drink," Lotario admitted.

"Don't you have your flask?"

"I'll get sand in it," he said with a shudder.

"What shall we do?"

"I don't suppose you'd close the door?"

Daisy rolled her eyes, snatched the cane from his hand, and used it to hook the knob from a distance and pull the door shut. "There."

"Chicken."

"Not as much as you," she said.

"I have no shame," he agreed. "Let's telephone my braver half. I'm not sure what to do."

THE BRAVER HALF

ISOBEL CLUNKED HER HEAD ONTO THE HALLWAY DESK AS SHE
listened to her twin's incoherent description of a dead body, a
lake of blood, and the trials of sand.

"Ari, I realize asking you to calm down is futile, but will you
just close your mouth for a moment?" She heard an audible
click over the telephone line. "You went to Carville alone?"

"No, Daisy's here."

She muttered something under her breath.

"What was that?"

"Nothing. Tell me what you saw."

"I told you, Bel. The fellow's throat was slit. And the
blood…"

"Yes, I know. You've told me. I need details, Ari."

"It was dark."

"Did you open the shutters?"

"I'm not going in there with that… bloated whale."

"Light a lamp in the doorway."

"I broke the lamp when I nearly drowned in the lake of
blood."

Isobel looked up to find Jin leaning on the table, listening in. The child was snickering silently. She shared a look with her daughter and propped her head on a hand. "Is he freshly dead?"

"Do you remember that deer you found when we were younger… the one that—" A gagging sound crackled over the line.

"Exploded. Yes. I do remember," she said. She'd happened on a dead deer and had decided to dissect it. It ended badly. "Were there marks on his wrists? A knife nearby?"

"Neither Daisy nor I are going to poke at a body, Bel. I telephoned you first because it's *your case.*"

The connection of the mind they shared wasn't diminished by distance—she understood what he meant at once. How much should he tell the police of the Shaw family? Did this writer's death have anything to do with the family's situation at all?

If her twin didn't suffer from necrophobia, she'd have those answers, but Isobel stopped herself short from voicing her frustration—everyone had their limits.

"I'll telephone Inspector Coleman. I don't trust anyone else with this. Can you wait for him at Mrs. Gunn's?"

He groaned. The smell of food would no doubt turn their stomachs.

"All right, what about *La Boheme*?"

"Is it safe to leave the body?"

"It doesn't sound like he's going anywhere, Ari."

He cleared his throat. "We'll be at the lair."

Isobel hung up the receiver and looked at her daughter. "Can you fetch a hack while I telephone the inspector? I want to have a look before the police trample everything."

Jin crossed her arms. "You cannot leave."

"Where's she going?" Sarah's head poked over the stairwell railing from a floor above.

"To poke at a dead man."

"Why?"

"Because Tweedledee and Tweedledum are at the crime scene," Isobel growled, snatching up the receiver.

ISOBEL VALUED HER FREEDOM—THE ABILITY TO COME AND GO as she pleased and answer to no one. But with her current limitations, leaving Ravenwood Manor took careful negotiating.

Jin was easily won over with the promise that she could come, too. Once Isobel had Jin on her side, Sarah caved in to their combined determination on the condition that Isobel take the tincture of morphia for the carriage ride.

And since Isobel could tell Sarah did not want to involve herself in another investigation, she asked her to remain behind to meet Mr. Meekins and Mr. Payne, whom she'd requested after receiving Maddie's cryptic letter. The discovery of a body only reinforced her feeling of unease. And any tough that Aisling's former pimp sent to threaten her (if Isobel's mental faculties weren't entirely gone) would quake at the sight of the ex-convicts.

The next obstacle was Margaret, who'd planted herself in the doorway. "I'm coming, too."

"All right."

Margaret blinked in surprise. "Really?"

"I need someone to shove me into the carriage."

"And a blanket. And pillows. And a *cane*."

Isobel flinched at the word. "My side was injured, not my leg."

Margaret plucked a sturdy umbrella from the stand. "How about this?"

"Fine. It's a sword umbrella."

"I've always wanted one of these..." Margaret mused,

fiddling with the mechanism. Before she impaled herself, Isobel snatched it from her hand.

Complicated domestic negotiations complete, Sarah helped her into a coat, and Isobel shuffled her way towards the waiting hack with Margaret carrying an armload of "necessities" like a hotel porter.

"I need to get my bicycle," Margaret said as she tossed in the blankets, padding, and a flask of water.

"We're going to Carville, not on a cross-country trip."

"I'm wearing riding bloomers. I'll get fined otherwise."

"Do you have a gun and a magnifying glass?" Jin murmured as Isobel settled back against the seat.

"I have my bicycle safety gun!" Margaret called cheerfully, giving her pocket a pat before trotting around back to fetch her bicycle.

"I forgot the magnifying glass. The damn morphia…"

"I will get it," Jin said before darting back into the house.

Isobel closed her eyes as she waited for the others to return, and soon they were rolling towards Carville. She felt every jolt of the undercarriage, and although she'd never admit it, she was beyond thankful for the pillows and blanket Margaret had packed around her.

The lure of an investigation was not the sole reason for Isobel wanting to make the trip—she longed to see the ocean. To feel its bite, to taste its salt, to be shaken by its roar.

She heard it before she saw it, a great crashing rhythm that invigorated her senses. Jin reached across her to push down the window so she could smell the salt-laden air.

Isobel laid her head against the window frame and stared out at the rolling white caps and choppy gray horizon. Seagulls floated in the air, battered by the winds, and going nowhere, their broad wings stretched but calm—never daring to fight the impossible power.

The hack rolled to a stop in front of La Boheme, and

Isobel remained in her seat, taking in the ocean air while Margaret trotted up to the entrance.

"What the hell are you doing here, Bel?" Lotario was blocking her view.

"Have the police arrived?"

"Did you even telephone the inspector?"

"I did. I left a message. Show me the horse car."

"Absolutely not."

"Ari, I'm here. I have little energy and I don't want to waste it arguing with you. So unless you're keen on poking at the body... just take me there."

Lotario frowned at her. "You look horrible."

"I took a dose of morphia. I don't feel much of anything."

"Atticus is going to kill me," he grumbled.

"Riot isn't here."

Lotario directed the driver to take the carriage as far as it would go on the hard-packed road, then to wait. By the time Daisy and Lotario caught up, Margaret had helped Isobel out of the carriage (after getting her bicycle down from the luggage rack) and they were strolling towards the more distant horsecars.

"It's good to see you, Miss Amsel," Daisy ventured.

Isobel glanced at the woman. It annoyed her that she couldn't place her. "I doubt Lotario agrees."

"Daisy, this is Margaret Ederle. Margaret, Daisy Reed."

"Call me Margaret."

"Daisy."

Margaret leaned her bicycle against her hip and shook hands. "You're looking green, Lotario."

"You will, too. Why on earth did you let her out?"

"I'd like to see you stop her."

"All you have to do is take away your arm and she'll keel over."

"I'm not her paid nurse," Margaret shot back.

Isobel caught Jin's eyes as the girl looked up at her in silent commiseration. She blocked out the banter of her escorts and focused on reaching the horsecar before the police arrived.

The sight of the lonely horsecar isolated from its neighbors pricked Isobel's instincts. She stopped to take in the ocean view, before gathering her energy to keep upright.

"My God, that smell," Margaret said, hesitating.

Daisy and Lotario stood some feet away, guarding Margaret's bicycle and huddling against each other for mutual warmth.

"Stay here."

"But—"

"I don't want your footprints all over," Isobel said, letting go of Margaret's arm. She tucked her umbrella under an arm to fish in her pocket for a battery light, but since her right hand was too weak to turn the knob, Jin stepped forward to open the door.

A stench of rot burst from the doorway, knocking Jin back a step and forcing her to press a sleeve over her nose. It was the sort of smell that crawled down the throat and lodged in the gut.

Isobel stood her ground and shone a light into the dark. A bloated corpse sprawled in the middle of the converted horsecar. It was sparsely furnished with a bed, desk, a washstand, chamber pot, and a few cooking supplies. The stench of human waste, decomposing flesh, and rotting food hit her like a wave. Small wonder Lotario hadn't ventured inside.

Isobel leaned a shoulder against the doorpost and tried to close off her sense of smell and taste. She did it when she swam—closing off her nose and throat to water, and only breathing when she had to.

A large amount of clotted blood pooled around the man. She was glad his face was turned away from her. His left arm was stretched forward, a smear of blood around his finger, while his right hand rested on a straight-edged razor with an elk horn handle.

Sand flies swarmed over the corpse.

She shone the light over the floor and saw where Lotario had slipped, broken the lamp, and caught himself. With care, she planted her umbrella on a clean floorboard and stepped inside and to the right, then opened a shutter that was on the sheltered side of the shack.

Sunlight illuminated a long room with a small potbellied stove in the back and a shelf of books and papers on the side wall. Keeping her eye on the floorboards, Isobel carefully picked her way around the corpse and blood.

She pulled a chair to a clean spot, sat, then used the tip of her umbrella to move his head. It flopped to the side, knocking loose a cloud of sandflies. The face was bloated, his black bushy beard soaked with blood. The gash on his throat was deep, made by a powerful stroke.

A noise interrupted Isobel's study. She looked up to find Jin standing in the doorway—the girl's eyes were wide with shock.

"Jin, go back to Margaret. *Now.*"

The girl did not argue but stumbled backwards and fled. She cursed under her breath. Not at Jin, but at herself. She should've known the reaction the blood would trigger.

Isobel pushed emotion to the side and tilted her head to squint at the man's left index finger. In the sunlight, the smear of blood had taken on a new shape—an upside down V or an A without the connecting line.

Voices came with a gust of wind, and a moment later, Inspector Coleman stood in the doorway—a silver-haired, studious looking man, with a giant of an Irishman looming behind him.

"Inspector. Sergeant."

"Miss Amsel. Care to explain yourself?"

"Not at the moment," she said, turning back to her inspection. "Sgt. Price, would you hand me the razor? Once you gentlemen have taken in the scene."

"Gawd almighty," Price said, stepping inside. He took a moment to open all the shutters.

"I don't see any other prints. The floor is a mess. Lotario broke the lamp when he slipped in the blood there."

Inspector Coleman used a handkerchief to pick up the razor. He studied it a moment, but the blood pattern had been obscured by the great quantity of blood that had pumped out of the man.

Isobel unfolded her magnifying glass to study the edge. "Inspector, could you get a closer look at that gash?"

"I don't think you ought to be out here, Miss Amsel."

"I'm already here, Inspector."

"Aye, but you can't even stand," Price grunted.

"I'm simply rationing my energy," she said, offering her glass to the Inspector. "Would you humor me?"

"This has to be a suicide," Price said.

"You will note the scrawl of blood by his finger."

Both men frowned at the shape.

"Anarchist?" Coleman asked.

"Might be a Hellfire Club symbol. Remember that one case we had…"

There was no way around the blood. Inspector Coleman gathered the ends of his overcoat, and Price shifted the corpse to get a better angle on the neck gash.

As the Inspector bent closer to peer at the edges, Isobel wiped clean a section of the razor, then ran her finger along its edge.

"A clean, powerful cut," Coleman said, straightening. "Most suicides will have a number of knicks as they work up the nerve."

"And this razor is dull," Isobel said, brandishing the blade at the officers. "This man has a beard, so he didn't bother sharpening it. There's also a roll on the edge that should've caught on the skin."

"Murdered then," Price grunted.

"Do you know who this man is?"

"Not for certain. I know who it's supposed to be—a Mr. Gary Mudd. Mrs. Gunn, or one of the other residents, should be able to identify him. And I believe that symbol was the beginnings of a star."

Inspector Coleman frowned at the shape on the floor. "A case of yours?"

"If you would be so kind as to help me out of here, I'll explain so you can conduct a proper search of the premises."

OF LIKE MIND

Isobel was beginning to envy caterpillars. She wanted nothing more than to crawl into bed, wrap herself in a cocoon of blankets, and emerge when she was whole and ready to fly.

Instead, she forced herself to walk downstairs.

Sarah was talking on the telephone, and as soon as Jin had pulled out a chair for Isobel to sit, the girl made a grab for the receiver.

"I want to talk to *bahba*."

"I'm speaking to him."

There was a brief struggle for control of the device before Sarah finally relented.

"Have you found them?" Jin demanded.

She frowned at Riot's muffled answer.

"I will come help."

The answer was clear, even to Isobel's ears. "Stay there with Bel."

Jin thrust the receiver in her face. "Here."

Isobel put the device to her ear and paused at the two sets of eyes staring expectantly at her. "Don't the pair of you have something to do? I'd like private word with my *husband*."

Jin blew out a breath, but Sarah had the good sense to look embarrassed. She grabbed Jin's hand and pulled her away. But Isobel could hear them lingering in the hallway to the kitchen.

"From the sound of it, I've had more rest than you," Riot said. His voice crackled with the connection, but she could hear the worry in his voice.

"It's been eventful."

"How are you feeling? You sound exhausted."

"Rein in that husbandly worry of yours."

"I have no reason whatsoever to worry about you. You're absolutely right, Bel," he said dryly.

"That's better. I can handle sarcasm. Dr. Wise was full of it."

"It's why Ewan and I get along so well. What did the good doctor have to say about your recovery?"

"That I'm stubborn. So no need to repeat that point. He also lectured me about taking my medicine."

"You're not taking the morphia."

"I took some for the carriage ride," she admitted. "And yes, I know, I sleep better with it, but it fogs my brain and I'm a little too tempted to drink the entire bottle, if I'm to be honest."

There was a pause of silence over her confession.

"Perhaps it's better you don't."

"I thought so too. Now if you've finished fretting over my health—"

"One moment."

Isobel waited.

"All right, now I'm done."

"Smart ass."

"I find asses to be superior in intellect to horses."

"Don't tell Jack that. He'll get jealous."

"Together we make a jackass."

Isobel groaned. "Sacramento is rotting your brain. Shall we get down to business?"

"I think my pun drove the eavesdropping operators away. What did you discover?"

The telegram she'd sent had simply read: Missing you. -B

She hadn't wanted to risk anything more, but the overly sentimental message had successfully relayed the intended information: I've discovered something new. We need to talk.

Isobel told him about the discovery of Mr. Gary Mudd. "Coleman and Price conducted a thorough search while I waited outside. There were papers burned in the wood stove, but nothing salvageable. He would've been killed around the same time the U.S. Marshals paid you a visit."

"It could be a coincidence."

"He was a witness to a crime."

"Oh?"

"So were the Whites." And since it didn't matter if someone was listening in on the parts that the U.S. Marshals already knew about, she relayed the past events in Maddie's letter without telling him about how she'd received the information or where the women were currently staying.

"But if Mr. Mudd was a witness to the crime... Why wait this long to kill him?"

"I was wondering that, too," she admitted. "Lotario is following up on that line. It may be coincidence, but given this new development, I've asked Meekins and Payne to loiter about the property. And... I believe your new hire had a visitor."

"Is she all right?"

"It rattled her nerves, but she's keeping tight-lipped about it."

"I'm not surprised. She's out of her element, and trust doesn't come easy."

"With reason."

"Sarah's idea of inviting the Umbrella Defense Club to meet at the house might not be a bad idea."

"Hmm, it's true… a dance hall full of combatant women would drive away the boldest of men."

"I'll telephone tomorrow if I'm able."

"How are you enjoying Sacramento?"

"I didn't find a horse I liked."

"Did you know Ewan has a sister?"

"Several."

"A niece by the name of Mary Bennet is staying at the Western Hotel. Apparently, she's something of a connoisseur of fine dining if you should need a recommendation."

"I'm on a case, Bel. I hardly have time for laundry, let alone eating."

"Miss Bennet mentioned the dismal laundries in the city."

"It's all over the newspapers."

"Oh? Take care of your shirts, Riot. Make sure to eat, too."

"I shall wash my shirts and partake of the fine dining this city has to offer."

"I'd rather you wait for me."

"Until next time, Bel."

"You're a clever man."

"You wouldn't have married me otherwise."

She rang off with a laugh, and he smiled as he hung up the line—both at the sound of her voice and the information she'd relayed. He might've lost Grimm and Tobias' trail, but Maddie was tossing out breadcrumbs.

A STEP BEHIND

ATTICUS RIOT WAS GLAD HE'D TAKEN TIME FOR A BARBER AND A shoeshine when the doorman of the Western Hotel gave him a once over before opening the door. He removed his gloves and slapped them into his hat as he strode across the polished marble floors of a grand lobby.

Maddie's two-week-old letter and Mr. Mudd's murder were troubling. This was no longer a matter of keeping Grimm from the gallows—the entire family was in grave danger.

If those U.S. Marshals caught up with the Shaws, not a single one of them would see the inside of a courthouse. If Lily had only told him…

If wishes were horses…

Trust was a precarious thing. But Riot didn't think it was the issue in this case. Surely Lily trusted him—they were business partners, after all. And while this business was messy, Lily knew he brushed the wrong side of the law often enough, so her secrecy was born of something else.

A need to protect. Surely. She had her own family on the east coast—a family with means and connections. Yet she hadn't turned to them, or perhaps they'd turned their backs on her.

There were gaps in Maddie's narrative. What happened in that cave after the children fled for their lives? What became of Nathan Shaw? And what had Lily been subjected to?

The mind was a complicated mechanism. Riot knew this as fact—his own had shoved aside memories of Ravenwood's murder to protect itself, to survive. For three years he hadn't been able to face the darkness, and when he'd finally dragged those memories into the light, the revelations had shaken him to his core.

No, his instincts told him it wasn't a matter of trust, but pain and suffering that had left her shattered. Lily Shaw could not speak of it.

Riot didn't expect to find Lily and her daughter still at the hotel, but he hoped the girl had left him another breadcrumb.

"Can I help you, sir?" the hotel clerk asked.

"Is Miss Mary Bennet still in residence?" He pushed his agency card across the counter, and as he hoped, the man took one look at the name, and turned towards the wall of pigeonholes.

"This was left for you, sir."

Riot plucked up his card and the envelope, and walked off to lean a shoulder against a pillar. He chose the spot on purpose—behind a fern with a view of the glass doors and the lobby.

Mr. Riot,

My employer, Mrs. Fairfax, has become restless in Sacramento. Grief has that effect. I regret I could not catch up with you to show you around the city. But I can recommend several fine restaurants—The Western Hotel, The Occidental, and for plain cooking that will take you back home, The Railyard Kitchen. Mr. Michael brews a hearty ale from the ice melt south of the Yuba: Rió Luna.

Please give Uncle Wise my regards.
With fondness,
Mary Bennet

There it was again. A mention of the moon. Moon River. Running without a moon. Was Maddie's first cryptic message pointing to a running river as well? The South Yuba River? Riot tucked the letter away and strode out the hotel doors, slipping on his gloves as he surreptitiously searched the busy street.

A life of threat had attuned him to danger, and the touch of eyes sent his instincts vibrating with awareness. He was being followed. Riot hailed a hack, tossing out a random street as he climbed into the carriage.

He edged to the side and against the seat, keeping clear of the windows as he searched the traffic. A cab followed, keeping a discreet distance behind, but taking every turn with them.

He told the hack driver to pull to the side, and watched the following hack roll past. But the passenger was obscured by a window shade—probably quickly pulled down.

The following hack turned a corner. Riot paid his fee and alighted, trotting down a narrow lane. He wasn't as familiar with Sacramento as he was with San Francisco, but the lane spit him out onto another street with a garden across the way. He cut through it, hailed another hack, and went to meet Tim at the stables.

Jack was there; Tim was not. He saddled the horse, changed into something more practical, and went in search of the *Railyard Kitchen*. It was a quaint restaurant that boasted of home cooking and simple fare. Riot took stock of the street as he dismounted and draped the reins over the stock.

As the name suggested, the restaurant was close to the rail yards, between a union hall and a hotel. A mixed crowd of laborers, porters, office clerks, and fettlers loitered on the street.

Riot gave Jack a fond pat, and removed his hat to step

inside the crowded restaurant. The tables were long and cramped, but the waiters hoisting large trays overhead had smiles and a running stream of banter for the patrons.

He wove his way towards a waiter whose bald head gleamed like polished wood. "Just grab a chair, sir," the man said, flashing a smile.

"I hear Michael makes a good ale."

Whatever Riot had expected, it wasn't the reaction he got —the waiter nearly dropped his tray. He caught the tipping end in time to prevent a disaster, but looked visibly shaken.

"Not anymore," the man said.

Riot cocked his head as the man hurried away. Why the fear?

He watched the ripple effect his question was having on the waiters, one gaze catching that of another, until the ripple ended with a glance towards the back. Riot wove his way towards the kitchens and lingered in the corridor until the waiter emerged.

The man hesitated, gripping his tray like a shield.

"Why not anymore?" Riot asked.

He wasn't sure why Maddie sent him here, but he had a suspicion, so he played along.

"Michael is dead."

"Murdered?"

"I got to get to work. It's in the newspapers."

Riot held out a card. "I'm looking for a friend—Mary Bennet."

"I don't know anything about her."

"I'm not with the police. I'm trying to help the girl. Did Michael take her somewhere?"

The waiter hesitated. "He arranged travel for people."

Riot nodded. "And he was murdered?"

"Beaten to a pulp. The cook found him dead in the garden when he went to open up. No one saw anything, no one heard

anything—not surprising with the trains so close by. I don't
know anything else."

"How many days ago?"

"Three."

"Did a pair of U.S. Marshals come by here before he was
found dead?"

"Not that I saw."

"One would've been white, weathered and rough. The
other a Negro, a real dapper fellow."

The waiter blinked in surprise. "I served them lunch."

Riot tipped him a dollar, and left.

30

WILD CARD

A FAMILIAR FACE WAS WAITING FOR RIOT AT THE STABLES— that of a gray-haired cowboy sitting on a hay bale, long legs stretched out, hat pulled low, and a cigarette dangling from his lips.

"I'm too old to play cat and mouse," Liam Taft said without looking up.

The Pinkerton agent looked relaxed, but his hand was dangerously close to his holstered gun. He pushed up the brim of his hat to eye Riot, who was as equally relaxed on the saddle.

"You were following me," Riot said by way of greeting.

"That obvious?"

"There's a reason I'm still alive."

"Same reason I'm here."

"Instinct."

Liam took a thoughtful drag on his cigarette. "It's like an itch. That feeling of being watched. Same with a case—I got an itch I can't scratch, and I came here looking for answers."

"You think I have answers?"

Sensing tension, Jack stepped lightly to the side, eyeing the cowboy like a bull about to charge. Riot gave the horse a pat and dismounted, keeping one eye on the Pinkerton agent.

"Why else would you be here? How's that young wife of yours?"

"Frustrated with her recovery. How's Mrs. Taft?"

"Happy to be back in Oregon."

"Except you're here."

Liam flicked his cigarette to the ground and placed his boot over it. "So I am."

"The itch?"

"That whole business with the racetrack and Carson… It was too neat."

"I agree."

"Left me with questions."

"You could ask your partner for answers. He's the one who shot Carson, and the only witness to that shooting is on the run."

"The boy is a wanted man."

"So he is."

Liam spread his hands away from his holster before taking care to stand. When he was on his feet, he met Riot's eyes. "Sam told me he had some business left in the state."

"What business was that?"

"Didn't say. Sam hasn't said a lot of things, like why he didn't arrest that boy when he recognized him." Liam smoothed his drooping gray mustache. "I'd just gotten nice and resettled at home when I got word he's working with U.S. Marshals to track down the boy. Now why would he do that?"

"Do you have reason to distrust your partner?"

Liam's jaw worked. "Hard thing to contemplate."

A noise twitched Liam's squinting eyes, and in a blink he spun and drew his revolver, but Riot's gun had already cleared the holster the moment he twitched. Tim stood at the corner of the stable, his gun at his hip, half his body shielded by the building's wall.

Liam cocked his head at Riot, noting the angle of his gun pointing not at Liam's back, but at the source of the noise. There was a gleam of amusement in his dark eyes. "Not one of us pulled the trigger. Fancy that. Instinct's a funny thing."

Liam holstered his gun the same instant Riot lowered his, then Tim uncocked his own.

"Or we're just old and tired and don't feel much like shooting a man anymore," Tim grumbled, stomping forward to check the interior of the stable.

"Something wrong?" Riot asked.

"I might have to scamper."

Riot's gaze flickered to the swipe of blood across the old man's trousers, to the bowie knife on his belt. "I take it you weren't satisfied with your laundry?"

Tim flashed his gold teeth before turning his pale blue eyes on the Pinkerton. "Why the hell are you here?"

"We were just working towards that."

"He was following me," Riot said.

"Dumb luck," Liam muttered, settling back down on his hay bale. "I was tracking Sam and spotted you. I needed to make sure you weren't working with Sam."

Tim caught Riot's eyes. There was a question there—one Riot didn't know the answer to. But Riot wasn't ready to lay down his cards just yet.

"How far did you trace him?"

"There's a reason the Pinkerton symbol is an open eye. It's true: we never sleep," Liam said, tapping his badge. "We have eyes and ears across this country, on every railroad, train car, you name it. So when I got word that Sam had put out an alert for not just that boy, but for his family too, I started thinking of cattle—how you cut a cow from the herd when you need to work with it."

Tim settled on a bale opposite, and took out his pipe and tobacco pouch. "Same with rounding up men. Separate an outlaw from his gang, pick them off one by one."

"Let me ask you something, Mr. Tim. Did you talk to that boy before he took off?"

"Grimm told me what he'd overheard about a female detective being shot. I went off to ring the agency and when I got back, he was gone. By the time we sorted things out with Miss Bel, the entire family was gone."

Liam gave a slow nod. He didn't look happy. But then the man never betrayed much emotion at all. He was a hard one to read—even for a man of Riot's skill.

Could they trust him?

"What do you plan to do when you find your partner?" Riot asked.

Liam rested his elbows on his knees and gazed at his boots. It was a long moment before he met Riot's eye again. "I've got a hunch—nothing more. As much as I'd like to ignore my instincts…" He turned his head and spat. "I can't turn my back."

Riot led Jack into the stable to fresh feed, and removed his bridle and bit so he could eat easier. It gave him time to think.

Tim wandered in to join him, resting his arms on a gate. A public stable house wasn't the most private of places to talk, so he kept his voice low. "If he's playing us, he's one sly son of a bitch."

"*Keep your friends close; keep your enemies closer*," Riot quoted under his breath.

"Agreed."

"How hot are you?"

"I didn't like the words coming out of the laundry manager's mouth. Typical predator. All bluster and bravado until someone with grit comes along."

"Were Lily and Maddie working there?"

Tim nodded. "He claims they assaulted him and stole the cashbox. He had some choice words for the pair. Fellow nearly lost his eye."

Riot's gaze flickered to Tim's knife.

"The eye was Miss Lily's handiwork. From what I gathered from the other women, Mr. Abberton finds his work stressful and needs a woman's touch to ease his workload."

Riot knew that look in the old man's eye. "Is he still alive?"

"I persuaded him to drop the charges."

Riot knew enough about the old man and his sense of justice to not ask any more questions. Despite all appearances, Tim was far from harmless and had a strong dislike for men who preyed on women and children. No one expected an amiable old man who brushed five feet to turn into a maniacal leprechaun with a blade.

"I traced them to the station—the ticket taker remembered them both. Bruised, looked half-starved, and filthy. Bought tickets for Oregon."

And then they'd checked into an expensive hotel to throw off the authorities. Given Maddie's wording, he suspected Miss Lily was posing as a white woman in mourning—easy to drape a veil over her face. And Maddie, her maid. No one would look for two battered, poverty-stricken Negro women in the Western Hotel.

They were good.

"Have you eaten today, Liam?" Riot called from the stall.

"Coffee."

"Let's find a place to lay our cards on the table."

————

THEY WERE SOON TUCKED INTO THE CORNER OF A QUIET saloon with decent fare. After they'd placed their orders, Riot brought Liam up to speed on the Shaw's situation: the contents of Maddie's coded letter to Ewan Wise, the murder of Mr. Mudd, the updated sketches of Grimm, and the brutal murder of a man who had a reputation for arranging transportation.

While Riot told him most of the facts, he withheld anything that might pinpoint the Shaw's current location. He wanted to see what the Pinkerton would make of the situation first.

Liam listened without comment, polished off his meal and a beer, and finally reached for his tobacco pouch. He rolled a cigarette, then scraped a match across the table and put it to the end while Tim did the same with his pipe.

When smoke wafted around their heads, Liam sat back. "I know the pair."

"You don't sound surprised."

"Angel and Eli… one name doesn't go without the other. Thick as thieves." Liam's gravelly voice came close to a growl.

"Have there been complaints about them?" Tim asked.

"Complaints? Hell no. They get the job done. They were after the Holden Gang for years—picking them off one by one. Clay was eventually cornered." Liam cocked his head in thought. "1894… 95? He was holed up in a fort on a hill—they had to bring in a cannon."

"Was he captured alive?" Riot asked.

"Official reports say no, but I know for a fact that certain powers that be wanted him alive."

"Why's that?"

Liam shrugged. "They're outlaws—train robbery, stagecoach, banks."

"Large reward?" Tim asked.

"Enough to set a man up for life—better than our pay, and certainly better than the U.S. Marshal's. Hell, we Pinkertons get our expenses paid and then some—but marshals have to buy their own grub for their prisoners."

"Only the Pinkertons don't accept reward money," Riot said.

"You have it in one."

So why was Sam Batten so keen on helping the U.S. Marshals? Did they offer him a cut of their reward money?

"I knew a fellow operative who worked the area—he said reports don't tell the half of what goes on in Indian Territory. But unless you can prove it..." Liam shook his head in dismay, a line of smoke seeping from his cracked lips.

"It's the Shaws' word against Angel and Eli's, which makes me wonder about the writer Mr. Mudd," Riot said.

"So what's your plan?" Liam asked.

Tim stared at the man through a haze of smoke. "That depends on your definition of justice."

Liam took a napkin and used it to polish the badge on his vest. "The boy has a warrant on his head. I can't make promises, but given the circumstances, his age, and if the testimony of his mother and sister matches up... I prefer to hook the bigger fish."

The Pinkertons threw a lot of weight around. At the very least, Grimm would live to stand before a court of law.

Riot inclined his head in understanding. "Does *Rió Luna* mean anything to either of you?"

"Moon River," Liam said.

Tim's bushy brows shot up. "Why?"

Riot handed him Maddie's latest crumb, and after Tim read it, he began to cackle. "Smart girl. There's a lodge called Moon River Ranch up near Truckee."

Riot tossed down some coins. "Let's hope the Shaws didn't tell Mr. Michael where they were headed."

31

PRINTED IN BLOOD

AFTER THE DEBACLE WITH THE DEAD BODY, DAISY REED WAS left feeling useless. It didn't help that Lotario hadn't gone near the corpse, either.

Even the athletic Margaret had kept away, and the scarred little girl had taken one look at the carnage and gone off to sit by herself in the sand. What had surprised Daisy was Lotario's response to that—he'd gone over to sit beside her. On the sand. Lotario *hated* sand.

Meanwhile, Isobel Amsel Riot had strode into the horsecar with barely a pause except to study the gruesome scene.

Daisy did not know why she felt the need to win the woman's approval—Isobel was only a few years older than herself. And she was rude. But there was something about her —a presence that wasn't born from charm or beauty. Daisy might be able to charm a roomful of men, but Isobel Amsel could send them scurrying off to their corners.

Daisy stopped in front of a printery tucked in a narrow lane that stank of rotting vegetables. She was happy she'd asked Garrett to join her, though the color of his skin made him just as likely a target of idle toughs as her sex.

"This might be another dead end," she said.

"The police will begin to suspect you if you discover another dead body lying on the floor."

"Lord, I hope not."

"From your lips to God's ears."

He opened the door for her and a dull clink of metal signaled a broken bell at the top. *A&A Press* didn't appear to be promising printery for an aspiring author, but from what she'd read of the works of Mr. Gary Mudd—aka Jasper, Serge Tremble, and Chandler Pascall—he seemed obsessed with deflowering young virgins.

Since Daisy's former employment catered to men with those very fantasies, she found Serge Tremble's lurid works a sad testament to the male sex's lack of imagination and preoccupation with their own anatomy.

The books published under his pen name of Jasper were pretentious literary disasters, while Chandler Pascall presented himself as a world traveler and collector of stories.

The office was cluttered with stacks of paper, pamphlets, dusty samples of bindings, and one large, oily machine clunking away under a cloud of cigar smoke. A sallow-faced man with ink-stained fingers stood nearby, hurrying to change out the paper as the machine clinked and pressed.

The man looked from Daisy to Garrett, who leaned an elbow on the counter to thumb through a volume of font samples. "Can I help you?" the man hollered over the machine.

Daisy only smiled at him—she wasn't about to carry on a shouting match with the press machine. As she hoped, he got the point and held up a finger.

Garrett cocked a brow at a stack of illegal pamphlets behind the counter on female remedies, then slid over another from a waiting stack to place it under her nose.

"They're so organized these days. Want to attend? It says there will be refreshments."

Daisy leaned closer. "I wonder what organized anarchists serve at their meetings?"

"One would hope it's at least a pitch-in." Garrett found himself shouting into a suddenly silent room. The machine had gone inert mid-sentence.

Daisy laughed.

"What's that now?" the man demanded.

Her smile didn't faze him. He stepped forward, scowling at the pair of them. "We were wondering what refreshments would be served at the anarchist's meeting."

"The food's brought in," the man said, cleaning his hands on a rag before extending it over the counter. "Oliver. Publisher, typesetter, and anarchist."

"That's quite the list of qualifications," Daisy said. "I'm only a hopeful writer. This is Garrett, my editor."

"Oh, aye? What size of an order can I do you for?"

"A client of mine has an order with you—Miss Reed here liked the work you did for him and was hoping to have the same done," Garrett said.

It was a shot in the dark. They'd tried five other presses, so when Garrett gave the various names of his client, and Mr. Oliver responded with a knowing nod and turned to a wall of shelves, Daisy felt faint with shock.

Oliver came back with a sheaf of papers without a leather binding. "Here's what I did so far. He pay you?"

Garrett cocked a grin at the man. "You know how these writers are…"

"Broke?"

"And forgetful."

"Mr. Mudd picked out a standard binding—nothing fancy. Gold lettering."

The title of the book was *Savage Gold* by Chandler Pascall. Daisy was surprised to see that pen name with the title. She'd expected anything printed at a press like this to be penned by Serge Tremble.

Daisy reached for the unbound copy, but Oliver pulled it away from her. "Have you ever heard of plagiarism?"

"I wanted to look at the quality of typesetting."

"I have samples." Oliver nodded to a stack. "There."

Splendid, she'd found the only press owner immune to her charms. But that was one of Daisy's specialties—she could assess a man in seconds and adapt. A pretty face and shapely figure didn't speak to him, but money would...

"Mr. Oliver. I'm afraid you won't be paid. Mr. Mudd has been murdered." And since he was an anarchist, she threw in, "Possibly by government men."

Oliver's brows gathered like a storm over his pale face.

"They burned documents. Or he did. We don't know."

"I think they were after this manuscript," Garrett added, reaching into his pocket to bring out a billfold. "How much does Mr. Mudd owe you for what you've done so far? We'd be happy to take it off your hands."

"Can you imagine what those officials would make of this press?" Daisy said, giving the anarchist pamphlet a conspiratorial nod.

Mr. Oliver needed no further convincing. Money was exchanged for the unbound book, and as they left Daisy tucked her arm through Garrett's, feeling rather pleased with herself.

They'd hit... something. It might be nothing in the end, but she had a hunch about those papers in the wood stove. Of all the books and papers and notebooks, why that particular stack?

"You know... if this turns out to be something," Garrett mused. "That shape Mr. Mudd was trying to draw with blood —it might've been an anarchist sign instead of a star."

"Or it could just be the name of the press."

"Either way, you'll get to tell Miss Amsel she was wrong."

Daisy grimaced. "I think I'll pass on that privilege."

THE AGENT

Tobias walked up to the ticket counter and pushed his fare towards the attendant. "Salt Lake City."

He showed off his two missing teeth as the man eyed him. "Traveling alone?"

Tobias inclined his chin towards the sling he wore for his arm. "I'm infirm. Do I get a special seat?"

The train clerk raised his brows. "No."

Tobias took his ticket, and was proud he hadn't looked at the wanted posters behind the man. It was disconcerting seeing his brother and some odd version of his mother and sister up on the wall, along with an assortment of bad sorts.

Assault and burglary? His ma? He could imagine it of Maddie—she had snuck into his room and confiscated his candy stash once.

Tobias took his ticket but hesitated—should he tell Grimm about the wanted posters for their mother and sister? It didn't look much like them.

After some consideration, he tossed down his rucksack and followed it onto a bench. Only a conductor came over to shoo him off, pointing down the platform to where other Negros waited.

Tobias dragged his rucksack off while the station attendant brushed off the bench, and went to stand with the other waiting passengers.

There was nowhere to sit, so he tossed his rucksack on the dirt and followed, crossing his legs. His stomach rumbled. Tobias looked around for someone selling something from a cart; he wasn't sure when the train was coming since he didn't have a pocket watch.

He looked at a family—a mother with two small children and a baby on her hip. She handed each a slice of an apple, and he just about started drooling.

The little girl dropped her slice. The mother bent to wipe it off and the little boy toddled away, drooling on the snack.

Tobias hopped to his feet and rushed over, steering the child away from the tracks and back to his mother.

"Billy, you stay with me. Thank you, young man."

"No problem, ma'am. I'm traveling alone. I just got myself to mind."

She frowned at him. "How old are you?"

"Practically a man."

"Are you?"

"Yes, ma'am. Broke my arm. Can't work at the ranch. Got to head home to family."

Billy tried to dart away again, and Tobias distracted the toddling boy by showing him his splint. "Don't suppose you know when the train's coming?"

"The train to where?"

"Salt Lake City."

"Shortly."

"They got food on the train?"

"A dining car, but not for us."

"Oh."

"There's usually someone selling something."

"Do you need help minding your children, or want me to carry your baggage? I just have a sack to manage."

"That's kind of you."

He thrust out his hand. "James Brady."

"Mrs. Neville."

Tobias went to retrieve his sack and pulled out a bit of twine he'd been working with to show the boy how to play cat's cradle. He was too young, but he drooled with amazement.

Mrs. Neville smiled, then bent to open up a basket and handed Tobias an entire apple.

"You are an angel, ma'am. I got a hole in my stomach."

"I thought so. You help me with the children and bags, and they'll be a sandwich for you."

A train soon rolled to a stop, spitting off smoke and steam and a hissing racket of noise. The baby started crying. The girl clung to her mother's skirts, and Tobias's charge tried to run the other way.

Tobias wrangled the boy back—a simple task after working with cows—and picked up the luggage to follow the mother inside.

His arm hurt, but he used it anyway to carry a lighter load. Since the carriage they were assigned to didn't have luggage racks, everyone stuffed their belongings around their legs. Tobias sat next to the little boy, who smushed his face to the glass as if the platform they'd just been on had changed into something amazing.

Mrs. Neville handed Tobias a sandwich.

"Thank you, ma'am."

"Meeting family, I hope?"

"My sister."

Grimm had been specific: Don't tell anyone you have a brother. Or a mother. Just like he'd been specific about buying a ticket for Utah, but getting off at Truckee.

"But I have to have a mother, Grimm. Everyone does," Tobias had argued.

"Just don't mention going to meet her."

Tobias soon joined Billy with his face pressed against the window as the horn blared and the chug of wheels grew steady.

A porter came to check the cars, then a conductor for tickets. Billy was soon passed out from the rocking when the train stopped at a station.

"They got candy for sale?" Tobias asked the porter.

"Dining car."

Tobias lifted Billy's eyelid. He was asleep in that unnerving way of small children, with twitchy eyes rolling from side to side. "Would you like something, ma'am? I think he'll be all right to leave for a bit."

"We're not allowed in the dining car."

Tobias shrugged. "I get told off all over the place."

He took off down the aisle, marveling at the way it rocked as he bounced his way off seats to wrestle open a door. There was a toilet in a little closet. He stepped inside, shut the door, and opened the seat. A wash of cold air blew up in his face and his mouth dropped open at the train tracks speeding under the hole.

Not precisely a toilet. Tobias wrinkled his nose. All this time he thought it was dogs going all over train tracks.

As he emptied his bladder, he hoped the little boy or girl wouldn't come in here alone—they were likely to fall through. He wiped his hands on his pants and went in search of candy.

The connections between the train cars were the best part. He leaned over the chain, watching the clacking wheels roll over the track, and then leaned farther out to look at the locomotive. A gust of smoke hit him in the face. Tobias reeled back, coughing, and staggered into the next train car.

One more car and the carriage changed. The seats were

padded with upholstery and carpet and curtains. And there were racks over the seats for luggage. The passengers stared at him as he passed; some glared.

He smiled at all the white folks and kept walking. "Going to buy some candy," he said to the porter, who stopped him at the next door.

"Just head back to your seat. I'll get you some. Do you have money?"

Tobias dug into his pocket even as an old lady pulled her handbag closer to look inside.

Tobias showed the man what he had, but before the porter could take it, the old woman batted at his hand. "None of that. I have some here." She handed him a paper packet of licorice.

Tobias thrust the coins at her.

"No, no. I've a sweet tooth, but not for licorice. Now if those were peppermint sticks…"

Tobias grinned, showing off the gaps in his teeth. She did the same. Maybe he ought to watch his sweet tooth. She appeared to have lost hers.

"Thank you, ma'am."

"How'd you break your arm, young man?"

He told her, and since she seemed to enjoy the story, he made a tale of it.

"You come visit me again if you get restless. It's a long trip for me."

"Yes, ma'am."

Tobias walked back to his seat, much cheered by the generosity of folks. Sure, there were some rotten apples, but Tobias didn't pay them any mind—he liked to keep an optimistic view. He chose to look for the good in people.

An apple, a sandwich, and a bag of licorice. He stopped to talk to another porter (who accepted a piece of licorice) and by the time he was done, had found out everything there was to know about being a Pullman porter. How the tipping could be good, and how it was like sailing over land and drifting into a different port every day.

Tobias also learned that times were changing. The old ways of cattle drives were dying out. Cattle were moved in trains and ranches were fenced by the devil's rope. Cattle should roam free, the porter said. Just like men. A lot of old cowboys were hiring on with Mr. Pullman.

"I'm gonna be a U.S. marshal. Or a detective," Tobias told the man.

"That right? But that don't pay as well."

"Really?"

The porter shook his head. "With the way you handle people, you could earn a heap of tips."

"I don't handle people—I just talk with them."

The porter flashed a smile. "You got the gift."

"Most just say I got a big mouth."

"Same thing sometimes. It's all how you spin it."

Tobias considered this as he bounced his way back to his seat. If his plans to become a U.S. Marshal fell through—he thought he might like to be a train porter.

More stops, more waiting, and Billy woke up, which made the time pass as Tobias tried to keep the child occupied while they seemed stuck at a station. There was only so much looking out the window at the train conductor smoking on the platform one could do.

Then the train started moving again with a blare of horn. And climbing, up and up, towards the white-capped Sierras. His ears started hurting, Billy started crying, and Mrs. Neville gave the children each a stick of gum to chew. Tobias chewed until his ears popped and after that they didn't hurt anymore.

The train car got cold, and snow sparkled all between the trees. Tobias thought he'd seen snow before, but he only had a vague impression of coldness. He was five when they came to Ravenwood Manor, and while he thought of it as home, he also wanted to get out more—his mother never went anywhere. It was maddening.

Now, finally, he understood why they never joined in the community or the churches or could go to public school.

Tobias wondered what would happen to his family—where their new home would be. His thoughts turned to Jin and Sarah, and he got sad. Not that he didn't love his brother and sister; it was just Jin and Sarah were close to his own age—the first friends he'd ever had. And they'd become family.

Jin and Sarah had no blood relatives of their own. They'd been adopted by Mr. AJ and Isobel, but they were a family, all mixed up and different colors. Why shouldn't someone be able to make their own family? Blood might be thicker than water, but water kept you alive.

He was lost in thought when he sensed a presence looming over him. Without looking up, Tobias dug into his pocket for his ticket. Hadn't he just handed one over?

He held it up and looked at the figure looming in the aisle for the first time. The carriage had gone quiet, and even Billy peeled his face from the window to turn around. A wiry white man with longish brown hair stood looking down at Tobias. He had his thumbs hooked in his vest, and a revolver and ammunition at his belt.

"Tobias White?"

Tobias' eyes darted to the side. "James Brady."

"Yeah. Sure. Atticus Riot sent me to fetch you."

Tobias' eyes widened. "Really?"

"Really. Come on. You hungry?"

"Is he on the train?"

"No, but Tim has eyes and ears everywhere."

Tobias beamed. His message had worked! Mr. AJ had been looking for them. "Is Miss Isobel alive?" he asked as he shouldered his rucksack.

"She is."

His heart felt lighter than it had since they'd fled Raven-wood Manor. "Sorry, Mrs. Neville. My, erm… uncle sent someone for me."

Mrs. Neville eyed the man. "Are you sure you're all right?"

Tobias nodded. "Sorry, I can't watch Billy anymore. You want me to pay for the sandwich?"

"No, that's fine. You take care of yourself. What did you say this man's name was?"

Tobias looked at the man, who looked familiar.

"Sam Batten, ma'am. I'm one of his uncle's agents."

"He's a detective," Tobias explained. "I'll bring something back for you, Mrs. Neville."

Tobias waved goodbye and walked off with Sam Batten, feeling pleased as pie.

33

THE HOPPER

T<small>OBIAS</small>' <small>OPTIMISM DEFLATED WHEN HE WAS ESCORTED PAST THE</small> dining car and into what looked like a private car. Two men were sitting in there—a weathered white man and a polished Negro man.

Tobias liked the polished man's reefer jacket and white hat. He liked the way his boots shone, and every piece of clothing was in its place. And then he remembered where he'd seen Sam Batten before—he was a Pinkerton, who Mr. AJ had been working with.

"Amazing what a network of agents can do," the white man said with a smile. "You look like your mother, boy."

Tobias hesitated. He looked from man to man, then recalled Grimm's description of the men who'd taken his family from their home. The men who'd pursued them all these years.

"Angel Davren," the polished man stood up, offering a hand and a pearly white smile. "This is my partner, Eli Blake. And you know Sam Batten here."

Tobias swallowed down a sudden swell of fear. "He promised me candy."

"Right."

The train clicked and climbed, and the air became colder, the snow-covered mountainside blinding. No one went off to get him candy.

"So you're taking me to Mr. AJ?"

"Why don't you have a seat?" Eli suggested.

Tobias sat. The moment he set down his rucksack, Sam Batten picked it up and started rifling through its meager contents. Tobias minded, but there wasn't much he could do.

"Can I see your ticket?"

It wasn't really a question. Eli made it clear there was only one answer, so Tobias handed it over.

"Utah?"

Tobias tossed himself back against the seat, kicking his feet in the air. "Sure. You ever been? I hear it's all right. Some lake that isn't a lake, all barren and a heap of Mormons. You know they can have more than one wife? I heard that, too. Can you imagine having more than one wife? I mean one seems bad enough, don't it? But they'd get to fighting and arguing over who has to do what and—"

"Where's your mother and brother?" Angel asked.

Tobias shrugged. "I don't know. I've been working at a ranch. Only I broke my arm. We got separated."

"Then why are you heading to Utah?"

"Because it was the farthest I could travel on my fare. Train travel costs money, you know?"

"What are you planning to do once you get there?"

Tobias rubbed his chin in consideration. "Get a job. Maybe as a Pullman porter. The man back there said I got the 'gift'. But what I really want to do is become a lawman." He leaned forward to squint at the edge of a shiny badge on Angel's vest.

The train climbed. The carriage was empty, and the three men loomed around him. He was as scared as could be, so he looked out the window, and spotted an icy river raging in a gorge below. "Say! Look at that. What river is that?"

"Where'd your mother and brother go?"

"Like I said—we got separated. Police chased off Grimm. Ma and Maddie didn't want to be cold, so I wager they went somewhere warm. Can you take a train to Hawaii?"

Tobias was aware of a movement out of the corner of his eye, but he kept playing dumb. Eli had tensed, Sam had chuckled, and Angel put a hand on his partner's arm. The man relaxed.

"Tobias," Angel said.

Tobias looked the man in the eye. The man had friendly eyes—there wasn't anything wrong about him, nothing to show he'd ruined Tobias' life and made his mother miserable.

Tobias wondered if Grimm had been telling the truth. What if these were just lawmen doing their job and his brother was really some kind of criminal running with a bad gang? It was hard to think ill of Mr. Angel Davren.

But there were also little things—tells, Mr. AJ would call them. The way Eli had tensed, the way Sam Batten had plucked him from his seat, and taken him off alone, then searched through his things without asking.

"So, are we headed back to San Francisco?" Tobias asked.

"That depends on you," Angel said. "Do you know your brother Josiah is a wanted man?"

"I saw a poster. Did he steal some candy? Or maybe a horse?"

"He's murdered men, including a U.S. Marshal."

Tobias scratched his cheek. "I don't know... he's too slow for that. Not the brightest. How come it took you so long to get him?"

"He's more slippery than he looks," Angel said smoothly. "What do you plan on doing once you get to Utah? Are you supposed to meet him there?"

Tobias considered his limited options. The optimistic part of him said they wouldn't do anything to an eight-year-old boy. But then a vision of Jin's scarred face flashed across his mind and he recalled her distrust of adults and Sarah's account of the men who'd come for her. No, he knew it to his bones—men hurt children all the time.

His mind seized on the badge, and he folded his arms, leaning back on the plush seat.

"So let me get this straight… you want me to help you find my brother?"

The men exchanged surprised glances.

"That's right," Eli said. "It's the lawful thing to do."

"If I'm being lawful, I need to be deputized as a U.S. Marshal. Otherwise, I'd be betraying family. Now, if I'm a marshal, then I'm conflicted and only doing my job, like Old and Young King Brady. Law before blood, and all that."

"I'm afraid you're too young," Angel said.

Tobias shrugged. "Guess I'm too young to capture criminals."

Eli knocked some ash out on a tray before climbing to his feet. "Repeat after me…"

Tobias stood at attention in front of the man who'd terrorized his family.

"I, Tobias Shaw, do solemnly swear that I will support and defend the Constitution of the United States against all enemies…"

Tobias repeated the words, and each part after.

"…foreign and domestic; that I will bear true faith and allegiance to the same; that I take this obligation freely, without any mental reservation or purpose of evasion; and that I will well and faithfully discharge the duties of the office on which I am about to enter. So help me God."

"So help me God," Tobias parroted.

"All right. You're deputized."

"Where's my badge?"

Angel looked at his partner, a smile creeping up at the edge of his lips. Eli rooted around his pockets, grumbling, until he pulled out a battered tin star to pin on Tobias' coat.

Tobias took out a handkerchief to polish it. It looked like it had dry, crusted stuff on it. When his handkerchief came back with a coppery powder, he thought it might be blood. Neat.

"Right. Mr. Batten promised me food. I haven't eaten in days."

Sam took off with a grumble, and Tobias sat down with the two U.S. Marshals, waiting for instructions.

"Tell us everything that happened once you left Raven-wood Manor."

Tobias took a deep breath. Starting at the beginning was always hard—where to start? There were a heap of begin-nings, so he started with Jack stealing apples, because, as he told the men, he was a lawman now, so he had to come clean. From there he went on to Grimm trying to drag him out of the fort, and him dragging his feet, and no one telling him anything on account of his loud mouth. And did they know his name wasn't Tobias White?

He ate and talked; he talked and drank, then ate some more. And even told them about how his sister and mother got sick of him and took off in the middle of a wetland.

The men stared. He was talking. He was telling them everything—from the blisters on his feet, to the hole in his stomach, to his sister's annoying habits of being cheerful. To jumping out of trains, and waking up in places, and no, he didn't know any of the names—no one told him on account of his big mouth.

Finally, Tobias asked to use the toilet.

"Why don't you get to the part where your brother parted ways?"

"How about I piss on the seat?"

The three men let him go. Inside, Tobias locked the door and pressed his forehead against the wall for a minute. He knew what he had to do. He opened the seat, bracing himself against the gust of cold air that blew in his face. White ground sped underneath, but the train had slowed on account of the grade and the snow on the tracks. It wasn't going nearly as fast as usual.

He took a deep breath as he gazed down the toilet. Tobias had always been small. He was like a beanpole and his head could fit between places. Until recently, it had fit through the railing slats at Ravenwood Manor. After he got his ears stuck, he stopped sticking his head through the slats. But this toilet... Billy could fall in it.

Trying not to think about the sides of the thing on the way down, he stuck his head inside, then farther down to his waist to get a look at the undercarriage.

He grabbed a bar and squirmed and turned until his shoulders worked free—the rest was easy. His boots hit the tracks and slid over the freezing snow. Tobias held on tight, but the metal bar was like ice and his hands burned as he was dragged under the train. Frantic, his broken arm quivering with pain, he let go, and dropped into the snow.

Tobias flattened himself like a pancake, keeping his eyes closed and his arms flat as the train roared over his face. It seemed to go on forever, the engine, the horn, the metal machinery threatening to crush him. Finally the racket stopped, and he opened his eyes to a gray sky and a wilderness covered in snow.

Tobias rolled over to watch the train fade out of view. When it was gone, he stood up, dusted off snow and studied his surroundings. The train tracks carved a path along a steep mountainside that plummeted into a raging river. All around, no matter where he looked, there were only snow-covered pine trees and more snow.

It was about that time he started to shiver.

"Good one, Tobias," he muttered. "Real smart. Way to think things through."

But at least he was a Deputy U.S. Marshal now, with an official badge. Cheered by the thought, he popped a piece of licorice into his mouth and started walking.

Things could be worse.

34

FROM BAD TO WORSE

THINGS CAN ALWAYS BE WORSE, HIS MOTHER ONCE TOLD HIM. But what amazed Tobias was just how fast they got worse.

In under an hour, he was shivering so violently that he feared he'd crack his teeth, so he started jogging along the tracks. The afternoon turned colder, and the sun vanished, and flurries started stinging his cheeks.

His lungs burned, his lips cracked, and tears froze on his cheeks.

Tobias kept moving. He didn't know where he was headed, or how far away the next town was, but he knew he'd die if he stopped.

This was worse than when he'd hopped in the back of a wagon to rescue Jin. *Why did I get off the train?*

Flurries landed on his lashes and caught in his hair, and the sweat on his back was cooling to ice. He wanted to lie down in the soft snow and just rest for a time.

Tobias squinted through the flurries at a darkness ahead—a deep hole of black. A tunnel. Tobias made his legs move until his lungs burned, but as soon as he took cover inside the tunnel, the wind stopped biting. It was warmer in there. He slowed, the air puffing in front of him, hands thrust in his pockets and fingers curled into frozen fists. He couldn't feel his toes.

Tobias walked to the other end of the tunnel and peered out into a sheet of gray—night was coming and he knew he was going to die.

MOON RIVER

THE LITTLE CABIN WAS WARM AND SMELLED OF BISCUITS AND coffee. Maddie snuggled into the chair with a book in her hand as pine logs crackled in the hearth, but try as she might, she couldn't focus on the words.

I should be thankful.

Her mother was kneading bread at the counter of a small kitchen. They'd worked all day at the Moon River Lodge. When they'd finished their cooking for the day, they hung up their aprons and made the short trek to an outlying cabin near an icy stream.

The cabin had a kitchen and sitting room in one, two bedrooms, and an outhouse out back. Her mother talked about fixing up the little barn for chickens and maybe keeping sheep or goats.

Lily talked of everything except her sons. Constantly working, cleaning, keeping busy, so she wouldn't have to think of Grimm and Tobias, and why they hadn't arrived.

That was the problem with splitting up—the aching worry. And there was nothing either of them could do without risking exposure.

Patience. That was always best. And hope.

Maddie set the book aside, and shrugged on a coat to fetch more wood from the shed. Even though winter was giving way to spring, there was no telling when a storm might blow in enough snow to trap them inside for a week or more.

The Moon River Lodge was a sprawling retreat, and although the winter season wasn't as busy as summer, it still attracted a crowd looking to take in the beauty of Lake Tahoe.

The manager of the lodge was the son of a friend of Miss Shaw—Ravenwood's old housekeeper. The son welcomed them like old friends, and knew enough not to ask questions. It didn't hurt that Lily's cooking could win a blue ribbon at any fair.

But were they safe there?

They didn't know if the U.S. Marshals were on their trail, but her mother was careful, always assuming those men were still hunting them.

The only time Lily had started to let her guard down was at Ravenwood Manor.

Maddie gathered an armful of wood, and turned to leave, when a shadow loomed off to the side. She froze. A bear? Surely they were hibernating, but it was closing in on spring—

"It's me, Maddie."

The hoarse voice made her drop her load. She rushed at the shadow of her older brother, and Grimm crushed her in his arms, and even swung her around once before setting her down.

"You're freezing. Get inside."

In answer, Grimm handed over his rucksack, then bent to gather the split wood. The front door opened, spilling light onto the snow, and their mother stood in the doorway with a rifle.

"Maddie?"

"It's Grimm."

Lily's breath caught. She waited for her son to unload the wood before pulling him into a rib crushing hug.

"Sit down. Get those wet clothes off. Maddie, pull the wool blanket off the bed."

"I'm fine, Ma. Just rode through the pass in a drafty boxcar."

His eyes were sunken and his cheekbones stark, his clothes muddy and patched, even frozen solid in places.

"Where's Tobias?"

At his mother's question, Grimm's mind knocked back into gear. He searched the cabin, expecting his little brother to jump out from behind a table. "He's not here?"

"No."

"What happened?" Maddie asked.

"We had to separate… They have my wanted posters all over the place. Yours, too, though they don't look like you. The marshals don't know what Tobias looks like, so I gave him train fare to Truckee, to make his way here…"

"He's eight years old, Grimm."

"Nearly nine." Grimm defended. "He did well at the ranch until he broke his arm."

Maddie gripped her mother's shoulder and pushed her down into a chair before she toppled to the floor.

"You left him?"

Grimm looked stricken by the accusation. "I… no. It was cold, Ma. He was hungry. I had a hard journey ahead… I thought he could just take a train, and he'd be more comfortable."

"He probably got distracted and is walking around Truck-ee," Maddie said.

"He knows where he's supposed to go."

"How long ago did he leave?"

Grimm glanced at his fingers, curled with cold, and nails caked in dirt. "He should've been here by now."

"I told you to watch him, Josiah. I told you——"

Grimm stood up. "I'll go find him."

"Sit down," Maddie snapped. "And Ma… that's not fair. Grimm was right to send Tobias on the train—no one knows what he looks like. For God's sake, he's been running wild all over San Francisco with the Riots. It's not like he can't manage himself."

Shocked silence met her outburst—from Grimm and her mother. But Maddie had had enough of everything in the past eight years.

"You're right," Lily said. "I'm sorry, Josiah. I—we'll make inquiries in town. Mr. Beigert knows everyone around. He'll be careful."

Lily rose and went off into the kitchen, where they heard the gentle sounds of her preparing a tray. Maddie studied her brother, and worried he might be sick on the floor.

She seized his hand; it was trembling with cold. "You did the right thing, Joe. Tobias might've frozen to death with you. He's so small and thin."

Grimm hung his head. "At least we'd know where he is. I can't do anything right."

"I wouldn't be here without you. You remember, don't you? That Night?"

Grimm raised his head to meet her eyes, and she saw that he was haunted with the memory of it. Of course, he remembered. She doubted there was a day that went by when he didn't regret every choice he'd made from that day on.

"We'd have been better off with me hanged," he whispered.

Maddie shook her head. "Do you really think they'd have stopped there?"

"No."

"Then you think those marshals are still after us?" she asked.

Grimm stared into the fire. "I do."

"Why?"

"I shot his brother."

"Blake wouldn't let pa tend his brother. He burned down the hotel before his brother was fully dead. There's something more… There *has* to be. And Ma…" Maddie glanced towards the kitchen and lowered her voice. "She's gone into herself, like before."

Grimm caught his sister's eye with a look as severe as his name. How could he ever forget those days of waiting for Clay to come back with their parents?

Five days later, Clay Holden had brought back their mother and baby brother. Only their mother was a ghost—all her life and spirit was poured into the squalling infant.

"Where's pa?" Josiah had asked.

Lily shook her head, staring in confusion at the infant at her breast. Josiah looked at Clay, who was haggard and bloodied. "Where's my pa?"

"Dead."

Maddie saw it in her brother's eyes—that word. He was thinking about it now, worrying over Tobias. "You remember what Clay called Tobias before ma got around to telling us his name?"

Grimm huffed out a small laugh. "*Foshi losa.*" It was Chickasaw for grackle, the loudest bird in the territory. "Stuck for years."

"If we weren't in hiding, I'd still call him that," Maddie muttered, taking his hands to warm them between her own. "Can you keep a secret?"

Grimm looked at her like she was crazy. He'd learned that lesson long ago—keep your mouth shut.

"Weeks ago, I sent a letter to Dr. Wise to pass on to Mr. Riot, then left another at a hotel in Sacramento."

"You shouldn't have—"

"I'm sick of this."

"You can't drag the Riots into this."

"We need help."

Their mother returned with a tray and set it down beside Grimm, then reached for her heavy coat. Maddie hopped up to put hers on, too. "I'll be fine, Maddie."

"I won't let you go alone."

"I'll take the rifle."

Maddie trotted out after her, anyway. The air was crisp, the scents of pine and snow invigorating as they puffed along a trail with only a hooded lantern to light their way.

It wasn't a long walk, but with the stars obscured and the forest closing in, the thawing of the snow and its muffling of noise, Maddie felt like they were alone in some vast wilderness.

And that would've been fine. Aside from bears and cougars, and who knew what else, it was people who made her afraid. And the dread of wondering whether they were actually alone out here.

THE BLAZING LIGHTS OF THE LODGE WARMED MADDIE, ALONG with the piano music coming from the windows. There'd be a blazing fire in the river stone hearth and soft chairs to roast beside, but the great lobby wasn't for them—they went straight to the staff entrance.

It was locked this time of night, so Lily knocked softly while Maddie shivered on the steps. A scrape of a peephole, then a lock sliding to the side, and the door opened.

Mr. Beigert himself answered, ushering them inside the mudroom. "Two men checked in. They were asking Sally about the pie you cooked earlier," he whispered. "Wanted to give their compliments to the cook."

"Ma's pies are the best," Maddie agreed.

But Mr. Beigert shook his head. "It was the *way* they were asking—"

"Did Sally give my name?"

Mr. Beigert shook his balding head. "No, no, she avoided their questions."

Lily tightened her grip on the rifle. Sally's evasiveness would only raise suspicion and confirm she had something to hide. Their names didn't matter—they were using fake ones.

"The younger fellow mentioned it was the same pie a niece of his bakes."

Maddie narrowed her eyes. "This fellow... Did he give his niece's name?"

"Mary Bennet."

Maddie grinned so hard her dimples showed.

"What is it?" Lily asked.

"I don't suppose the gentleman in question wore spectacles?"

"He did. And Sally said he was far too charming."

"Did he give a name?"

"Mr. Collins."

Maddie laughed, while her mother was looking at her like she'd gone insane. "What have you done, girl?"

"It needed doing, Ma."

Ten minutes later, Maddie walked into one of the private smoking rooms, and all her pent up fear and worry rushed to the surface when she spotted the man waiting inside. Impulsively, she rushed into his arms and he returned the embrace with avuncular affection.

Atticus Riot put his hands on her shoulders and stepped back to study her face. "Of all the Bennet sisters, I would've pegged you for Jane rather than Mary." His voice was low and full of warmth, and her vision blurred with tears.

"Is Miss Isobel..." she hesitated.

"She's alive, and healing at home."

Maddie shuddered with relief.

"Are you both all right?" This question came from the other man in the room—bald, tough as leather, and with a bushy white beard.

Tim opened his arms in invitation. Maddie's cheeks hurt from smiling, and she felt shaky with relief. But one look at her mother burst her bubble of joy.

After Lily had shut the door, she hadn't moved—her back was to it, and there was no warmth in her eyes.

"Ma, I—" Maddie took a step towards her mother, but stopped at the silent rebuke she received. "I thought it was time we try something else."

"You shouldn't have involved them," Lily insisted. "There is nothing *else* to do. And there's nothing they can do!"

"You've been running so long you don't know what else to do." As soon as the words were out, Maddie clicked her mouth shut in shock—she'd never used that tone with her mother.

Riot spoke into the heavy silence. "Your mother isn't running from the marshals, Maddie. She's running from the past."

Lily's eyes blazed with anger. "Don't presume to know my mind, Mr. Riot." It was like a whisper of steel through the air.

Riot caught her eyes with his own, and didn't let go. "I don't know your mind," he admitted. "But I have dark corners of my own."

She shook with fury (or maybe pain), then she broke eye contact. "You don't know who's after us."

"We know most of it," Riot said.

"And then some," Tim added.

"A pair of U.S. Marshals paid us a visit."

"They came to the house?" Maddie asked, glancing at her mother in shock. But Lily wasn't surprised by the news. It only confirmed what she already knew.

Maddie felt a sudden surge of guilt for ever doubting her

mother—ever wondering if she wasn't just being paranoid. With that realization came another dread. "Tobias is missing."

At her blunt statement, whatever had been holding Lily together seemed to unravel, and she sagged against the door. Riot was at her side, helping her into a chair, pressing brandy into her hands. "What do you mean, he's missing?" he asked Maddie.

"I think Grimm best tell you."

NO LONGER ALONE

"I FIGURED IT'D BE SAFER THAT WAY—THERE WERE NO WANTED posters with his face. The marshals don't know what he looks like…"

Only Tobias was missing.

Grimm had finally stopped shivering and looked better for the tray of food he'd eaten. His long fingers fiddled with the mug between his hands. But at the sight of Riot and Tim walking through the door, some of the strain had left his eyes.

They weren't alone. Not anymore.

Tim huddled on a stool by the hearth. Any closer and he might as well be sitting in it. His pipe smoke mingled with the fragrant pine logs.

Lily hadn't said a word—only stared into the flames. Distant and quiet. She'd barely touched the mug Maddie pressed into her hands.

"I'm afraid they know what he looks like," Riot said.

Grimm looked up in confusion. "We were so careful. How did they track us?"

"You're too talented for your own good, boy," Tim said. "Word got around about your horse charming."

"Shit," Grimm muttered.

Lily didn't even stir to correct his language.

"Don't heap any more blame on yourself," Riot said. "Sam Batten is looking for you, too."

"The Pinkerton at the racetrack?"

"The very same."

"But he told me to run…"

"And now he seems to have taken up with Eli Blake and Angel Davren."

Lily flinched at the sound of their names. That movement wasn't lost on Riot—he studied her for a moment, his eyes softening with understanding.

"What happened after I ran to find a telephone?" Tim asked.

"He knew my real name, said he recognized me and knew I had a bounty on my head. Since I helped him stop Carson, he did me a favor and gave me time to run."

"Did Carson reach for a gun?" Tim asked.

Grimm stared down into his mug. After a time, he looked up and gave a shake of his head. "Everything happened so fast… At first, I thought so, but then… No, Sam shot Carson in cold blood."

"Why would he do that?" Maddie asked.

"I suspect Sam was in on the racetrack scheme," Riot said. "He was there to make sure Carson didn't rat out the bigger fish."

"And who's that?"

Riot lifted a brow in a kind of shrug. "We don't know. That's for Liam Taft to sort out once we lay hands on Sam Batten."

"No one will believe me," Grimm said.

"Probably not," Riot agreed.

Grimm straightened and set aside his mug to look Riot square in the eye. "I understand if you have to arrest me and take me to the authorities, but I need to find Tobias first."

Tim snorted. "Grimm, who the hell do you think we are? Do we strike you as law-abiding folk?"

"You'll get in trouble if you don't hand me over. I've killed lawmen."

Riot leaned forward to grip the young man's shoulder. "We're not turning you in."

"I'm tired of running. I'd rather it be you."

"Delivering you to Judge Parker won't stop those men. You're all witnesses to their corruption."

"It doesn't matter what we saw," Grimm argued. "They wear badges. It's our word against theirs."

"Not necessarily. There was a writer by the name of Mudd at the Mineral Springs Hotel. Do you remember him, Miss Lily?"

She didn't stir.

Riot knew where she was—deep inside of herself, trying not to remember, trying to avoid the dark corners of her mind. The places where pain lurked.

"I haven't heard that name in years," Grimm whispered, wiping his eyes.

"I remember him," Maddie said. "He kept to himself."

"He was found murdered in Carville a few days back."

This statement snagged Lily's attention. She stared at him in disbelief.

"When you disappeared, we started making discreet inquiries. After the marshals visited us, I threw Ravenwood Agency on the case. My—" Riot caught himself. "Lotario's agents traced a bill to a small press in San Francisco, where they found an unbound novel about the Holden Gang."

"But it's just a book," Maddie said. "That won't stand in court, will it?"

"It sheds light on events. And on the investigation that

Zephaniah Ravenwood began for Mrs. Shaw, who I think was an aunt of sorts to your late husband."

"But *why*?" Maddie demanded. "Why did they come after us in the first place? Why burn our hotel down? Why take us all?"

"The title of the book is *Savage Gold*."

Silent tears spilled down Lily's cheeks, but she didn't notice them. She was somewhere else—somewhere dark, in the cold, and begging to die.

"Miss Lily," Riot said, taking her hands in his own. "Your son is missing. I know you don't want to remember, but the more we know about those men, the better chance we have of finding Tobias."

Lily gave a shake of her head. "It's not that. There hasn't been a day that's gone by that I don't relive it. I couldn't..." She stopped herself, glancing at her children.

"They're old enough to know," Riot whispered. "They need to hear it—what parts you can tell. You're not alone anymore, Miss Lily. You don't need to carry the burden alone."

TOBIAS

1892

THE MOMENT JOSIAH DISAPPEARED INTO THE CRACK, NATHAN turned to his wife. She gripped the side of the rock with a desperate plea in her eyes—don't let my babies fall.

He looked towards the cave entrance where the marshals were arguing about what to do next. No one was facing the back of the cave, but that would change soon enough.

Nathan peeled his wife's hands from the rock and drew her to the back of the cave, where a black hole belched out a rotting stench.

"I won't leave you, Nat."

Nathan took her head in his hands. There wasn't time for goodbyes or long embraces—no amount of time would be enough to spend with the woman he loved.

"You have to," he whispered. "It's the only way. Once they see the children gone… they'll tear you apart to get at me. This way, they'll just take me with them when they go after Holden."

"And if they don't?" She held onto his forearms like she'd never let go.

"I'll break," he said hoarsely. "You know it. I'd rather risk you to the pit of snakes down there than those men. Please. *Please.* I'm begging you to leave me. Just this once."

Silent tears streamed down her cheeks as he pressed his lips to her forehead and crushed her in his arms, searing the feel of her in his mind—her soft body, her warm scent, her love. He wanted to hold on to that feeling and nothing else.

He kissed her then—slow and urgent, drawing in her breath like it was his last. "Tobias," he whispered in her ear.

Nathan felt her smile. "That's worse than your last choice."

"I'll just have to come up with a better one. Come on, my girl, into the cesspit with you."

"So romantic."

There was a partially covered mine shaft at the far end of the cave. Long abandoned, it was nothing more than a rubbish pit for human waste, animal bones, and anything that a camp full of men needed to toss down to conceal their presence.

A stone partially covered the cave in, but there was enough room for his wife to squeeze through. Nathan pressed his medical lantern into her hand along with matches, then listened to the men at the cave entrance, waited, and when he was sure one of them was about to raise his voice in a shout, he dropped a heavy rock into the shaft.

It landed instantly with a thud and a whisper of slithering movement over rock. There were bound to be snakes down there, but it was cold, and he prayed they'd be sluggish.

Nathan helped his wife sit on the edge, then he got on his belly and gripped her hands. She was heavy with child, but he could always lift her with ease. Carefully, slowly, and dreading the moment he'd have to let her go, he lowered his wife into the mine shaft.

Their palms pressed together, her fingers clutched his, not wanting to let go… with a final squeeze, he shook her free.

———

LILY FELL ON A HILL OF FILTH: RAGS, TRASH, BONES, AND human waste. Something slithered over her hand and she froze.

Stay calm, she told herself. It was pitch black in the shaft, but she was aware of slow, creeping movement. Despite the possibility of poisonous fangs sinking into her flesh, she found the thought of life down here comforting rather than terror inducing.

Animals made sense; men did not—not when they had a mind to be worse than animals.

"*Shaw!*"

The shout echoed down the shaft, and Lily closed her eyes to the fury in that name. She couldn't risk lighting the lantern. Not yet. With glacial care, she found her footing in the cesspit and climbed to her feet with a grimace. The landing was softer than she cared to think on, but she was heavy with child, and any bump or jolt, or even rolling over, was hard going in her current condition.

"Where's Shaw!" the booming demand made her bite back a cry of fear.

Just keep calm, she told herself. But standing in a mine shaft on a heap of bones and waste with a whisper of long bodies moving at her feet tested her courage. It wasn't fear for herself —it was fear for those she loved. She was here, helpless, and her family was in danger.

The snakes were nothing compared to the thought of her children, alone in the dark, running away from lawmen to seek refuge with a gang of outlaws.

What a twisted world.

But when Eli Blake's harsh voice came again, concern for her children was replaced with a growing dread of what she'd tried to ignore—the fate of her husband.

"You know something, Shaw."

"I told you they probably moved after I left."

"Clay moved after you sent your boy back, didn't he? And he took you along to their new camp."

"Clay's son couldn't be moved—"

Smack! Flesh pummeled flesh.

"You think we don't know what a cold fire looks like? That damn fire is four days old!"

"Clay didn't want to be spotted. They snuffed it out."

"Grab his little girl."

Lily held her breath as she listened to the echo of boots overhead. The darkness above blazed like a sun, and she shrank back from the approaching lantern light.

"They're gone, Eli!"

"What the hell do you mean, they're gone?"

"His woman and brats aren't here. That's what I mean."

"That's not possible. Dammit, Tucker, I told you to watch 'em! Where'd your mutts go, Shaw?"

"As you say, sir, they're gone," Nathan wheezed.

A crack echoed off the stone, then a heavy weight hit the ground.

"There's a crevice here. They might've climbed out," someone said.

"Git up there and look for them!"

"We can't fit."

"Then git on a damn horse and find them!"

Sounds of rapid activity followed: thudding boots, the creak of leather, and beating hooves as riders sped away.

"Dr. Shaw," Angel Davren said in a cool voice that was more terrifying than a shout. "I suggest you tell us where Clay moved his camp to."

A weighted silence followed—a deathly stillness where Lily imagined the two men facing off. She knew, deep in her bones, that Nat wouldn't be standing in defiance, but with that insufferable look on his face when he knew he'd won. No matter what that triumph was about to cost him.

Nathan Shaw met Angel Davren's gaze with a light in his eye and a quirk of his lips. A split second later, Angel Davren tried to wipe that smirk off his face with a fist.

At the sounds that followed, Lily bit down on her hand, and squeezed her eyes shut against the darkness.

Snakes slithered around her feet, but she was too numb to feel them, too sick to care. It was a full fifteen minutes of pounding flesh and cruel laughter before Nathan Shaw screamed in agony.

That scream broke her, but not her husband. Lily Shaw slid to the muck with the taste of blood and tears on her tongue as the sounds of torture ripped out her heart.

———

SOUNDS ECHOED IN THE CAVE. WORDS. HER NUMB MIND couldn't make any sense of their meaning. It was like a different language. It was the silence between those words that she understood—her husband was dead.

Lily knew it in her bones. She felt as cold as death.

"They'll bring the kids back…"

"…we'll track 'em at first light."

"How do you hide that much gold?"

"What should we do with 'im?"

"…mine shaft."

That last pierced the fog in her mind. First came a shape that landed with a rattle of metal. Nathan's medical bag. Clothes fell next, and finally a lump of flesh landed with a crack.

Lily pressed against the stone wall as light illuminated the shaft. Her husband stared back, his neck bent at a horrible angle, his face swollen with bruises and cuts and blood, his naked body and hands mangled and broken.

She stared at those hands. Every finger was broken. The nails pulled off and his fingertips stumps of blood—those gentle, strong hands that had caressed every inch of her body, that had held her, that had warmed her, and saved so many.

Lily put her fist to her mouth and bit down hard.

"Smells like shit down there. Ain't nothing but rubbish and rattlers."

She wanted to scream. Wanted to rage. Instead, she stared at her husband's mutilated hand.

The light left, the voices drifted away.

Lily sat shivering in the dark.

It might've been an hour, a day, a month… the world just stopped. In the end, it was the baby who kicked her out of her stupor. The child was restless in her belly, pushing against her rib with a foot, its head bumping against her womb as if trying to propel itself free.

She shifted. Then recalled the lamp.

Did she want to see?

Did she care?

Lily used the slick rock to pull herself up. She pressed her face against the stone, teeth chattering, and tried not to be sick. She fingered the scalpel her husband had pressed into her hand.

A clean slice along both wrists…

The baby drummed its feet against her rib. She took her hand away from the scalpel in her pocket and pressed it to her stomach.

Tobias.

Lily fumbled around for the medical lamp, and got it lit with shaking hands. The small candle of warmth felt like the sun in this dark pit. She swallowed, braced herself, and turned to her husband.

He lay in filth, all twisted. Snakes slithered around the far edges, towards the back, but mostly they didn't like the rot the gang had tossed down there any more than she did.

Lily gathered her strength and left the stone. Trying not to look at his wounds too closely, she straightened his legs and folded his hands over his broad chest. She laid a shirt over him, shrugged on his coat, then sat and laid his head on her lap, stroking his brow.

For a precious minute, she convinced herself he was asleep. She wanted to stretch alongside him and wait for her own death. They'd be together that way.

The baby kicked again.

Tobias.

Their unborn child wouldn't see the light of day.

Lily looked down into the face of Nathan—he hadn't sacrificed himself so she could die. He wanted her to live. He wanted more for his unborn child.

"And what if it's a girl, Nat?" she whispered.

No smile. No answer. Nothing.

Emptiness shoved her forward, and she wept silently over his body until she was drained of tears.

When she looked up, she spotted a rattlesnake slithering over his shin. Instead of fighting with nature, she picked up the lamp and climbed to her feet to study the shaft. She gave a rotted timber a kick, before wrestling it from the muck, then used it to prod the ground as she delved deeper into the shaft.

The ground didn't feel solid. There were crevices and gaps, and a hollow noise in places like wooden planks underfoot. Lily studied the walls. The stone was uneven, not smooth, and if she weren't full with child, she could've pulled herself up in desperation. But now...

Lily set down the lamp, and knocked the rotted branch

against the stone wall to check for nesting snakes. Nothing hissed in return. She set the branch aside, and reached for a hold, then tried to wedge her boot against another.

Her balance was off, the extra weight substantial, but she might be able to manage.

The muscles in her stomach stretched and tugged until they felt like they were tearing. She climbed up to the next hold, and another, but her strength gave out and she slipped.

Lily hit the ground and staggered back, tripping and falling onto the body of her husband. She smelled blood. But it was better than the other smells, so she buried her nose against his cold flesh, panting with exhaustion.

Lily struggled to her feet, gathered her strength, and tried again. But on her second attempt, when she fell, a gush of warm liquid rushed down between her legs.

"No, God, please, not now."

But Tobias Shaw was keen to start his life.

SAVAGE GOLD

1901

"You gave birth to Tobias in a cesspit?" Maddie asked in shock. The doctor in her was outraged—the unhygienic environment, the risks of infection and disease tumbling through her mind. The daughter in her was horrified.

"I didn't have much choice, Maddie. I've always said Tobias is trouble. He was born kicking and screaming into the worst sort of it."

"They tortured pa to death?" Grimm's voice was a painful rasp.

"Yes."

This last word seemed to drain her of speech. Riot's face was utterly blank, but his eyes were gleaming with cool rage. He cleared his throat, gave her hand a quick squeeze, and rose to root around the shelves until he found a medicinal bottle of brandy. He poured her a glass, and pressed it into her hands, then did the same for Grimm and Maddie.

Tim hadn't stirred from his place by the fire, not even to

refill his pipe. But after she'd taken a fortifying draught, he leaned forward to knock the ashes into the hearth.

"How long did you stay down in that pit, Miss Lily?" Tim didn't ask the other part of the question: How long did you stay in the dark with your husband's corpse?

She swallowed and seemed to collect herself. "I didn't know if Maddie and Josiah had reached anyone... If they were alive or dead, or if help was coming. I won't lie, I thought about using that scalpel on myself. But then the contractions started... I don't know how long I was down there. Two or three days, maybe."

Time enough for a body to bloat, for the flies and bugs, for the stench to set in—

Lily took a long draught of brandy, the glass shaking in her hand. Maddie squeezed in beside Lily to wrap her arms around her shoulders. "Clay found you?"

"If you two hadn't reached him—" She looked at her son. "If you hadn't kept your sister safe, Tobias and I would've died down there."

"If I'd kept my mouth shut, you wouldn't have been down there," Grimm said. "Pa wouldn't be—" His voice cracked with emotion, and he surged to his feet, hands clenched in fists.

Riot gripped the young man's arm. "Those marshals came to the hotel because they already suspected your father had gone off to treat Clay's son. They were waiting for him to return. It wouldn't have mattered one way or another—you and your family were hostages the moment those men rode up to your hotel."

Grimm's world shook—the foundations of the past eight years began to crack under Atticus Riot's calm voice and reason.

"He's right," Tim said. "Angel and Eli are a pair of ruthless sonofabitches. Pardon my French."

"I thought Holden's men attacked the Turners... They had

badges. They were the law." Grimm shook his head in disgust. "What took Clay so long?"

"You knew Clay as well as I did, Grimm. Careful as always, he and Slim made sure they didn't attract attention. He was a good man, too—whatever they say about him. When it came to women and children, at any rate."

"What happened to Holden?" Riot asked.

"What happens to every outlaw," Lily sighed. "Grimm had a bounty on his head for murder, so we stuck with the gang. I wasn't really… there. Clay watched out for us like we were his own and never asked for anything in return, but eventually, the law caught up to us."

When Lily fell silent, Grimm took up the narrative. "We were staying in a fort he'd built on a hill with some of the gang, three logs thick, with a well and a garden. Clay was a crack shot, a gunsmith, a carpenter… A lot like you, Mr. Tim."

"Only a lot taller," Maddie said, wiping the tears from her eyes.

Tim huffed out a laugh.

"He was cunning, too," Lily added. "Always had a plan. When the marshals caught up to us with a posse the size of a small army, he already had an escape tunnel. He sent us through with some other women and children, barred the door after us, then stayed to buy us time."

"Hanged?" Riot asked.

"He went out fighting. And then, one by one, his gang was all tracked down and picked off. We've been running ever since."

Tim studied his empty pipe. "And I wager not a single outlaw in his gang ever saw the inside of a courthouse."

"No."

"I don't understand that part," Maddie said. "Plenty of wanted men have families and children. Their families aren't usually hunted by the law. Those men who met up with Eli and

Angel… they were the ones who attacked the Turner Ranch, weren't they?"

"I think so," Lily said. "And I think… looking back… those men used to run with Holden's gang, but I can't be positive. As I said, I wasn't all there for a couple of years—I barely remember Tobias as a baby. Everything was a fog. I recall looking down at Tobias in my arms and wondering who he belonged to."

Grimm sat down on a footstool. "Wyatt, that's Clay's son, once told me the gang had split up over some disagreement. He got shot during the breakup."

"It's not uncommon for outlaws to band together for a job, then split ways," Riot said. "Which brings me to Ravenwood's housekeeper—Mrs. Eleanor Shaw."

Lily gave a bitter laugh. "Is that what she claimed to be?"

"I assumed…"

"Eleanor just said that, so no one would talk."

"Were they…?"

"No, I don't think so. Friends, maybe? She valued her independence."

Riot cocked his head in wonderment. For someone who'd worked with a man for decades, he'd missed an awful lot. But Zephaniah Ravenwood guarded had his privacy with a vengeance. Apparently, his "housekeeper" did, too.

"Regardless, Bel put the names together and started digging through Ravenwood's journals. Mrs. Shaw wasn't convinced your husband was guilty of committing the crimes reported in the papers, so Ravenwood started looking into the case. He made inquiries in Indian Territory. A month before your hotel was burned down, a train was robbed. It was carrying one hundred thousand in gold bullion."

Grimm's head snapped up, but Lily showed no reaction to the revelation.

"Unmarked. It was being transported in an armored

boxcar with a new safe that the railway boasted was unbreak-able. But the shipment of gold disappeared. It never made the papers, because the railway company didn't want word to get out that it wasn't as secure as they claimed. Rumor said it was the Holden Gang, but Ravenwood suspected they had inside help."

"The marshals were in on the train robbery?" Maddie asked.

"That's the story of Mr. Mudd's *Savage Gold*," Riot said. "And it fits with what we know—Angel and Eli strike me as a methodical pair. They might've planned from the beginning to double-cross Holden and take the gold for themselves."

Grimm's amber eyes blazed in the dim. "All this was over some damn gold?"

"People murder for a lot less."

"And they think we know where it is?" Maddie asked.

Lily began to laugh—a sound bitter and full of pain. "My God, what fools. My hotel was worth half as that."

CAT AND MOUSE

Atticus Riot found Liam Taft in a saloon. He sat with his back to a corner, sipping from a tumbler beside a bottle of whiskey as a piano was drowned by voices.

With a sweep of his gaze, Riot assessed the room—who was harmless, who was a threat, which man was likely to throw a punch, which men were intoxicated, and who wore a gun. He wove his way through the crowd, eyeing the long black braids tacked to the wall behind the bar. Queues—souvenirs from when the inhabitants of Truckee burned down their Chinatown and drove the Chinese out of town.

Never mind, they were the same men who risked their lives to carve a railway through the Sierras. Without the railroads, there'd be no Truckee. Fear was a twisted thing.

Liam poured another whiskey as Riot took a seat beside him to watch the crowded saloon. "You ever feel like the world is just too damn fast now?"

Riot accepted the whiskey. "Since I was a boy." A boy who hadn't had spectacles—one whose world was a blur of movement and noise, and a confusing mess of brutality. "It definitely feels smaller."

Liam raised his shot glass before drinking, then set the empty glass down, and reached under his coat. "Progress is a double-edged sword."

"How so?"

Liam tossed two missives on the table. "I wired our San Francisco office. Our train security guards filed these reports a few days ago."

Riot read the missives: *A Negro boy spotted on tracks on tunnel closest to Truckee. Suspected train robbery attempt.* And the second: *A Mrs. Neville, a Negress, reported a Negro boy by the name of James Brady missing on the train from Sacramento. A white man claiming to be a friend took him away before Donner Pass. Inquiring about boy's safety.*

"Did you find your family at the lodge?" Liam asked.

"Tobias is missing."

"Thought so."

Riot understood what Liam meant by a double-edged sword. "If we have this... then so does Sam. Any sign of him or the U.S. Marshals?"

"Sam's the type to fit in. Average height, ordinary looking, he knows how to blend when he has a mind to. But the marshals stand out a bit more. A conductor confirmed that a white man and a Negro man disembarked at the Truckee station."

"Did you file a report about your suspicions with one of your principles?"

Liam poured himself another whiskey. "Would you report your partner?"

"Considering my partner is also my wife... likely not."

Liam gave a raspy chuckle, then sobered as he glowered at the whiskey in his hand. "I don't know how deep this goes. We don't have proof. Right now, it's just a hunch... Or is it more?"

"It's Grimm's word against Sam's," Riot said. "But he confirmed that Carson never made a move."

"Damn."

"These U.S. Marshals are a dangerous sort."

"Who isn't, in this business?"

"Before they killed Nathan Shaw, they tortured him for no other reason than sport."

"We got to find that boy."

"They're the type to use him as a hostage," Riot agreed.

"If he's alive."

Riot shied away from that thought. His neck itched with threat despite the wall at his back. And he wagered Liam felt the same—the marshals and Sam Batten were being careful—as careful as any skilled detectives. It was a game of cat and mouse. Only Riot was beginning to feel like the mouse.

Their enemies were in the shadows while they were sitting in the open.

"You think these wires are related?" Liam asked.

"Tobias has a knack for getting into trouble, then getting right back out of it. If he was snatched on the train, I can imagine him figuring out a way to escape."

"Into a godforsaken wilderness."

There was that. Riot tried not to think of the cheerful boy being out there alone in the cold. Though that was better than being in the hands of Eli and Angel.

40

HANSEL

A TRAIN WAS APPROACHING, AND TOBIAS DECIDED IT WAS better to be caught than freeze to death. He stood in the middle of the tracks, illuminated by its lamp and waving his arms frantically at the approaching locomotive. It belched a black line of smoke and blared its whistle.

The train wasn't slowing.

Could the engineer see him? In the dark, in the flurry of snow, in the blinding white and cold—

Tobias threw himself to the side as the train plowed through the snowdrifts. A split second later, a wave of snow crashed over him, and he lay suffocating under its weight. At least it was warmer there. Though when he shifted, the snow moved too, and then an entire mountain of it dragged him down a slope.

Oh, hell. The steep mountainside, the trees, the raging river. Tobias fought against the snow, clawing his way to the surface and scrambling to find purchase. Something pounded the breath from his lungs, and he lay, fighting for breath. But he'd stopped sliding. He was plastered against a pine tree.

Tobias sucked in a frantic breath and wrapped his arms

and legs around the trunk until he was sticky with sap. The river raged down below. The train tracks sat far above. Slowly he warmed up, and thought this was a nice place to rest against the tree. But then he spotted something downriver. A line of smoke.

A fire?

Tobias roused himself and slid to another tree, then another, until he came to a flat ridge on the slope. He clawed through the snow towards the smoke, but every step was hard fought, and with each step he slid down a little more towards the river.

"Help!" he hollered. But there was no way anyone would hear him over the river's roar. He trudged onwards, until he spotted a cabin at the river's edge, nestled in pine trees.

The sharp snap of a twig brought him around, and he turned in time to watch a furry form rise from the trees. The form loomed over him, and his gaze traveled up and up its furry body to a great bear's head glowering down at him.

Tobias screamed himself into darkness.

TOBIAS WAS COLD. HOLLOW. BUT HE WAS SOMEWHERE DRY. Fire crackled in his ears, and he lay in a cocoon of fur.

He'd been eaten. He was sure of it. If Jonah could spend three days in a fish, then little boys could boil in a bear's stomach. But didn't bears have teeth? And claws?

Tobias cracked open an eye. Bears, he knew for a certainty, did not make fires. And that was a fire—a cheerful one in a river stone hearth.

The smells coming from a pot hanging on a hook made his stomach growl. He sat up, shivering slightly, to find that save for a blanket, he was naked. His clothing hung near the fire, steaming in the heat.

A shadow moved in the room, and a hunched figure wearing furs and wool neared.

Tobias tried to retreat, taking the fur blanket with him, but he hit a wall of rough timber. The man who came into the fire's light was woolly gray, with wild hair and a beard threaded with bone trinkets and a skull necklace. Birds?

His hands were gnarled, missing fingers, and he held a wooden bowl with steaming sludge filled with chunks of something.

Tobias stared at the man. The man's wild green eye stared back. His other eye, the missing one, was a shallow crater of pink flesh under a bushy gray brow. The man grunted and thrust the bowl at him.

When Tobias accepted the bowl, the man spun with a whirl of his furry poncho, then whirled back with a wooden spoon. He stuck the spoon in the bowl and retreated to a stool by the fire, where he slid a giant bowie knife from a sheath and began sharpening it.

Tobias gulped.

Firelight glinted off the knife, but he found he was too hungry to care. If he was going to die, then he'd rather die with a full stomach and warm bones.

Tobias shoveled the gruel into his mouth. It was meat. Venison. And though it'd never live up to his mother's standards, he just about wept in gratitude.

The man poked something in the fire with his knife, and plucked a round, flat disc from a stone. A hard, flat pancake of some kind. He held it up to let it cool, then passed it to Tobias.

"Thank you, sir."

The man grunted.

Tobias used it to sop up the last of the stew, and after he'd eaten every crumb, he tugged the furry blanket tighter around his shoulders and studied the room. It was square and had walls of large logs whose gaps were packed with what looked

like pine needles and mud. A table by the fire. A few pots, some
dented pans, a bow and rifle, and other odds and ends hung
from hooks, along with deer antlers and drying furs of raccoon
and beaver.

"You a trapper?" Tobias asked.

The man grunted.

It was obvious, he had to admit. "Or mining for gold?"

The green eye glared.

Tobias swallowed. "My name's Tobias."

The man grunted and went back to sharpening his knife.
Tobias looked hopefully towards his clothing, but they didn't
look dry. And where was he going to go? He could hear the
wind battering the walls.

In the end, he turned over and went back to sleep, warm
and fed in a cocoon of bear fur.

———

HE AWOKE TO AN EMPTY CABIN. TOBIAS SLIPPED OUT OF BED,
and snatched his clothes. They were dry. His arm hurt and his
stomach rumbled. There was a plate of dried meat and an
apple on the stool, along with a mug of water.

Tobias ate the offering, then poked his head out the door.
The river flowed, the trees were blanketed in white, and the
furry man was chopping wood.

Tobias didn't much care to venture into the cold, so he
went back inside and poked around the cabin. The man soon
stomped back inside, carrying an armful of logs. He glowered
at his guest, dumped the wood. And went out again.

When he came back, he had three fish on a line, all gutted
and ready to cook. He laid the fish on strips of wood to smoke
in the hearth, then baked more of his flat pancakes on the
rock.

When the man was satisfied, he sorted through some

branches on the floor, selecting some flexible, thin pieces from
the jumble. Then he picked up a ball of twine, and his hands
worked the twine into some complicated pattern like a net
between the branches.

"You got a name?"

The man frowned.

"Can't talk?" Tobias asked. "My brother was mute for eight
years. He could talk, but he just didn't want to. It's fine. I can
talk enough for the both of us. But it's nice to have a name,
isn't it?"

The man pointed a three fingered hand towards the bear
cloak.

"Bear?"

The man shrugged.

"All right. Mr. Bear."

The man gave a shake of his shaggy head and pointed
again at the bear's head.

"Just Bear?"

Bear turned to spit out some foul chewing tobacco into
a pot.

"I fell off the train. I need to get back to my brother in
Truckee. You know where that is?"

Bear set aside his work to rummage through clutter until he
came back with a book. He flipped through the tattered pages,
then handed the open book to Tobias.

Bear grunted, jabbing a gnarled finger at the chapter title.
Tobias swallowed as the man turned back to heap more food
into a wooden bowl. Fish, the flat bread, and dried fruit.

Bear set the bowl in front of him and took up his own.
Only Tobias didn't know if he had an appetite anymore. Bear
looked up from his dish, and jerked his beard towards the
book.

"You want me to read?"

Bear nodded.

"Maybe I should eat first?"

The man shrugged.

"Er… maybe I'll read a different one?"

Bear shook his head.

The book was Grimm's Fairytales; the chosen story was "Hansel and Gretel." Tobias frowned at the enormous cooking pot, and Bear caught his eye.

"You gonna kill me before you eat me, right?" Tobias asked with a shaky breath.

The man smiled, revealing pointed teeth and black gums.

41

A GRIM TRAIL

"WE'RE NOT POSITIVE THE BOY SPOTTED ON THE TRACKS WAS Tobias," Riot stressed.

As Lily began to read the missives, she'd put a hand to her stomach as if she'd been kicked. Maddie's face fell as she read over her shoulder, and Grimm started gathering his gear.

"Who else could it be?"

"There's a good chance it was him," Riot admitted.

Maddie glanced out of the cabin's frosted windows. The snow was melting into spring in the valley, but it was still freezing on the pass. "Maybe he took shelter in the tunnel?"

"Maybe so."

"I'm coming," Lily said.

"Miss Lily, I need you to wait here in case Tobias returns. He knows to check in at the lodge, and besides… that would leave Maddie alone."

"Grimm will be here."

"No, I won't," Grimm said. "I lost him. I'll find him."

The younger son missing and the older wanting to put himself at risk—Riot could see a war of emotions etched on the Lily's face.

"I need to look for him, Ma."

Tim was huddled by the fire with a blanket around his shoulders. He started to get up from his chair, but Riot put a hand on his shoulder, and gave him a long look. An entire conversation passed between the pair, but out loud, Riot simply said, "It'll be cold."

"I'll slow you down," Tim grunted in agreement and tugged the blanket closer.

"Or complain the whole time."

"Don't get smart, boy."

"Grimm, do you have a gun?"

"I have a rifle and a knife."

Tim shifted to unbuckle his holster. "Take mine." His own rifle sat by his knee.

Grimm buckled on the belt, then drew the gun, and skill-fully checked over the revolver. As Riot suspected, the young man knew his way around a gun.

"Be careful," Maddie said, stepping forward to give her brother a hug. "You too, Mr. AJ."

Lily handed her son his coat, hat, and gloves. There were no words to say—she squeezed his hand for a fierce moment before the two stepped out into the darkness of a new day.

THE FIRST RAYS OF SUN BRUSHED SNOW-CAPPED PEAKS, AND Grimm watched it climb ever higher as he waited with his horse. An entire group of seasoned settlers had been trapped by the snow, and those who hadn't resorted to cannibalism had starved to death. The pass was named after the Donner Party.

It made him sick to think of his little brother up there alone.

Grimm had named his horse Lyric because she was sensitive to noise. Her ears now tilted forward in alarm, and a moment later, approaching hooves crunched on snow.

Atticus Riot pulled Jack to a stop beside Grimm to gaze up at the peaks. "Do you ever wonder if they used the word 'party' ironically when it comes to that pass?"

"A different kind of food, to be sure," Grimm said.

"At least we're closer to spring."

"Can we trust Liam Taft?"

Riot cocked a brow at him. "We'll find out. We may be walking into a trap."

Grimm blew out a breath.

"I meant what I said in the cabin, Grimm. It wouldn't have made a difference if you'd kept your mouth shut. Your heart was in the right place."

Lyric shifted beneath him with a creak of leather. The silence of the early morning was thick and the dry mountain air filled his lungs, but Grimm was a halfway across the country —remembering, regretting, wishing he could take it all back.

"It's… I gave my word, and I broke it. My father knew it, and I never had time to prove myself otherwise."

Riot wasn't the type of man to offer sympathies where none were warranted. He was thoughtful for a moment, so quiet and still that Grimm nearly forgot the man was beside him.

"I don't even know my father's name——" Riot paused to clear his throat and adjust his hat. Jack huffed out a breath and side-eyed him as he did so. Impatient. Or worried?

Grimm waited.

"I doubt my father's a man I'd want to meet, but I would have liked to know yours. Nathan Shaw was a good man who raised a good son. I'd be proud to have a son like you, Grimm."

It was Grimm's turn to clear his throat.

"We all make mistakes," Riot said.

"Some are the worst sort, though."

"A wise man carries regret; a foolish man flings it to the side. You're no fool."

Grimm rubbed at an itch in his eye. "I'm trying."

"So am I."

"I don't want Tobias to be one of my regrets." The words wrenched from his throat like a harsh prayer.

"He's likely befriended a pack of wolves."

Grimm knew his little brother well enough to know it wasn't impossible.

Riot clucked his tongue at Jack to get the horse moving, and Lyric fell in behind, content to follow the gelding.

They rode to a train yard some distance from the station, where they dismounted and led the horses towards a train fitted with a Bucker plow—a machine propelled by multiple locomotives with a gigantic sleek wedge at its front that looked like a ship's bow.

"Stand up straight," Riot murmured at his side. "You have nothing to hide."

Grimm realized he was walking with his hat low, and his shoulders hunched, worried that at any moment someone would recognize him. He straightened, tall enough to see the top of Riot's hat. The detective had always seemed so tall to him, but he was half a foot shorter.

Liam waved them onto a boxcar that'd been added to the line.

"Liam Taft. Josiah Shaw." Riot introduced the pair once they'd settled the horses in the car.

Liam pinned Grimm with a hard stare. "Did Carson make a move before my partner shot him?"

"Carson had his hands up, sir. I had a gun on him."

Liam grunted like he'd been kicked. "Just so you know… I may have to arrest you, Mr. Shaw."

"As long as it's after this is over."

Liam offered a weathered hand. "Call me Liam."

"Grimm."

The older man's skin felt like leather, but he had a gleam in his narrow eyes. He was as hard to read as Atticus Riot. But Grimm had spent enough time with Riot to read his slightest twitch.

As the train whistle blew, Liam unbuttoned his coat and brought out a map, then pegged it to a wall with a folding knife. "I've arranged for the plow crew to drop us at the tunnel where a boy was spotted." Liam pointed to a spot on the map. "I'd wager a boy would walk along the tracks. Best chance he has of getting somewhere. But a fellow said there's an old trapper along the Yuba here. Crazy as heck, but still… parts of the pass aren't entirely uninhabited."

It was a chance. A one in a million chance that Tobias Shaw hadn't been dragged away by wolves or fallen into the river.

The train started rolling forward, multiple locomotives pushing the plow out front, powering through any snow drifts. If the tracks weren't too heavy with snow, they'd make good time—better than pulling a line of passenger cars.

"As good a place as any to start," Riot said. "Depending on the snowfall up in the pass, there may still be a trail."

No one said what was on their mind—that the trail likely led to the frozen little body of a lost boy.

42

DIVIDE AND CONQUER

BY THE TIME THE TRAIN SLOWED AT THE TUNNEL, THE SUN WAS
high overhead, making the snow glitter. Icicles hung from the
entrance, making it look like a giant maw with jagged teeth.

Riot squinted at the landscape, his spectacles catching the
light and piercing his eyes. He kept his brim low and wished he
owned a pair of tinted lens, even though they were usually
worn by people afflicted with syphilis. He'd have gladly taken
the hit to his reputation just about then.

They disembarked at the tunnel entrance, and one of the
crew handed Liam a red flag. "Wave this around and any train
should stop. The badge will help, too. I'll let the line know to
watch for you."

Liam touched his brim, and the train chugged away with a
great racket of noise that seemed to vibrate the snow on the
upper slopes.

Riot eyed the snow above them. He'd nearly died in an
avalanche once upon a time and wasn't keen to test his luck
again.

The track carved into the side of the granite mountain. A

slope high overhead, and another plunging down into the South Yuba. The river was already bloated with snow melt and spitting up white water and ice.

Riot handed Jack's reins off to Grimm, and took out his battery light. But when he thumbed the switch, nothing happened. It was too cold.

Liam frowned at him. "Don't tell me you have one of those horseless carriages, too?"

"Tim's keen on them," Riot said as he retrieved a hooded lantern from his gear.

"Where's the old bear?"

"Hibernating. His joints seize up in the cold."

Liam eyed the tree line on the slope below. "Why I brought the horses—figure you can drape me over the saddle when my bad leg freezes up."

Riot walked into the granite tunnel, taking a moment to appreciate the engineering feat and the army of Chinese laborers who had risked their lives in brutal conditions to carve a path through the Sierras.

With that thought, he lowered the lantern to study the train tracks and the narrow strip of icy earth on each side. "Here." His voice echoed in the tunnel as Liam coaxed his horse into the darkness.

Jack and Lyric followed Grimm inside without complaint, and the young man stopped to study the spot.

Riot traced a gloved finger over a scuff on a railroad tie. "A child-sized boot print. The child was balancing on the rail, lost his balance, and caught himself on the sleeper there."

Riot moved down the tunnel and pointed to a shallow concave bowl in the granite wall. "He rested here. Moved on..." Riot stopped just outside of the tunnel, then plunged down the slope without a word.

Grimm followed Riot down, his mind conjuring all the

dreadful possibilities: his brother ripped apart by wolves, frozen to a chunk of ice, starved—Grimm caught himself on the last. Tobias hadn't been missing long enough to starve.

"He jumped from the tracks, slid, and got buried in snow…" Riot looked up, searching the jutting rocks above the train tracks, but the glare from the sun was piercing, leaving him near blind from the brightness.

Liam turned, a hand on his gun, to search the mountain-side, too.

"What?"

"We're not the first to come looking for him."

"How many?" Liam asked.

"Hard to tell. These indentations are too deep for a child. Tobias would've been up to his waist to make these impressions. I wager they all used the same path to save themselves the effort of pushing through the snow."

Riot turned back to the slope that led to the river and pine trees. Snow was difficult terrain to read. Recent snowfall and shifting snowdrifts obscured tracks. The night froze the snow, the spring sun thawed it, then froze it again, leaving a slushy pile of ice.

"What do you think?" Liam asked.

"They may have picked him up here."

Grimm let out a shaky breath. "Then he's alive."

It was a possibility. The marshals weren't the type to be burdened with the responsibility of seeing a body properly buried.

Riot's eye caught on a mark farther downslope, but as he moved in that direction, the silence exploded in gunfire.

THE FIRST SHOT HIT GRIMM IN THE BACK, THE SECOND STRUCK Liam in the knee, and the third zipped through snow-laden pine needles to graze Riot's cheek and puncture Jack's saddle.

Riot slapped Jack out of the way as he wrenched the rifle from its saddle holster. He squeezed off a quick shot towards the tunnel and moved behind a tree trunk. Liam used his own horse as cover to reach Grimm, who was lying face down in the snow.

In the volley of blind shots Riot sent flying up the slope, another barked from behind, biting him in the arm. He cursed and spun, putting his back to a trunk.

Liam's horse went down with a scream.

"There's a shooter downslope!" Riot yelled.

"And two above," Liam grunted, dragging Grimm behind the dead horse.

There wasn't time to check on Grimm, wasn't time for conversation or debate. Riot plunged down the slope, slipping from tree to tree. They'd stand no chance with a shooter at their backs.

Another shot grazed him with a spray of snow and needles, but Riot kept moving until the top of the tunnel was no longer visible through the trees. He skidded to a stop against a sap-covered trunk.

A blur of movement darted from tree to tree, and Riot fired, pulling the lever in rapid succession, as he moved forward, each shot sending a spray of pine needles into the air.

The gunfire was oddly muted—a silent battle where heart and lungs and biting shots were drowned out by the river's surge. He rested a shoulder against a tree to reload.

The shooter was baiting him. Keeping just ahead, drawing him farther away from the others and depleting his ammunition.

Ordinarily, he'd be able to hear footsteps crunching in the

snow, but the river silenced everything, including his own heartbeat.

He had no idea where the shooter had taken cover.

A movement to the side had him diving down the slope. He rolled, hit a tree, and aimed. Only his spectacles were covered in snow. Riot fired anyway, then ducked behind a granite boulder rising from the river's bank.

The river had carved a path through the granite with relentless power and purpose, and snow covered the rock in patches, coating the granite with cascades of tiny waterfalls flowing to join the greater torrent.

A white hat rose from behind a fallen tree that had settled on a rock. "I hear you're a quick draw," a voice shouted.

Riot wiped the snow from his spectacles, but his efforts left the lenses streaked with moisture and blood. He'd dealt with his poor eyesight long enough to know damning it wouldn't change his lot.

"Quick enough to still be alive," Riot shouted back.

"That boy won't be if you don't drop your weapons and come out with your hands up."

Riot tightened his grip on the rifle. "The boy will also live if you're dead."

"Doubtful."

White hat and a Southern drawl—the man could only be Angel Davren. "I hear you're a quick draw, too," Riot said.

The conversation had to be shouted—their voices bouncing up the slope.

"I see I wounded you, and you pegged me. We can both sit here until we freeze, or the Undertaker's Friend and the Angel of Death can face off like men," the man crooned.

"I suppose you'll stand up first?"

"I'm no fool."

"And I don't trust your word."

"Now that stings. A man only has his word."

"Would you have given Nathan Shaw that same chance?"

"He went back on his—I don't much care for people who play me for a fool."

"So you and your men tortured him to death."

"I have no control over what others do."

"We know about the stolen gold shipment, Angel. You and Eli helped robbed that train. Then you betrayed Holden. We know you hid behind your badges to hunt down the very gang you worked with."

Silence.

"Your time of hiding behind the law is over—no matter what happens next."

Laughter rose from the behind the boulder. Riot risked a glance, noted the angle, and ducked back behind the boulder. He'd ended up on the verge of a steep granite slope. Dirt and twigs rolled down the granite to mingle with white water. He pulled off his gloves and flexed his fingers against the cold.

"What happens next… You should always know that, my friend. Never do anything without a plan, which is exactly why I'm none too worried about waiting this out. My friends are up top, and once Liam and Sam take that boy out, it'll just be you. We've been in control the whole time."

Riot's blood went cold. But no… Liam had been shot in the knee. Had it been a trick? Everything had happened so quickly.

Riot shoved that worry aside. He had to deal with his current one. "Like your plan for the train robbery: help Holden, then turn on him? Only that backfired on you when he hid the gold."

"Eli is taking care of that end. We're sure Mrs. Nathan Shaw knows where our gold is."

Had the telegrams about Tobias been a trick, too? Liam could've easily given the marshals their location, made up the telegrams about a boy being spotted to separate the group and draw them into an ambush, while Miss Lily and Maddie were left defenseless. It was a common tactic lawmen used to split criminal gangs. Divide and conquer.

Riot had led them right to the family.

He propped his rifle against the rock, and placed his hat on top, then tucked away his gloves. "Once gold fever gets a hold of a man, he can't see much beyond that—you killed Clay Holden without finding that gold."

"It's not a fever—it's about getting what's mine."

"You mean winning."

"We only get one life."

"Then how about you and I end this?"

As soon as he said it, Riot slid off to the side, stretching his body along the precarious granite slide. The rock was slick, without purchase, but there was a crack along the top that he crimped his fingers on to keep him from plummeting into the river below.

He moved as quietly as possible across the rock, edging to the side for a better angle on his opponent. It was a risk, but so was standing up and firing at a man as skilled as Angel Davren.

He needed better odds than chance.

"You first."

"How about we count to ten?" Riot shouted, throwing his voice back towards the boulder where he was supposed to be hiding. As he had once told Isobel, it was a useful trick—one easily pulled off with the confusion of noise.

"Sounds fair." Angel started counting down. One, two..."

Riot let go with one hand to reach for the gun at the small of his back.

"...three, four—" Angel dove to the side of his conceal-ment and popped up to fire at Riot's position—only Riot wasn't there.

Riot aimed and pulled the trigger—a split second before Angel spun and fired. A bullet hit the rock an inch from Riot's hand. Angel staggered forward, blood blossoming over his heart. Then he fell and rolled right down the slope at Riot.

The impact knocked three fingers loose. He clung to the rock with the remaining two, but as Angel rolled towards the river, he grabbed hold of Riot's ankle with his last strength, dragging him into a torrent of icy water.

LAZY COYOTE

LIAM TAFT CINCHED A BIND AROUND HIS LEG AS HE FROWNED down at the young man in the snow. "You just had to aim for my bad leg, Sam," he shouted up the slope.

"You're still alive," Sam called down.

Liam twisted behind his cover—his dead horse—and spotted Sam near the tunnel entrance along with another man of broad features and brown skin, who wore a round hat and duster. Jack Ebbs. The shots from below had stopped, and he wondered who would come walking up that hill. Atticus Riot or—

"Well, the boy's dead," he shouted. "You didn't think to cut your old partner in on whatever you got going on?"

"You want in?"

"I don't get paid enough for this shit," Liam hollered, before raising his rifle and making a point of putting it to the side. "You shot my horse."

"Wasn't me."

"Son of a bitch," Liam muttered. "That friend of yours up there going to shoot me, too?"

"Lower your rifle, Ebbs."

The man up on the tunnel lowered it, but he didn't step out from behind his cover. Liam raised his hands, then struggled to his feet, balancing on one foot and trying to ignore the bloody mess of his knee. "So you shot Carson to quiet him, then?"

"He would've talked."

"And all this is official?"

"More or less."

"Damn it, Sam," Liam said, limping up the slope. "All I want to do is retire—buy a little ranch and waste what days I have left with my wife and grandchildren."

"I didn't think you'd go for it."

"Who was pulling the strings on that racetrack venture—a principle?"

"You think I'm stupid, Liam?"

"I know you're not. I'm just pissed."

Liam staggered against a tree and used it to ease himself down, straightening his bloody leg. He was in the open, unprotected. If they were going to shoot him, they'd shoot him.

"How'd you get caught up with this lot?" Liam asked.

Sam stepped out into the open and walked forward to the edge of the slope, searching the mountainside for anyone else. "Where's Atticus Riot?"

"How the hell should I know? He took off down the hill. Do you have any whiskey? I'd prefer morphine…"

Liam could well imagine the shattered bones in his now ravaged leg—he'd be lucky if he didn't lose it.

Sam reached under his coat and tossed down a flask. Liam unscrewed the cap and drank it dry, then tossed it back to his partner. It landed with a thud between them.

"Didn't answer my question."

"Our goals are running parallel for the moment. I reported Grimm to get him out of my hair and keep him from talking about me shooting Carson." Sam shrugged as if it were common sense. What man wouldn't do that? "I knew I could find him later. But then I hear Atticus Riot is looking for him, too. I needed some help."

"You don't even know what you got yourself in the middle of, do you?"

"Don't care."

Liam twisted around to look his partner in the eye. "Is it Jim Hagen?"

Sam smirked. "You want a cut? You don't get answers—that's the way this arrangement works. I don't even have them."

"Sure, I'll take my cut."

"You, the law-abiding, by the book Pinkerton for his entire life?"

"I just want to see my wife again," Liam sighed. "But I doubt either of us will—you're in with a nest of vipers, Sam."

"They're U.S. Marshals after a bounty. What could—"

An approaching train deafened him. One moment, Sam Batten was standing over him looking smug, and the next he was lying face down in the snow with a hole in the back of his head.

"IT'S OUR ONLY CHANCE," LIAM HAD WHISPERED.

"They'll shoot you."

"If it's my time, then it's my time."

Then Liam Taft had struggled to his feet to play the bait. As soon as the wounded Pinkerton started limping up the slope, Grimm slithered to the side, keeping out of view. His chest burned, his left arm didn't work, and the handkerchief he'd stuffed under his vest was wet with blood.

He'd run with outlaws for two years and learned a lot of things in that time. Clay had treated him like a son. But that wasn't really the man's name. The Chickasaw had only taken it because white men forced his people to conform to their ways. They'd stripped his people of their heritage and culture, so he'd named himself something pliable. But his true name, *Nashoba Itakobi*, the Lazy Coyote, fit him best. A coyote was clever, a trickster—savior or villain—and the most dangerous sort were those who appeared helpless.

And nothing was more harmless than a dead man.

Liam Taft knew that, too. He'd lured Sam closer, got him off his high perch, so only the one man atop the tunnel remained. If Grimm could get a clean shot...

An approaching train rumbled on the tracks. Voices were drowned in the clatter of wheels, and Grimm flexed his left hand, feeling the warmth of blood dripping down his arm. He thought of his father. His mother. His family. He thought of everything those four men had done to them, and when the locomotive plunged into the tunnel, he darted up the slope.

The train rattled, the whistle blew, misting the air with snow and ice spray. Grimm hit the top of the slope, abandoned the rifle, and charged through the wave of snow to leap at the train. He caught an access ladder and scrambled to the top of a boxcar, his shoulder on fire.

The tunnel was coming fast. Wind whipped in his face, and ice bit into his cheeks. Jack Ebbs was turning, raising his rifle, his eyes widening as he pumped the lever.

Grimm drew his gun and fired.

THREE LITTLE PIGS

ELI BLAKE SMILED AT THE WAITRESS. SHE WAS YOUNG AND
rosy, her eyes bright with life as she returned his smile.

Eli raised the lapel of his coat to show his badge, and she
paused while clearing away his breakfast. "I'm looking for a
black-haired fellow with a white stripe at his temple."

Her lash flickered.

"You don't need to talk, miss," he purred. "Just nod. He's
dangerous... I understand you don't want to be accused of
turning him in."

Sally glanced over her shoulder, then brought out a rag to
clean his table. "There was a man here by that description. He
and another fellow—old and bald, with a white beard—they
went into one of the private smoking rooms and talked a while
with our new cook and her daughter."

Eli shook his head. "That's a shame. A real shame. Those
women might be killed."

Sally's forehead wrinkled in concern. "I don't think so.
They cooked your breakfast."

"Can I compliment the chef?"

"They're on break until supper."

"And where do they take their break?"

Sally hesitated, and Eli laid a firm hand over hers, pressing it against the wood until her face screwed with pain. "I don't know," she said with a gasp.

Eli released her hand. "Then I'm afraid it might be too late for them," he said as he stood to put on his hat.

———————

MADDIE COULDN'T EAT, SHE COULDN'T READ OR FOCUS OR DO much of anything. They'd cooked up a storm to distract themselves. And now she was left to wait.

Tim had escorted them to the lodge, waited outside in the cold as their guard, and walked them back to the cabin. Now he huddled by the fire in a blanket, looking old and worn, and tired.

The snow glittered with sunlight; the air was crisp, and the cabin inside felt hot and stuffy. Her mother sat in another chair, staring numbly into the fire. There were only so many things to clean and bake in a cabin this size. The sewing project on her lap sat idle.

Her mother's hands were rarely idle. Maddie found the stillness of her hands unnerving, and she tried not to think about her father's murder—tried not to imagine the suffering he'd endured and the screams her mother had heard.

Abruptly, Lily rose to make a fresh pot of coffee.

Maddie couldn't take the silence anymore. "I'm headed to the outhouse. And no, Mr. Tim, I'd really rather you not stand outside."

But halfway to the door, someone knocked.

Maddie glanced out the window. "It's only Sally."

"What does she need?" Lily asked, sounding tired.

Maddie cracked open the door. "What is it?"

"There was a man at the lodge. He said you were in

danger. That fellow you talked to last night is in trouble with the law."

It took a moment for Maddie to register her words and the concern on the woman's face. "This man, what did he look like?"

"Like a wolf," Sally breathed.

Maddie's blood chilled. But before she could move, the wolf himself stepped out of the trees with a smile creasing his weathered face. He had a gun in his hand. "We can do this the easy way, or I can blow your friend's brains out."

Sally fainted and fell flat on her face, blocking the doorway. Maddie couldn't even close the door. Eli moved forward with shocking swiftness and shoved Maddie backwards into the cabin. He aimed his gun at Tim, whose rifle was leaning against the hearth.

The old man looked startled, and blinked blurry eyes up at the gunman, then gave a wheezing cough that shook his brittle body.

"It's been awhile, Mrs. Shaw. Why don't you come out of that kitchen and stand over here with your daughter—unless you want her hurt."

Lily went cold with dread the moment she spotted the man —though older than she remembered, his skin was as baked as ever by the sun. There was a leanness to him, too, like the wolf Sally had called him. He looked rabid.

Eli kept the gun trained on Maddie as he kicked Sally into the cabin, and shut the door. The girl moaned at his feet and fluttered herself awake.

"You just lay right there and play dead," Eli said, moving the rifle beside the front door.

Sally didn't move.

"Kind of her to check on your welfare."

Lily had moved in front of Maddie, who stood in front of the hearth, her skirts pressed against the woodbin. If the room had been stifling before, now it was suffocating. Maddie's heart fluttered, climbing up her throat, along with bile.

Everything came back to her, and once again she was a seven-year-old girl watching her family spiral into disaster.

"What do you want?" Tim wheezed, another cough shaking his body.

"Mrs. Shaw knows what I want."

Lily closed her eyes. "We left the Holden Gang—I don't know where they are."

"They're in a grave," Eli said. "Every last one of them except you and yours. Your boys are close to one, though."

"What the hell have you done?" Tim asked.

"Tobias has quite the mouth on him. Sneaky little bugger, too."

Lily took a step back as if she'd been struck.

"And Angel is out there taking care of your boy Josiah and his detective friend, but you can save them, Mrs. Shaw. If you tell me what Holden did with the gold."

Out of the corner of her eye, Maddie studied Tim's rifle, leaning against the wall by the front door. Could she grab it in time? Raise it, cock it, and fire?

"I don't know what you're talking about," Lily said.

"That's a shame. The lives of your family are riding on it."

Lily steadied herself on the stone hearth, forcing Maddie to the side. Maddie realized her mother stood at an angle now, so her right hand was obscured from Eli's view by the combined expanse of their skirts... Her mother's fingers were slowly wrapping around a fire poker.

"Don't faint now, Mrs. Shaw. I've always wondered how you escaped that cave—clever of your husband. How'd he manage it?"

"I didn't escape."

The voice that came out of her mother was like nothing Maddie had ever heard—it was cold and calm.

Eli cocked his head.

"We sent the children up through the crack. Nathan lowered me down into the mine shaft, where you dumped his body after you mutilated him."

Eli barked out a laugh, the revolver raising for a moment towards the rafters. "You heard it all, then?"

"Yes."

"Angel was furious," Eli said. "He never likes it when his plans hit a rut in the road."

"My husband wasn't a rut."

"He offered the boys some amusement. You were going to be the main act—"

A furious rage consumed Maddie. She didn't think; she didn't hesitate—eight years of pent-up fury charged her body to action. Maddie snatched up a log from the kindling box and threw it at his gun. At the same moment, Tim sprang from his chair with a whisper of steel.

Before Eli could fire off a shot at the old man, Tim chopped a knife at his wrist. The gun clattered to the floorboards with a spray of blood. But Eli wasn't fazed by his nearly amputated hand—not like a normal man. Battle-hardened to pain, he brought his opposite elbow down on Tim's head.

The old man skipped back, knife raised to fight. But a length of iron speared Eli Blake's back, punching through his chest. He stood in shock, looking down at the fire poker as blood filled his throat.

Lily yanked him back by the hair, so his ear was level with her lips. "My husband's buried on that gold, you fool!"

Eli's eyes widened in realization before the life went right out of them.

45

A BITTER END

As Josiah Shaw stood bleeding over the body of Jack Ebbs, he wondered if he'd ever stop counting the men he killed.

Stopped remembering their faces.

The alternative sickened him, too. What happened if he stopped counting and stopped remembering? What kind of man would he be?

He hung his head.

Vengeance was a bitter draught.

But this wasn't revenge—Grimm hadn't shot out of vengeance, only survival.

He squinted through the sparkling landscape to the trees below, where he spotted Liam Taft sitting on his dead horse. The grizzled cowboy raised a rifle, signaling the all clear.

Where was Atticus Riot? Where was his little brother?

There'd be no questioning Jack Ebbs; he hoped Sam Batten was still alive. Grimm slid down the mountain slope to where Liam sat.

Sam Batten lay dead in the snow. He was on his back, his

hands folded over his chest. Liam sat in the snow beside his dead partner, smoking a cigarette.

"Rifle shot from above." The Pinkerton sounded defeated.

"I didn't—"

"I know," Liam said with a shake of his head. "I never took Sam for an idiot. Never trust a crooked lawman, boy. I reckon that fellow up there saw him talking to me and decided to cut ties. Who was it?"

"Jack Ebbs. He's dead," Grimm said, searching the tree line.

Liam twisted to look downslope with a wince. "I haven't heard anything."

"Did Sam say where Tobias was before he got shot?"

Liam gave a shake of his head.

Grimm followed the tracks down the slope to the edge of a river. He searched the ground, spotted the blood splattering the snow, and the boot prints on the edge of a slick granite slide that plunged into icy waters.

"Atticus!"

The only answer was a roar of water.

Grimm was no expert tracker, but he'd learned the basics while running with the Holden Gang. He found the spot where Riot had left his rifle, gouges in the rock where shots hit, and boot scuffs on the stone slide.

There was no sign of Atticus Riot.

A BADGE WAS A DOUBLE-EDGED SWORD. LIAM'S BADGE STOPPED the trains, flagged down help, and sent a dozen security agents swarming over the mountainside, dragging bodies into boxcars and tending gunshot wounds. A bullet had punched through Grimm's back and out of his chest, missing everything vital.

"Not your time to die," Liam had grunted.

Grimm had found Jack and Lyric huddled together. The painted pony was bleeding from his side. A bullet had punctured the saddle and sunk into his flesh, but not deep.

He led the horses back, helped Liam into the saddle, and trudged uphill. As easy as that.

And now he was dry, sitting by a potbellied stove in the guard's boxcar, but he couldn't stop shivering. He felt like Jack, who'd reared and resisted being led up the ramp without Riot.

And Tobias.

"I can't go back without my brother," Grimm murmured to the man at his side.

"Rest up. Heal up. Let the sheriff and Pinkertons look for him. As soon as we get back, I'll send some men out to track down Eli Blake. Your brother is likely with him."

Grimm rested an elbow on his knee and put his head in his hand. The pain in his chest was nothing compared to the ache in his heart.

Atticus Riot was likely dead. And so was Tobias.

46

SURRENDER

THE WHITE WATER REACHED UP AND SNATCHED HIM FROM THE
air like a ravenous wolf. Riot plunged into the river and was
pushed under by a body.

Not that he could swim.

He clawed at the body, pushing it under as his own
screamed in pain. He was being burned alive, dragged over hot
coals.

Riot broke the surface with a gasp. Desperation seized his
mind. The icy water held him in a viselike grip, cutting
through flesh and clamping down on his bones. His muscles
turned to lead. And he went under.

A boulder came quick. He smacked against it with a shoulder, bounced away to hit another as the river pulled him down
a furious path.

Calm. Calm.

You can swim, Riot. Stop fighting it.

Bel's voice came to him. Slightly mocking, impatient, but
with a smile in her eyes.

He gulped in air. Gave himself over to the pain, and went
under again, turning his feet towards the next boulder. His

clothes added some buoyancy, but not enough. His back scraped along a hidden boulder beneath the surface, then the river tilted alarmingly.

Everything was a blur. Gray shapes, white water, angry river. The pine trees were one long line of green along the banks. An alarming number of gray shapes were rising in the river ahead. And coming fast. He rammed one, bounced off, and caught the next with his boots, slipping to the side.

He tried to grab for the next boulder, but ended up face-down, being ripped downriver by a godlike force.

Riot twisted for the next rock, but his fingers were claws of cold and didn't move right. His fingernails only scraped across slick granite.

And then the world dropped away.

He was spit into a churning mass of white. He broke the surface, numb now, his eardrums feeling about to burst.

Swim sideways in a current, Riot. Stop fighting the water. You'll lose every time.

The ocean. A riptide. It was like a river, she'd said. He stretched out a hand, took an armful of water, and pulled it towards him. He edged sideways in the current.

The ice had burned his nerves numb. The pain was gone, but his muscles were cramping and twisting, yanking him under. Riot slapped his mind into focus. *Keep moving. Keep moving.*

Isobel would kill him, otherwise.

He sensed the moment the river gave up on him. His strokes came easier and the trees along the bank took shape. One boot touched the riverbed, then another. He tried to stand but his legs were clumsy, so he lurched towards a rocky bank.

Crawling, staggering, and stumbling, he left the water, hobbled over river rocks, and fell onto a bank of snow. Riot lay there panting.

The first shiver traveled down his spine, zipped along nerves, and wracked his body. His teeth started chattering.

Keep moving.

Riot struggled to his knees to find a rifle barrel in his face. The barrel was jerking violently with every chatter of his teeth. He followed the barrel up, to the furry hands that held it, to a chest of fur, and finally a bear's head.

Riot blinked. Then dropped his gaze from the bear's eyes to the bright green eye of a man. Wearing a bearskin cloak.

There was a shift of movement to the side, and a smaller furry figure stepped out from behind the man.

"It's Mr. AJ, Bear! Told you he'd find me."

Riot was sure he was hallucinating. He shook the water from his ears, and when he looked again, Tobias was standing in front of him, grinning. "You know there's an easier way down. You could've just used the path. And look here... I'm a Deputy U.S. Marshal now."

Riot yanked the boy into a hug.

47

DIGNIFIED FLIGHT

FOUR BODIES. AN ARREST. REPORTS OF A MISSING CHILD AND A massive search by Truckee lawmen, along with Pinkerton railway security. The brief newspaper article was more sensation than substance, and the facts were achingly bare. But Isobel had one that was impossible to ignore: There'd been no word from Riot.

As soon as she'd spotted the evening edition, she wanted to throw on a coat and race to the railway station. However, Margaret had battered her with sense—damn the woman. So she'd tasked Ravenwood Agency with making inquiries, since she didn't want to alarm the children. Isobel now waited by the telephone, idly throwing her knife into a wall.

As soon as the telephone rang, Isobel snatched up the receiver. "Ahoy there."

"Reports of my death have been greatly exaggerated."

"Riot." She slumped with relief.

"Don't faint on me, Bel. I can't catch you from here."

"I never swoon."

"It's good to hear your voice."

"You sound like you didn't expect to hear mine again."

"Never crossed my mind."

"What happened?"

He ignored her question. "What's that clacking noise?"

"The Umbrella Defense Academy is training in your dance hall."

"And you're not down there beating women over the head?"

"I was busy pacing the widow's walk. What the hell happened?"

"Eli Blake, Angel Davren, Jack Ebbs, and Sam Batten are all dead."

"Kind of them to die," she said.

"And you saved my life."

"Did I?" she asked, surprised. "How good of me."

"I intend to take up swimming with more enthusiasm."

"It was never your enthusiasm that was the issue, Riot. It was your focus."

"You are distracting."

"I'll let Jin know your pig and barrel tattoos work."

"She'll run out and get them."

"Not anytime soon. She's thrown herself into umbrella defense training."

"That's terrifying."

"Not as terrifying as you apparently nearly drowning. Did you lose your spectacles again?"

"I did," he sighed.

"I'll be a good little housewife and order you another pair."

"Make it two. I'll need one pair with tinted lenses."

"Have you picked up an illness I should know about?"

"I won't dignify that with a comment."

"Then tell me what happened."

He told her. She listened.

"We knew the pair were sly, so Tim and I were expecting an ambush. Tim stayed behind to play his old man act. Eli

Blake never expected him to move so fast. Liam was a wild card, though."

"Sounds as if Angel had you convinced he was on their side."

"For a tick," Riot admitted. "But it made no sense to shoot Liam when they ambushed us. He'd be better off getting the drop on us from behind. Angel was playing off my concern for Tobias."

"When they really had no idea where he was," Isobel mused. "So Sam got the same report as Liam, and they figured you'd put two and two together and go searching for him... And since Eli was white, he could blend in with the town better, so he stayed behind to ask questions."

"I believe so." The line crackled as Riot chuckled. "Tobias played a cool hand."

"I'm glad he's alive. And you. Everyone. Are you hurt?"

"I've thawed out enough to feel a graze or two. Though I doubt I'll be warm until you're in my arms."

"I have that effect on you," she said with a smile that he could hear over a mountain range. "What about the Shaws?"

"Maddie and Lily are physically fine. Grimm was shot, but the bullet went clean through. Tobias' arm is healing straight—the trapper who found him saw to that after he scared the piss out of him. And Jack is being overly dramatic about the bullet they dug out of his hide."

"So now what?"

Killing three U.S. Marshals and a corrupt Pinkerton doesn't exactly clean the slate for a wanted man.

"Grimm is in jail."

"Ah."

Riot cleared his throat. "However, Tim is working on something."

An image of dynamite, horses, and a masked old man

blowing out the side of a jail house flashed across her mind. "Oh?"

"He has a card up his sleeve that might help Grimm avoid a trial."

"A plea bargain?"

"Do you remember when the children were investigating that newspaper article that was written about the manor?"

"The one claiming you were running a whorehouse? Or was there another I missed?"

"That would be the one."

"I do."

"And do you remember what Tobias discovered?"

"I do."

"Tim had it traced."

"Did he?"

"Hmhmm."

There was a lot of meaning in that sound. Isobel didn't miss it. And so when her partner and husband said the next, she knew what he really meant.

"You'll have the police there shortly. I wouldn't want Watson to be trodden underfoot."

"No… we can't have that. He's quite harmless."

"I knew you'd understand, Bel."

"Until then, Riot."

The line went dead.

Isobel hung up the receiver and checked the grandfather clock in the hallway. He'd be napping in the library. She stood, and despite loathing it, picked up her cane—at least it was a sleek gentleman's stick with an ivory handle. And it had some semblance to an ice pick.

She walked into the library to find Mr. Harry Hughes snoring in an armchair by the fireplace with Watson draped over his lap.

Isobel prodded the man with the tip of her cane. "Mr. Hughes."

He jerked awake with a snuffle, and Watson glared at her for disturbing his cushion. "Mrs. Riot, er... I would stand, but Watson here..."

"I'm afraid you must," Isobel said. "I'm here to warn you, Mr. Hughes. Riot informed me that the police are on their way to search your rooms."

The man paled.

"All that cash in your wardrobe..."

"You know?"

"You've been found out," she confirmed. "But it's the money they'll be after. If you should happen to disappear again..."

"Oh." Mr. Hughes sat up a little straighter, then politely asked Watson to remove himself. "Yes, yes... the bank wants their money back. It was frightfully easy to steal it, you know."

"Robbery?"

"Dear me, no." The man chuckled, his stomach rumbling with mirth. "Just a bit of clever bookkeeping... No one even noticed it was gone for years."

"How much did you steal?"

"You don't know?"

"I'm only relaying a message."

"Oh, then. Well... a smidge over a million."

Isobel glanced towards the rafters. "You have a million dollars in your bedroom?"

Mr. Hughes shrugged. "Hasn't done me much good. I'll be sad to leave my comforts here."

"I'm not sure how much time you have," Isobel said.

"I should like to pack a bag."

"Not too heavy of one," Isobel said.

Mr. Hughes stood and turned to stroke Watson on his head

one last time. "You'll see he gets shrimp? He prefers Sun Fat's market to the Monterey market."

"The shrimp all come from the same ocean, Mr. Hughes."

Mr. Hughes and Watson sniffed at her.

"Watson will be fine," Isobel said dryly, eyeing the plump cat.

"I've always wanted to visit the Caribbean."

"I hear it's nice. And Mr. Hughes…"

"Yes?"

"It may help to know that your stolen money will save an innocent young man from being hanged."

Mr. Hughes beamed, shook her hand, and waddled off to pack a bag, which she was sure would be filled with stolen bank money.

EVER AFTER

THE OTHER EDGE OF A BADGE WAS THAT JOSIAH SHAW COULD no longer hide. The past had finally caught him. He lay on a cot in a cell, close to a wood stove, with plenty of clean blankets and good food.

Liam Taft had seen to that while the cogs of justice ground through a torrent of reports, telegrams, and lengthy telephone conversations.

There was nothing simple about his case—a Gordian Knot of corrupt lawmen, stolen (and unreported) gold, both noble and vile outlaws, and a string of murders, including Nathan Shaw.

Grimm was happy to rest. To finally stop running. For the first time in eight years, he was free of that crushing weight. Whether or not he faced the hangman's noose, he would die a free man.

No one could take that feeling away from him.

A turn of keys in the heavy door had him sitting up. The sheriff stepped aside, and Liam Taft came hobbling in, leaning heavily on a cane. His knee was padded with thick bandaging.

"I don't think you're supposed to be walking on that," Grimm said, climbing to his feet.

"Well, this is special." The edge of Liam's mustache twitched upwards as he slid a key into the cell lock. "You have some visitors."

The cage door swung open, and his family swarmed in after. He was nearly knocked over by his little brother. "Tobias," he breathed, lifting the boy up with one arm and crushing him against his chest.

"Gah, I'm not a little kid anymore, Grimm. Put me down."

"Look little to me."

Tobias squirmed free and landed on his feet. Maddie came next to wrap her arms carefully around him, and then his mother, who stood on her tiptoes to bring him down to her level, so she could kiss his cheek.

Grimm spotted Atticus Riot leaning against the doorpost, and Tim rocking back and forth on his heels, smoking a pipe, with a twinkle in his blue eyes.

"Mr. AJ." Grimm stood stunned, a dozen questions on the tip of his tongue, but as usual Tobias filled in the silence.

"I'm a Deputy U.S. Marshal now," Tobias said, polishing a badge on his chest with his sleeve. "I already solved a bank robbery—with Mr. Tim's help. We traded some stolen money I found for you. Though I'm not sure you're worth a million."

Maddie whacked the back of the boy's head. "If you keep polishing that badge, you'll put a hole in it."

"You can't strike a U.S. Marshal."

Maddie groaned.

But Grimm was stunned. The world under his feet was tilting—too much was happening, too quickly. He needed time to think, to take it in. To make sense of the words tumbling out of his brother's mouth.

His mother took his arm. "You're free, Josiah. Let's get something to eat."

He stared down at her, then looked from the sheriff to Liam, and finally to Riot and Tim. "How…?"

"Turns out you're not worth a million dollars," Riot said. "Not in the eyes of the powers that be—considering the complicated nature of events and the trade Tim made on your behalf. The U.S. Government wiped your slate clean in exchange for the money. You're a free man."

Riot stepped forward to offer a hand. "It's good to finally meet you, Mr. Shaw."

Before Josiah could think of a response, Tobias moved between them. "Turns out Mr. Hughes was a bank robber— not a fancy one. He just moved some numbers around. Makes me think I ought to pay more attention to maths. Anyhow, I was doing some investigating and found his stash. So you kind of owe me, Grimm…"

Tobias talked the entire way out of the jailhouse, but Grimm didn't mind. It was the only thing keeping him on the ground.

They walked to the Moon River Lodge, where they settled in for a fine dinner. Tobias finally quieted because his mouth was full of food. And Grimm listened as Riot filled him in on his fight with Angel, and finally Maddie recounted what happened at the cabin.

His mother was silent. She ate little and every time she looked his way, her eyes shimmered with a mix of emotions.

Grimm placed a hand over hers and shared a knowing look: I wish he was here, too.

Lily dabbed at her eyes with a napkin.

"I don't get it, Ma," Maddie finally said. "You've known about that gold this entire time? You even knew where it was?"

There was only family in the private dining room. Liam had stayed behind to fill out more damned reports, as he so eloquently put it.

Lily took a moment to compose herself, rearranging her

napkin on her lap. "I didn't know the gold's history—the details of it. But when I was down there in that mine shaft, I searched through the rubbish looking for something that would help me climb out. When I first landed down there, I felt something hollow underfoot, and when I cleared away the garbage and muck, I found several strongboxes. The lock was broken on one, so I opened it and had a look inside. It was too heavy to lift, and there wasn't anything in it of use to me."

"You mean the gold is still there?"

"It's lining your father's grave, Maddie."

"Do you want to retrieve it?" Tim asked. "It's gold bullion, untraceable, from an unreported theft. You could use it to pay for Maddie's university." And a heap of other things.

Lily looked at her children and saw her answer mirrored in their eyes. "Thank you, Mr. Tim, but it's blood money. We won't have anything to do with it. My husband is at peace. We'll let him be."

Riot stood with a bottle of wine to refill glasses, and even poured some into Tobias's glass. Then he set the bottle down, and raised his glass to the table. "To Dr. Nathan Shaw."

"And to family," Lily added, tapping her glass to his.

"To family."

THE END

CONNECT WITH AUTHOR

If you enjoyed *A Grim Telling*, and would like to see more of Bel and Riot, please consider leaving a review. Reviews help authors keep writing.

Keep up to date with the latest news, releases, and giveaways. It's quick and easy and spam free. Sign up at www.sabrinaflynn.com/news

HISTORICAL AFTERWORD

Only a fraction of my research finds its way into my historical mystery series, but extensive research helps to give me a more accurate view of the past so I can write more realistic fiction. I especially look for source material that breaks with the common narrative of mainstream history that's taught in schools.

I've lost count of the number of times I've heard 'cowboys weren't Black.' Western movies would certainly have anyone believing that. The entertainment industry has long excluded people of color from western films, or limited their roles. But thanks to a number of associations like the Black American West Museum and Heritage Center, deliberate voids are being filled.

I've come across statistics stating 25%, 35%, 60%, and even up to 80% of cowboys were Black. Even taking the conservative estimate, think of all the western movies you've ever seen, and now imagine them with a fourth to half of the cowboys portrayed by Black actors. Our perception of the Wild West changes in an instant. This is why it's important to be accurate in history and fiction.

I'll highlight just a few names I came across while researching (it's hard to pick only a few)...

An expert rodeo cowboy by the name of Bill Pickett invented 'bulldogging'. Although cruel by modern standards and later banned, it involved leaping from horseback onto a running steer, rolling along its back, grabbing its horns, and wrestling it to the ground. He didn't stop there... Bill then bit the bull's sensitive upper lip and would flip it onto its back using only his teeth. His act was a huge success for rodeo shows, and he often performed alongside Will Rogers.

Nat Love (aka: Deadwood Dick), was a cowboy brimming with swagger. He was born into slavery, freed after the Civil War, and left starving and trying to support two families at the age of thirteen. For twenty years, he drove cattle, fought off thieves, was shot thirteen times (but never crippled), was frozen and thawed out, captured by a tribe and escaped, and had a tendency to rope things that shouldn't be roped, like a cannon and a moving steam engine. When trains replaced cattle driving and the lifestyle faded, he became a Pullman Porter and wrote an autobiography of his wild life. And although some claim his autobiography is full of tall tales, there's nothing in it I haven't come across in other research.

Jesse Stahl is considered one of the greatest bronc riders. At a time when bronc riders rode a horse to exhaustion (instead of the 8 seconds of today), his ride on Glass Eye is legendary. And he made iconic the hat-in-hand bronc riding pose.

At a time when wild horses were caught by shooting the stallions and running the herd to exhaustion, Robert Lemmons took a novel approach to capturing them: he won their trust. Born into slavery, he was freed when he was seventeen and began working for a Texas rancher. But he had no use for the brutality involved in rounding up wild mustangs. Instead, he worked alone and slowly took over leadership of a herd through weeks of living rough and earning their trust by acting like a mustang. When the herd accepted him as its leader, he simply led them to a corral.

There are horse whisperers today, but Robert Lemmons is known as the "most original mustanger" and likely the first horse whisperer.

One of the many women Lily Shaw is loosely based on is Annie Box Neal—a multiracial Cherokee, Black, and white woman whose family moved from Indian Territory to Arizona. She married, rode shotgun on a stagecoach with her husband, and eventually, through savvy business choices, built the opulent Mountain View Hotel on their 3N Ranch in Arizona. At a cost of $90,000 to build, it was "Tucson's Favorite Mountain Resort and Health Sanitarium." It featured gorgeous gardens, a 9 hole golf course, carriages, bicycles, and horses to rent. It was called the "Epitome of Western Opulence."

Not many have heard of U.S. Deputy Marshal Bass Reeves. But he's a larger-than-life legend who should be every bit as well known as Wyatt Earp, and he certainly had a more interesting life. There are too many stories to fit into this Afterword. Described as "rough-and-tumble-fighter, boastful and lusty," he wore a big black hat and sported a bushy mustache.

Bass was a great detective and a master of disguise, and often tricked outlaws and arrested them without a shot fired. Bass would round up and bring in large groups of wanted men and women at one time, and he claimed to have arrested more than three thousand criminals in his twenty-seven-year career as a Deputy Marshal. He even arrested his own son for murder.

There were outlaws aplenty of all races in Indian Territory. Black, Native American, white and every mix in between. Every detail woven into this narrative has a spattering of truth behind it.

Clay Holden is based loosely on an infamous Cherokee by the name of Ned Christie. Ned was a blacksmith, gunsmith, sharpshooter, and jack-of-all-trades who built a fort (three logs thick) on a hill now known as Ned's Fort Mountain. He evaded capture for five years, until an army of U.S. Marshals finally brought in a cannon. It's the first and only time the U.S. Government has used a cannon to capture a civilian.

What of poor (or rather, rich) Mr. Harry Hughes? He was based on some history, too. In 1896 the Pinkerton's came to San Francisco to enter into contracts with local corporations, but they were also hunting a thief. A Chicago bank cashier stole $152,000 from his bank without raising the slightest suspicion. The bank didn't find out the money was gone until sometime after the man disappeared. As far as I could discover he was never caught, but slipped away on a steamer headed elsewhere.

Angie Debo, Ph.D. was an American historian who wrote thirteen books about Native American and Oklahoma history. But the start of her career was surrounded by controversy. Why? She told the truth. Instead of praising the history of white settlers and glorifying the land rushes, she shined a spotlight on the betrayal and exploitation of Native Americans by the U.S. Government and wealthy white Americans.

When she wrote "And Still the Waters Run" she was dropped by her publisher and barred from teaching by the wealthy and politically powerful of Oklahoma. She never did find a permanent teaching assignment, but she did eventually find a publisher for "And Still the Waters Run" and many books afterwards. She was eventually recognized and respected for her work, but even today, American history as taught in schools tends to gloss over the betrayals and paint the land grabs as a triumph of white settlers.

The Indian Removal Act of 1830 forced tens of thousands of Native Americans from their lands into what is now Oklahoma. Thousands of people died during the forced march. One Choctaw leader called it a "trail of tears and death."

Before it became a state, Oklahoma was known as "Indian Territory" and was inhabited mostly by five main tribes: Cherokee, Chickasaw, Choctaw, Creek (Muscogee), and Seminole. The U.S. Government promised the tribes that whites would not be allowed to settle in their territory, and that the land grants would be theirs "as long as the water runs, as long as the grass grows."

The Five Tribes were dubbed "civilized" because they adopted many Anglo-American cultural traits such as Christianity, centralized governments, and English literacy. This assimilation was largely because of the concerted efforts of the U.S. Government to erase Native American culture and tribal traditions by forcing children to attend white-run boarding schools and abandon their identity and culture.

The Five Tribes had their own laws and police force: the wide-ranging mounted Lighthorsemen, local sheriffs, and the consolidated Union Agency Police. Some Native Americans served as Deputy U.S. Marshals and Special Railroad Agents, such as Sam Sixkiller.

Many Native American tribes were accustomed to taking slaves during warfare with other tribes, so many tribes of the southeastern states started enslaving African Americans. While the tribes varied in their views of slavery, the Choctaw and Chickasaw were reportedly most like white slaveholders. Greenwood Leflore, an influential Choctaw leader (and later a Mississippi Senator) reportedly owned four hundred slaves and five plantations, though he sided with the Union during the Civil War.

The Five Tribes largely supported the Confederacy during the Civil War because many hadn't forgotten the Union government's forced removal of their people, and the Confederacy promised them full recognition as a sovereign, independent state.

After the Civil War, the U.S. Government drafted new treaties with tribes that had supported the Confederacy. The Reconstruction Treaty required the abolition of slavery. The formerly enslaved were called Freedmen. Some tribes adopted the Freedmen into their tribe, others offered limited citizenship rights, but all of them required a "By Blood" (some tribal ancestry) stipulation. Mixed ancestry and interracial marriage were common in the Five Tribes. However, many rights and laws were reversed later on, and some descendants of the Freedmen are still fighting to be recognized as full tribal citizens today.

And most have seen the photograph taken of the massive number of wagons and horses in the 1889 Land Grab. The U.S. Government went back on their treaties when white Americans realized that land in Indian Territory was valuable. The government gave away 1.9 million acres of Indian Territory to white settlers, despite their agreement of "as long as the water runs, as long as the grass grows."

History on a whole is a mess of injustice. There's good and bad in every race, and all the gray in between. It comes down to individuals. Just as today, people of every race committed atrocities against their own kind and other races.

The Cherokee proverb at the beginning of the book is a running theme of this book (and really the series), so I'll leave you with the full version of a grandfather teaching his grandson about life:

"A fight is going on inside me," he said to the boy. "It is a terrible fight and it is between two wolves. One is evil—he is anger, envy, sorrow, regret, greed, arrogance, self-pity, guilt, resentment, inferiority, lies, false pride, superiority, and ego.

"The other is good—his is joy, peace, love, hope, serenity, humility, kindness, benevolence, empathy, generosity, truth, compassion, and faith. The same fight is going on inside you—and inside every other person, too."

The grandson thought about it for a minute and then asked his grandfather, "Which wolf will win?"

The old man simply replied, "The one you feed."

ACKNOWLEDGMENTS

No book is written entirely alone. So a huge thank you to the following: To my dog Kelly, who has sat with me for every single word of the past twelve books. (She may have some attachment issues.)

To my teenagers, who put up with (do they have a choice?) my absentmindedness and shuffling around the house talking to myself.

I bounce plot ideas off them now, too. Poor things.

To Giovanna Donnithorne-Tait for help with the horses. And to the usual suspects of early beta readers: Alice Wright, Merrily Taylor, Lyn Brinkley-Adams. Your feedback and encouragement keeps me writing!

To Kerie for her enthusiasm. And to Tom Welch, my editor, who gives every book a polished feel. I don't know what I'd do without you!

And of course Gus. For regularly anointing my office with his fragrance and chasing me out into another room. For his hoover vacuum-like ability to gulp up everything I drop. For all his ER visits. And for all the times he's punched me in the stomach because he's so happy to see me. To say nothing of nearly breaking my knees every time I get the mail, because once he gets running, he can't change course… You're special, buddy.

ABOUT THE AUTHOR

Sabrina Flynn is the author of the **Ravenwood Mysteries** set in Victorian San Francisco. When she's not exploring the seedy alleyways of the Barbary Coast, she dabbles in fantasy and steampunk, and has a habit of throwing herself into wild oceans and gator-infested lakes.

Although she's currently lost in South Carolina, she's lived most of her life in perpetual fog and sunshine with a rock troll and two crazy imps. She spent her youth trailing after insanity, jumping off bridges, climbing towers, and riding down waterfalls in barrels. After spending fifteen years wrestling giant hounds and battling pint-sized tigers, she now travels everywhere via watery portals leading to anywhere.

You can connect with her at any of the social media platforms below or at www.sabrinaflynn.com

GLOSSARY

A man for breakfast - a murdered body found in the streets at dawn.

Avó - grandma in Portuguese

Bai! - a Cantonese expression for when something bad happens (close to the English expression, 'shit')

Bahba - Dad

Banker - a horse racing bet where the bettor believes their selection is certain to win

Between Hay and Grass - teenager

Blind Pig - an illegal drinking establishment

Bong 幫 - help

Boo how doy - Hatchet Man - a hired tong soldier or assassin

Bull - an officer of the law

Capper - a person who is on the lookout for possible clients for attorneys

Chi Gum Shing 紫禁城 - Forbidden Palace

Chinese Six Companies - benevolent organizations formed to help the Chinese travel to and from China, to take

care of the sick and the starving, and to return corpses to
China for burial.

Chun Hung - a poster that puts a price on someone's
head

Dang dang - Wait!

Digging into your Levis - searching for cash

Din Gau 癲狗 - Rabid Dog

Dressed for death - dressed in one's best

Faan tung 飯桶 - rice bucket or worthless

Fahn Quai - White Devil

Fettler - a person who maintains railway lines

Kwei - Foreign Devil

Fence - a person who knowingly buys stolen goods to sell
at profit.

Graft - practices, especially bribery, used to secure illicit
gains in politics or business; corruption.

Hei Lok Lau - House of Joy - traditional name for
brothels at that time

Hei san la nei, chap chung! 起身呀你個雜種！- Wake
up, you bastard!

Highbinders - general term for criminals

Kedging - to warp or pull (a ship) along by hauling on the
cable of an anchor that has been carried out a ways from the
ship and dropped.

King chak - the police

Lardon - a thief

Lo Mo - foster mother

Mien tzu - a severe loss of face

Mui Tsai - little Chinese girls who were sold into domestic
households. They were often burdened with heavy labor and
endured severe physical punishments.

Nei tai - you, look

Neta - Portuguese for granddaughter

Ngor bon nei - I help you

No sabe - Spanish for 'doesn't know' or 'I don't understand'. I came across a historical reference to a Chinese man using this phrase in a newspaper article. I don't know if it was common, but it is a simple, easy to say phrase that English speakers understood.

Pak Siu Lui - White Little Bud

Sau pan po - 'Long-life Boards' - coffin Shop

Si Fu - the Master

Siu wai daan 小壞蛋 - Little Rotten Eggs - an insult that implies one was hatched rather than born, and therefore has no mother. The inclusion of 'little' in the insult softens it slightly.

Speeler - a gambler

Slungshot - a maritime tool consisting of a weight or "shot" affixed to the end of a long cord, often by being wound into the center of a knot called a "monkey's fist." It is used to cast a line from one location to another, often a mooring line. This was also a popular makeshift (and deadly) weapon in the Barbary Coast.

Sock Nika Tow - Chop Your Head Off - a very bad insult

Wai Daan 壞蛋 - Rotten Egg

Wai Yan 壞男人 - Bad Men

Wattles - ears

Wu Lei Ching 狐狸精 - Fox Spirit

Wun Dan - Cracked Egg

Wun... ah Mei - Find Mei

Yiu! 妖! - a *slightly* less offensive version of the English 'F-word'.

Made in the USA
Las Vegas, NV
29 September 2022

56223155R00208